I0661703

NYCTOPHOBIA

LEE BROWN

Epigraph Books
Rhinebeck, New York

Book & cover design: Amy Manso
Front cover photo: Ian Wickstead

ISBN: 978-1-960090-06-5

Library of Congress Control Number: 2023903226

Epigraph Books
22 East Market Street, Suite 304
Rhinebeck, NY 12572
845.876.4861

*This book is dedicated to Nancy Paterson
who in a life that was much too short,
managed to bring a mass murderer,
Slobodan Milosevic, to justice at the
International Court of Justice at The Hague.*

CONTENTS

Coulro

The clowns were running at me like a storm of Technicolor nightmares. They took high steps, with their knees almost hitting their chins, exaggerated by the huge red and yellow shoes they wore. Their clothes were every color of the rainbow; all too big or too small. The music under the tent was screaming for them and as their clothes rippled, it made me feel like paint was dripping off their shoulders.

When they were out of the big top ring into the hallway, they slowed to a walk like a team heading back to their locker room. As they got closer I thought I saw tiredness in their eyes, almost as if they had just come out of a coal mine elevator at the end of their shift.

I was standing on a round elephant pedestal looking down at them as they started to pass me. I couldn't really see facial features through all of the grease paint, big red noses, yellow forehead stars and blue cheeks. So I screamed.

"Fulbright!"

A couple of the clowns looked at me.

"Corky Fulbright!" Now all of the clowns looked at me, except one on the other side of the hallway.

■ ● ■

"Yeah, you. You! Corky Fulbright!!"

The clown with orange, curled hair under a ratty fedora started to run. That had to be Fulbright. I jumped down, pushed my way through the other clowns and went after him. His size 24 pink and yellow sneakers didn't help him much. I tackled him and put him on the ground trying to get him under control. We started rolling around in the sawdust and after about ten seconds I felt the first of the clowns kick me in the leg. There was another kick. One kicked me in the stomach. I lost my breath and I was starting to lose my grip. My hands slid down from Fulbright's knees to his ankles, while he yelled, "I'm not Fulbright." I heard a little boy holler, "Mommy, that man is trying to hurt the clown."

Then I saw a bright red shoe, with a yellow flower on it about twice the size of a large watermelon, stomp down on my fore-arm. Fulbright was struggling to get up while I was still holding his ankles. I let go of one ankle and managed to pull my hand-cuffs out of my jacket pocket. I slapped one end on the ankle I still had a grip on. I closed the other end on my wrist.

I started to yell "police," but as I turned my head my face was met by a fluorescent pink glove that covered a good-sized fist. My face dropped to the ground and my mouth filled up with sawdust.

Fulbright had made it to his feet and was dragging me like a ball and chain into the sunlight. Punches and kicks were raining on me like a monsoon. Someone yelled, "What the hell is going on here?!" Fulbright just kept on going with a step and a yank of the idiot's arm.

A bright yellow bulb, that resembled a nose, fell in front of my face. Then a whole clown fell in front of us with his eyes closed. Fulbright stopped. I glanced to my right and saw another clown sitting on the ground holding his face. The kicking and punching stopped. I could hear Andy yelling, "He's a detective, asshole!" When I managed to look up, I could see Sharp standing over me growling, "Any of you other clowns want to go to sleep in the grass?" I rolled over spitting out sawdust, just in time to see the biggest of the clowns take two steps forward. Sharp faked with his right shoulder and put a left hook in the clown's ribs. The clown twisted sideways, tried to keep his feet, and then went down on one knee, panting. The other ten clowns started moving away.

Suddenly a really small clown in baggy everythings, that were too short everywhere, came out of nowhere running right at Sharp. I tried to yell "look out," thinking the clown would hit Sharp in the back of the head with the horn he was carrying. But my tongue wouldn't work with sawdust all over it. Whatever sounds I made tripped on my teeth, dripped down my chin and I started choking. The little short clown stopped behind Sharp's back, blew his trumpet at Sharp's head, changed direction and ran off to hide behind the other clowns.

Sharp ducked at the horn blast, spun around, turned back and stomped a foot at them. All of the clowns started to half turn in retreat, except for the one that was still unconscious and the one on his knee, who was now grinding his teeth.

Sharp bent down over me and while he was unlocking my cuffs, with a smile bigger than an elephant's head, said, "Why'd y'all provoke this little ruckus with a gang of fanatical clowns, anyways?" I glared at him while I tried to get the rest of the sawdust out of my mouth with my dirty fingers.

When I stood up I saw that Andy had Fulbright's arm twisted up behind his back. Sharp tossed Andy my set of cuffs and he caught them in his left hand. All the time Fulbright was talking at 120 mph, insisting his name was Patterson; that he'd been a clown for fifteen years; where we could find his mother; who his sister was.

■ ● ■

Then I heard that same little boy say to his mother, "What are those mean men doing to the clown?"

The mother caught our stares and charged off, dragging her son away while the kid insisted they had to do something. A huge cheer erupted from inside the big top just as some overweight security guard staggered…

"He's not here! You said he'd be here!"

I shook my head a little and then focused my eyes on my client.

"Look, Mr. Blakeslee, I told you to be here at 12:30. You came half an hour early. My watch says 12:25. And since you're sitting right across from me, would you mind speaking in a normal voice. In kindergarten they call it your 'inside voice.'"

"My watch says 12:32 and you weren't paying attention to me."

Of course I wasn't paying attention to him. I wanted to throw Blakeslee out of the office. Maybe through a window, since we were on the fourth floor. That would have been very satisfying. He was pushy in a condescending, arrogant way and he made it obvious that he had money. I was not happy about the three or four phone calls he made to me every day. I was not happy about him sitting in my office for the past twenty-five minutes because he didn't want to sit in the waiting room.

I stared at him with some attitude. He stared back at me from someplace where intelligence clearly wasn't valued.

"You know, the clock on the wall still says '12:26.'"

Blakeslee blinked his eyes twice to adjust part of his brain. He started looking around my office for the clock.

"What clock? I don't…"

We both heard the door to the main office area open and close. I stopped smiling. I looked at my watch dramatically. "I

■ ● ■

suspect that is Mr. Foreman."

I stood up and went to the doorway of my office. Foreman was standing by the entrance door looking around. He was wearing a very nice, bluish-grey suit that didn't seem to fit him or match the brown shoes he was wearing. His hair was longish and combed straight back, not really matching the suit or the time period we were living in.

"We're going to be in here, Mr. Foreman."

Foreman walked toward me slowly, glancing out the reception area windows. He paused to stare back at Sharp's office. It figured; two of them. One couldn't wait and brushed his teeth in between the soup and the main course. The other had a world of time that he apparently had to squander. Some of it he obviously needed to waste before he got to my office. But, he was on time. I didn't feel like waiting for the end of Foreman's meander across our reception area, so I went back into my office and sat down at my desk. Blakeslee had a frown on his face with a matching squint that made me think he was going blind.

When Foreman finally made it to the door, I stood up to introduce the two, though I suspected they already knew each other. The next ten seconds felt like a firecracker went off and a new universe exploded out of it.

Blakeslee yelled, "That's not Foreman!"

Foreman's eyes grew big and I followed his gaze to Blakeslee. Blakeslee already had his hand in his jacket. I could see him pulling a gun out.

"Whoa! Blakeslee, what the…"

The first shot came from Foreman. My head snapped back to him. He looked more scared than I felt. The second shot came from Blakeslee and plaster started dropping down on my head almost immediately. I turned back to Blakeslee in time to see him catch three more bullets with his chest, fall over the chair he

■ ● ■

had been sitting in and take his last shot when he hit the floor, missing my foot, but blowing one of the casters off my desk chair.

When I looked back at the doorway Foreman was gone. For a second I felt I was having an out of body experience. My ears were ringing, but I thought I heard the main entrance door open. I became aware of myself standing in a slight crouch behind my desk. My arms were extended straight out in front of me. My palms were facing the doorway like I was trying to block stones thrown at me by some little kid. I stood there frozen, feeling like an idiot. In the next second I felt like the sanitation department had dumped half a ton of raw shit on top of my head.

Rage finally broke through. I ripped open the bottom drawer to my desk and popped the button Mojica had installed that dropped a Colt down to where I could grab it.

I ran out of our office like I was going to catch somebody who was probably already in the next state if he had a moderately slow car. Out in the hallway I tried to push the stairwell door open. It was blocked. I looked at the elevator bank. One car was on the ground floor and one was on the way up, so obviously he ran down the stairs.

I walked back into the office reception area and stood on the carpet staring at my open office door. I glanced at Andy's office next to mine. He had stacks of books. He had clocks and photos. He had a chess set on a small table in the corner. I looked into Sharp's office and it was like looking at a page from *Good House-keeping – Southwestern Edition*. He had framed black and white photos of the Rio Grande and a few arroyos. There was a beautiful Mexican tapestry on the wall. He had really nice wooden furniture. Mojica's office had so much stuff in it that it looked like a five and dime, but it sure felt organized. There was so much stuff you felt like you wanted to go in, sit down, and just look

■ ● ■

around. My eyes wandered over the reception area. Elaine made it look like you were actually walking into some place important. The rug was impressive. Her computer made us look serious. She had art prints on all of the walls and managed to mix in framed posters of Eugene Debs and Frederick Douglass, which I had to admit, I did appreciate. I still wondered how much she had spent fixing the place up. Then I looked at my office knowing all I had in mine was a desk, three chairs, one small filing cabinet and a dead guy lying in a pool of blood under a large, arched window.

I sat down on my quasi-partner, kind of secretary, Elaine's desk. She was at lunch or I never would have sat there. I picked up her phone and punched in the number for the police. I stared out the reception area window and thought that for some reason it didn't seem like it was very warm out. The desk sergeant listened to my story and told me not to leave.

I heard the elevator door open and close. The thought crossed my mind, 'How could they get here that fast?' I realized it was Elaine's footsteps coming quickly. They slowed down and then they stopped just outside the office door. Elaine's head popped in and out and in. She sniffed the air, came in slowly with her hand inside her backpack. She stopped about three feet away from me and whispered, "What's going on?"

I stood up, turned my back on her and walked to my office. Elaine followed until she pulled up beside me in the doorway. We stood there for a few moments in silence. Blakeslee was on his back with a pistol in his right hand. Maybe a Beretta, or a knock-off. His right leg hung over the wooden chair and I was surprised at how bright his sky blue socks were. Or did they seem bright next to the blood pooling by the wall? It was the first time I noticed that the floor was uneven.

"Was he a client?"

"Yeah…he's already paid up front." I kept looking at Blakeslee

■ ● ■

and then noticed that Elaine was staring at me with a frown.

"Even though I'm glad his bill was paid in advance, I was more wondering if you knew who he was. And I'd really like to know why he's lying dead in your office?"

"Where'd you want him to be dead, Elaine? Out in the reception area next to your desk where all the other bodies ended up?"

Elaine walked away from me toward her desk. "Well, Mr. Jerk, did you call this in?"

"Already called."

She stopped suddenly, turned around and walked back over to me with her hand out.

"What?"

"Since you are one of the only two black detectives in town, I suggest you give me your weapon before the boys in blue get here."

I handed her my gun. Puzzled, I asked, "Who's the other one?"

She looked at me like I was mostly dumb.

"Raoul."

"Raoul? He doesn't even have a license."

"Doesn't seem like he needs one, does it? And I think you should sit on the couch. I'd hate to have them come up with a reason to shoot the only witness."

"Reason?! If I sit down they might shoot me for intent to stand up."

I gave her half a smile and crossed the room to our waiting room couch. Now I could hear the elevators coming and I began to dread the idea of spending the afternoon answering questions for the police.

When the first two uniforms came through the door, Elaine was on the phone with Andy. "You better get back here as soon as you can. We have a body in the office and the clowns just got

■ ● ■

here."

One of the cops I recognized immediately. I was surprised at how long it took him to yell at me. All of about four seconds. My acquaintance from the bakery, ol' Officer Somebody.

"You! Stand up over there and put both hands on the wall!"

As I stood I noticed Elaine sit down and bend over slowly to make sure the video recorder was on. Neither of the boys in blue seemed to notice.

"Get them up!"

"Not even going to ask what happened, are you?"

"I said get them up!"

The other patrolman finally spoke. "There was a call about a shooting."

Elaine craned her neck toward my office. "Dead guy back in the corner office."

"Why don't you get up and show me."

Elaine got out of her chair and walked back to my room. The cop passed her while she stood at the doorway. I could hear him calling in a homicide on his radio.

My cop. My dear old racist friend from the bakery patted me down. He grabbed one arm and twisted it behind my back. I heard the metallic click of the cuffs as he snapped one end on.

Elaine turned and got loud in about a second. "What the hell are you doing? He didn't shoot the guy!"

"Shut up!"

The second cop came out of my office to announce that my former client was definitely dead. I could feel the cuffs going on much tighter than they needed to be. Then I got a punch in the kidneys with Officer Somebody's gun butt. He pushed me to the floor with his knee. Calvin Livingston. That was his name. Good ol' Calvin.

Elaine went ballistic. "What the fuck do you think you're

doing, you bastard. He didn't do a damn thing and…"

"Cuff her, Dave!"

"You sons of bitches! You think you'll get away with this?!"

Officer Dave put cuffs on Elaine and pushed her back over to her desk.

"Sit down. You keep your voice down or I will take you down to the station and keep you overnight. Wouldn't that be inconvenient?"

Elaine sat down and summed up the situation for him.

"Fuck you, you pussy bitches."

I couldn't help myself. "That's really, really sexist, Elaine, and demeaning to women." Elaine started to laugh until Officer Calvin put his foot on my neck and said, "Shut up, darkie."

Elaine jumped up cursing. Officer Dave said, "Well, that's enough of that so we'll be taking you in." Elaine's cop grabbed the middle of her cuffs and lifted. Elaine breathed out heavy, "You bastard." He lifted higher.

"You want to say anything else besides 'I'm sorry'?"

From my position on the floor it looked like Elaine's eyes started to tear and at first I thought she was going to apologize. She nodded her head and the cop let her arms down a little.

"Fuck you, you pimply, puss-faced racist cocksucker!" He pulled up hard and Elaine screamed in pain.

"Was it worth it? Huh? Are you done now?"

"Go ahead, bitch…break my arm. Owwww!

"Don't have to do that. How'd that feel?"

Officer Somebody wasn't paying too much attention to me now. He was watching the show with Elaine and his partner, so the pressure of his shoe on my neck was kind of relaxed. I wanted to tell Elaine to shut up, but by the way she was acting I was pretty sure she thought she was on the fast path to martyrdom and she didn't want to be slowed down any.

■ ● ■

With all of the excitement and Elaine's hollering, no one heard the elevator until the doors closed. It got real quiet. I could hear the one step shuffle and I knew it was Sharp. He came through the office door, cane first, and then stopped at the edge of the carpet.

Officer Calvin said, "Who the hell are you?"

Sharp smiled with one corner of his mouth and said, "I'm someone who pays cash money rent to walk into my office here whenever I want to."

"You have identification?"

Sharp broke into a full smile, "Of course I do and why the hell are you resting your spit-shine Florsheims on my associate's neck?! Move that foot!"

Very deliberately the shoe slid to the floor.

"And now, if you want to see my I.D., I'll reach for it here in the front of my jacket."

I wondered if it was the Texas accent that had my cop mesmerized, or if he was intimidated by Sharp's stare. Whatever it was, it always amazed me that people seemed to act when Sharp spoke.

Officer Somebody walked over to Sharp to look at his I.D. He started nodding his head and Sharp said, "Look, I'm going into my office to make a phone call, if that's okay." The officer nodded some more and then walked back over to me. Sharp stopped in the doorway to his office and asked, "By the way, did either of you shoot or maim anybody?"

I said, "No."

Officer Somebody said, "We don't know that. We have a body in the room over there and we don't know who did what."

Sharp's laugh sounded like a knife cutting someone's neck. He disappeared into his office and I could hear him punching the phone. After a few moments I heard Sharp say, "Louise, how

■ ● ■

are you?...Ah'm getting' better, leg feels better, but this here is kind of an emergency. We have two cracker policemen in my office roughing up two of my partners and we need Mr. Daniels or one of his associates over here quick to bring some righteous sanity back to our part of the western hemisphere...Ah would appreciate that greatly."

Sharp walked back out into the reception area and leaned on his cane with a smile.

My cop was apparently angry. "Fuck you, gimp. Sit down over there."

Sharp was still smiling. "You know what? You dumb, boy... just dirt ass dumb. Not a pebble up in there, is there?" Sharp sat down. "Some day, maybe soon, you are going to meet me somewhere when you are not in uniform."

"Are you threatening me? I'm a police officer, gimp."

Sharp smiled.

Officer Somebody's face went red. "Are you threatening me?!"

"The basic rudiments of the English language escape you, don't they? You dumb, boy." Sharp shook his head like he felt really, really bad. "You just plain dirt dumb."

■ ● ■

Glass

I watched him sitting on the edge of the bed. His back was
sweaty. His elbows were on his knees and he was holding his
hands together. He was looking at the floor. I'd seen this pose
about a hundred times before. He craned his head back so he
could look at the ceiling. Seen a lot of guys do that, too.

He stood up and pulled his wallet out of his back pocket.
He's already paid, so what's he doin'? Maybe he's going to give
me a tip. Jesus Christ. Or maybe he's checkin' to see if I robbed
him some way while he was layin' on top of me. He was gentle
though. As big as he is, I wasn't expectin' that.

Why's he keep running his fingers over the edge of the window?

"What's with the window?"

"The window is screwed closed."

So fuckin' what, I'm wonderin'. Damn. Now he's got tears
runnin' down his face. What the hell? Is he gonna tell me I
remind him of his mother or some fuckin' thing? Or worse yet,
he'll say somethin' stupid, like he wants to marry me. Why'd he
put his wallet on that rickety little table? Oh, shit.

"You okay?"

■ ● ■

"Nah. You know why?"

I have no idea, but I feel better now that he's sliding his feet into his shoes. I thought he had some crazy idea about jumping. But if the window won't open, I don't have to worry about that.

"You know why I'm not okay?"

"No." Looks like he turned off the tear faucet, but I don't like that he's walking toward me now. Might be time to get out the mace or start running. He's really starting to look weird.

"Because I'll never make it to heaven. You're about as close to heaven as I will ever be."

I need to get my stuff and get out of here. Damn…now he's smilin'.

"Thank you for letting me see what heaven might have looked like."

Yep; you; God; St. Peter; the local prostitute…fuck my stuff! Time to go! I'm leavin'.

He's turned away from me. Let me grab my stuff. Oh shit! He's runnin' at the window and he dives right through the glass. I can see the soles of his shoes as he goes through the window. I can still see his shoes. How's that?! His one leg is caught on something. He's hanging there. Should I try to pull him back in? I start to walk over to the window, but he's kicking with one foot and spraying glass around the room.

"Hold on! I'll help you. Stop kickin'." He's pushing with one foot against the ledge. I can hear cloth ripping. I reach for his foot and his shoe falls on the floor. I think he says "No," and then he's gone. Fuck! I pick up his shoe by the shoelace. It starts to twirl. I hang it outside the window. Then I drop it after him.

What the hell am I doing?! I gotta get out of here. Take the wallet, stupid. Take the wallet.

I throw the wallet in my bag and grab my jacket. Maybe I should grab the condom out of the trash. I think about it for

■ ● ■

about two seconds, and then I grab the condom, the wrapper and drop them in my bag. I'll have to clean my bag out later. Stop looking around. Get out of here, stupid! Just get out!

The hall is empty and dark. Empty 'cause it's two o'clock in the afternoon. Dark 'cause the cheap bastards who run this place won't invest in some 60 watt light bulbs.

Damn! The elevator is coming up. Take the stairs, stupid. Take the stairs.

I'm going down the stairwell as fast as I can, and of course, I gotta' fucking trip. I grab the railing with both hands, but I'm almost upside down. My head is about six inches from the stairs. I pull myself back up and I'm bouncing down the stairs two at a time. At the ground floor I stand still, bent over, trying to catch my breath. I have to pee, damn it! I push the door open just a little to look in the lobby. Nobody. I push the door wider and I see someone run past the entrance door out on the sidewalk.

I walk through the lobby past the clerk's desk. He's gone. He's probably outside with the gazers. I go out the door and turn left, away from the crowd. I can see the diner four blocks down. I'll piss there and get a coffee. Wait for the crowd to evaporate.

As I cross the street, I look back at the crowd of people and someone is pointing in my direction. I turn my head and keep going. Where the fuck is Louie when you need him?

I need one more block to make it to the diner. I glance over my shoulder and two guys in ties are crossing the street a couple of blocks back. Shit!

In the diner the first person I see is that drunk, Jocko. Is he the only one in here? I grab a napkin and write down Louie's number. Where the hell is Holly?

"Well, well, well. Good afternoon, Madam. How is the transitory emotional therapy worker doing this afternoon? It's a pleasure to see your radiant eyes smiling at…"

■ ● ■

"Shut up, Jocko. Is Holly working today?"

There's Holly coming out of the kitchen fixing her hair that looks like shit.

"Holly, can you let me out the back and call Louie for me and…"

"I'm not getting involved in anything you're involved in."

"Come on! Don't shake your fuckin' head."

There's Jocko starin' up at me with those runny eyes. "Jocko, take this and call the number and tell somebody I need help at DeForest and Third."

"Just somebody or…"

"Shut the fuck up, Jocko! Don't let anybody see that note. Make the call in ten minutes. You got that?!"

"Of course, darling. I can…"

I grab Holly by the arm. "I'll give you ten dollars to unlock the back door and let me out."

Holly snatches the ten, shakes my hand off and says, "Come on."

When we go to the back I hear Lester holler. "Hey, Lisa. What the hell are you doing back here?"

I turn to look at him and see he has a huge smile on his face. "I'm going to see you on Friday, honey."

"I'm probably all booked up."

"Oh come on. You haven't been booked up since grade schoo'."

"Fuck you, Lester. Holly, let me out of here and don't give the cops my name."

Holly is looking at me like I have flies pourin' out of my mouth. She unlocks the back door and I slide out into the alley. I pull a garbage can over to the fence at the end of the alley and turn it upside down. Then I run to the entrance to the alley and peek around the corner just in time to hear the screen door

■ ● ■

of the diner slam shut. I run next door to Phipps Taxi Service. Standing in the garage entranceway, a voice behind me makes me jump.

"Hey, Lisa!" Billie Neale starts laughing.

"Shit, Billie. You scared the hell out of me."

"What the heck are you whispering for?"

I peeked out at the diner. "You got a cab in there?"

"Yeah. Two that don't run right now. Everybody else is out on the street."

"Damn it."

"You hiding from someone?"

I looked up at Billie, who was now standing about two feet away from me.

"Yeah."

"A guy?"

"A couple of them."

"Heck, I can take care of that if it's just two guys. No big deal."

I turned my eyes back to the diner as I spoke. "I think they're cops, Billie." When I glanced behind me, I saw Billie was already about fifteen feet away heading back to his mechanic's bench.

I heard the metal screech of the diner's back door. I ducked back into the shadows by some old empty kerosene barrels. I heard the cry of the diner's screen door as it opened. After a few seconds I could hear their voices. I couldn't understand what the first one said. The other one said, "I think she may have gone over the fence."

"Let's go get the car then. Maybe we can spot her." They were coming closer.

"Not if she lives in the neighborhood…or has a place to hide around here."

"Maybe she's in this dump."

■ ● ■

I could see Billie walking back up the ramp toward the garage door.

"Hey, fella's. Need a cab?"

"Nah. You see a girl run past here or maybe heard someone in here a little while ago? You know...got her a cab?"

I was afraid to breathe. I could see Billie shakin' his head.

"Haven't seen anyone. I did hear a small ruckus in the alley a little while ago. Couple a cats screamin' and a garbage can got knocked over, I guess."

One of them said, "Heard all that from inside there, huh?"

"Fuck no. I was standing where you're standing. I needed some air. You a cop or somethin'?"

"We're 'or somethin'.'"

"Oh yeah? What's 'or somethin'?"

"FBI."

"Okay then. If you don't need a cab, I'm back to work."

I watched Billie walk back down the ramp toward his work bench.

One of the two guys said, "Stupid, greasy bohunk. Do you think we should look around this dump?"

"Nah. He's probably too stupid to lie. Let's go back in the diner and see if we can get a name."

I thought I could hear them walk away. I was listening hard and then, "That's not a very good hiding spot." I banged into the barrels and it sounded like the roof was coming down.

"God damn it, Billie. Why the hell are you scaring me like that?!"

"It's fun?"

"Drop dead." I brushed myself off. "Are they gone?"

"I don't know. Maybe they went back in the diner."

"Well, could you go look?!"

"Sure, Lisa."

■ ● ■

Billie came back in about two seconds.

"You didn't even look in the diner!"

"Didn't have to. They're about two blocks down on the other side of the street. They're heading for the crowd out in front of the Dixon. Looks like an ambulance and a couple of cop cars. You know what happened down there?"

"Why the hell would I know?"

"You're in there enough to know everything that's going on in there. Two FBI agents are looking for you. You're hiding back in the kerosene cans in a dark corner. You must know something about something."

I tiptoed over to the garage door.

"They're gone, Lisa."

"I'll see you, Billie. I wasn't here, okay?"

"Sure."

I ran for the alley and stopped to look in my bag. I pulled out the condom and the wrapper and dropped them on the ground. I took out the wallet, pulled the bills and threw most everything else away. Credit cards are always a problem. I snapped the wallet closed and dropped it in a small pile of trash. I hurried over to the trash can and climbed up. I hiked my skirt up to my waist, hooked my leg on the top of the fence and pulled myself up. Then the applause started. I lost my balance for a second and almost fell. I looked back up the alley and there was Billie, clapping his hands with a big grin on his face.

"Hope you liked the show, asshole."

"Lookin' good, girl. Lookin' good."

I shot him the finger and dropped down to the other side.

■ ● ■

Jocko

It was 7:30 now. The police and forensics were gone. The others had talked things over for a couple of hours. I didn't seem to have much to say. We looked at the video tape a few times and I struggled with being furious each time. Apparently the machine had been recording even when Blakeslee came in. So now we were all familiar with what Foreman looked like, and which cop did what. Elaine said we should take the video to the papers and T.V. stations so that the city could see how their police force treated its citizens. I wasn't sure I wanted the whole city to see me on the floor with a cop's boot on my neck.

Petrulich said we should turn the tape over to the police as soon as possible so that we weren't accused of withholding evidence. Andy wanted to know how quickly Mojica could make a dub. Heeks said he'd have two done in an hour. Petrulich and Andy said they'd deliver one as soon as the first one was finished. Everybody had a lot to say, except me and Sharp. Sharp talked, but I think he was sitting there with both hands on top of his cane waiting for me to say something. So I said I needed to take a walk. Everybody looked at me. Sharp nodded his head, looked away and I walked out.

■ ● ■

I took the stairs down because I didn't have the patience for the elevator. I went through the lobby and had my usual flashback to the shootout where we almost lost Sharp. When I got to the sidewalk I really started thinking about the cop standing on my neck, like I was his hunting trophy. I had a hard time thinking that people would see me in that position. Then I thought about the Freedom Riders and I started to feel ashamed. They got the shit kicked out of them and a lot of them went back for more. Here I was thinking about being embarrassed because people would see some cracker cop holding me down with his foot. 'Grow up, tough guy. You can't always be tough.'

I wandered on the sidewalk for a little and then stopped in front of the store that still had a Robot Commando in the window. Somebody had put a sign by its feet that said, "Vintage." Next to it an old black and white television was playing. It looked like Reagan was giving a speech. The T.V. had a sign that said, "Like New!" I was close to laughing, but I had to admit, the reception was really sharp.

I slapped my right arm against my leg and looked around. I decided to walk to my favorite diner, "Jackie's. If it wasn't for my anticipated destination, the stroll would have been depressing. Most of the streets on the way were grey quiet. They gave you the feeling the city was abandoned. In reality it was only an early evening Wednesday. But for a few blocks it felt like the city had no light in it. Everyone was just waiting for black...and was intent upon hiding from it.

After about twenty minutes I could see "Jackie's," about six blocks away. The street lights were finally coming on and two blocks in front of me was the Dixon Hotel. There were a few guys out on the sidewalk, which seemed odd. Usually everybody was inside doing what they did, or everybody went some place else. The Dixon wasn't the kind of place where people congregat-

■ ● ■

ed out in front to invite police activity.

Someone came out the front door with a bucket and threw water on the sidewalk. The men out front danced out of the way while screaming at the bucketeer. As I got closer I could see it was one of the night clerks and now he was swearing and pointing up the street and then down. The men started moving away while the night clerk stood in the doorway to the hotel.

A couple of the men passed me, each one muttering to the other at the same time. I noticed the water in the gutter had a pink tinge to it. The clerk I recognized as a real jerk from a time when Andy and I needed some information. Of course, maybe if I worked ridiculous hours I would act like a jerk, too. But I guess I just acted that way with normal hours.

But I was curious. I stopped in front of the clerk thinking he might look at me, and give me a little information.

"What happened?"

"Gee, Nosey...Ya' missed the show?"

I was kind of taken aback. He still wasn't looking at me and I felt like grabbing him by the neck and dropping him in the gutter unconscious. My right hand turned into a fist.

"Yeah. I guess I did. What was the act?"

The clerk finally looked at me with disgust and frustration swirling on his face.

"A guy did a half gainer through a sixth floor window and tried to land on the soft part of the sidewalk. He missed."

I wanted to say something, but whatever I had to say wouldn't be appropriate. Even if I said I was having a bad day too, I doubt I could say anything that would dent his. With the women worried about the cops being around, business would go elsewhere and the clerk wouldn't get his cut.

"Sorry." I turned to finish my walk to Jackie's.

"Sorry for what?!"

■ ● ■

I turned back to him.

"You're right." I started off for the diner again. Behind me I heard, "Pfft." The middle finger he was flashing me probably wasn't worth the effort.

The screen door to Jackie's diner screeched as I pulled it open. I stepped in and immediately saw Jocko staring at me from a booth. He looked strange. He actually looked like he wasn't drunk. I half-smiled and he waved me over.

I walked over kind of slow. "What's up, Jocko?"

He looked around like he was lost and didn't expect to see himself here.

"I believe I need to talk with you or one of your associates."

"Okay. Let me order a coffee. You want something?"

"Any fluids of any kind may disrupt my thought process at the moment." He looked up at me like he was scared. "You know, I'm not used to this way of feeling. It's frightening."

I noticed his hands were trembling. "Be right back." I took a step toward the counter and looked back over my shoulder at Jocko. Somewhere he had borrowed a serious frown from someone. I really wanted to know what had him so shook up. "Where's Holly, Jocko? She out back?"

"I believe she has gone home for the evening. Margot is in the restroom."

Margot suddenly burst out of the Ladies room at the far end of the hall past the counter. She reminded me of the woman who gets shot from the cannon in the circus. She was brushing the wrinkles out of her lime green uniform, and then she ran both hands down the sides of her face while looking at the floor.

"I'm sorry. Sorry. What would you like?"

Nobody wanted to look at me it seemed. I smiled. "A 'Hi.

■ ● ■

How are you?' maybe?"

She finally made eye contact and her head snapped back.

"Oh! I'm sorry. Sorry. I didn't know it was you. What would you like?"

"Just a coffee, Margot."

"Sure. Okay. You want me to bring it over to you?"

"Nah. I can wait."

"Okay. I'll bring it over there to you."

"Then I won't be able to get it since I'll be over here waiting."

"Huh?"

I smiled at her.

"Never mind, Margot. Bring it over to me. I'll be the guy sitting across from Jocko."

Margot strained her neck around me so she could see him. "Really?"

"You know what? Wherever I'm sitting, just bring the coffee there, okay?"

"Sure."

I moved over to Jocko's booth trying to make my eyebrows fall back to their normal position after the exchange with Margot.

"So what's up Jock?" He must have been home at some point during the day. His body stench was mild so he must have remembered to shower.

He looked around the diner again and then said, "I believe I have lost my faith in humanity."

I chuckled. "You told me that, years ago."

"Today confirmed it."

"Is that why you're sober…or close to it?"

In response Jocko slid a small pile of cards across the table to me, then pulled them back as Margot put a cup of coffee and the cream in front of me. When she walked away, Jocko pushed

■ ● ■

the same pile over to me again.

I started to say 'what's up?', but instead I scanned the driver's license on top. I slid that off and an I.D. purporting to be issued by the F.B.I. appeared. I looked up at Jocko. He pointed to the stack of cards.

"This is why I needed to talk to you."

The name on the F.B.I. badge matched the driver's license. I slid that off the pile and turned it over. Next was an I.D. from the U.S. State Department. I picked up the F.B.I. card and compared photos. Same guy; different names. Then a Diner's Club credit card matching the driver's license. Then another driver's license with a new name. A University of Chicago staff I.D. Another name, same face, matched the second driver's license.

"Where'd you get these, Jocko?"

"Out in the alley."

"Right here, by the taxi garage?"

He nodded.

"How'd you manage to find these? Did you see something?"

Jocko clenched both hands in fists and then spread his fingers out flat on the table.

"Maybe I should have that coffee."

"Hey, Margot." Margot did a little hop back from the counter and spilled sugar all over the counter while trying to fill a sugar shaker. She looked all around the diner and then said, "Yes?"

"Can we have another coffee over here and a grilled cheese sandwich?"

"You want it over there?"

Jocko whispered, "Sad, isn't it? She's such a sweet child."

I glanced at Jocko and then turned back to Margot. "Yes, Margot. Over here."

"Sure."

Two men walked into the diner after the screen door

■ ● ■

screamed. Jocko put his hand over the pile of cards.

"I don't think we should be indiscreet." He pulled the pile to his side of the table and laid his arms over the cards.

"Jocko..." I watched the two men sit down at the counter. "Where'd you get these?"

"I thought I told you. In the alley."

"What were you doing in the alley?"

"Looking for Lisa."

I leaned back in the booth staring at Jocko. Margot brought over a new coffee and put it on the table. "Who is this for?"

"For him."

"Sure."

I watched Margot walk away. "Lisa who?"

"Lisa. The pretty woman of the night. Holly's sister."

One of the two men at the counter said, "That's a lot of sugar." Whatever Margot said made the two men laugh. Margot moved behind the counter looking confused at her own joke.

I turned back to Jocko, who had a pint bottle of Irish whiskey leaning over his coffee cup.

"Jocko, you can't wait with that a little so you can tell me your story first?"

"I don't think I should. I believe the story will have more flow if I have some coffee to steady my nerves."

I sighed. "Just tell me the story, will ya'?"

I watched Jocko take a satisfying swallow of coffee. He pulled the bottle back out of his jacket pocket. I reached across the table and snatched the bottle from his hand. Jocko's mouth opened and he stared at me like I had slapped his mother.

"Tell me the story, Jocko, or I'm going to accidentally drop this bottle on the floor."

"But I needed to make more room in the cup."

"Don't put so much cream in next time. Tell me the story and

■ ● ■

you can have bottle back. Where'd you get this stuff?"

"At Delphino's over on…"

"Not the damn bottle." I shuffled through the cards again. A credit card I missed that didn't match the names on either license popped out at me. The name matched an I.D. for 'International Land Surveyors,' with addresses for San Francisco and Langley, Virginia.

"Well, I was sitting at that table and Lisa came in very quickly. I greeted her, but she was looking for Holly. She asked Holly to call Luis for her…"

"You mean Louie…Louie the pimp?"

"I guess so, now that you've reminded me. Holly refused and then Lisa wrote down a number on a napkin and handed it to me with a handful of change and told me to call that number in ten minutes and I was to say she needed help at Third and Dorchester and…"

"Take a breath, Jock."

He frowned at me and took a swallow of his coffee.

"Lisa gave Holly ten dollars to let her out the back and asked her not to tell the police she had been here. They went out the back and seconds later two men came in. They asked Holly where Lisa went and Holly just hooked her thumb over her shoulder. A woman in need…her sister…and she's ratted out like a fleeing Jew in Nazi Berlin! And you wonder why I have lost all faith in humanity. I…"

"Finish the story, Jocko."

"I am pointed in that general direction if you could refrain from interruptions."

"They knew Lisa by name?"

"No. They just asked where the blonde had gone."

A woman came in and sat in the booth farthest away from us. Jocko tilted his head and stared at her. I snapped my fingers

■ ● ■

in front of Jocko's face. He looked at me like he forgot who I was. I opened the bottle of Irish and poured a slug into Jocko's cup.

"Ahhh…so you finally noticed the beans were a little weak."

"Jocko…"

"Oh yes. One man was lead to the back of the kitchen by Holly and the other one went out the front. I waited ten minutes and then walked down the street to the phone booth. I saw the men talking to Billie the mechanic in the garage. Then they left. Billie came back outside while I was walking back from the phone booth. Mere seconds later Lisa ran out of the garage and went down the alley. Billie walked over to the entrance to the alley and started applauding for some unseen reason."

Jocko took a long slug from his coffee. "It is still a very weak cup of coffee, if you've noticed." Jocko stared at me and I stared at him. "Billie went back into his garage. When I got close to the alley I could see a crowd and police cars outside the Dixon Hotel. A man passed me and told me someone went out a very high window in an unauthorized manner. He thought it was a suicide. But I started to wonder if someone thought it wasn't suicide. I went into the alley and managed to find a discarded wallet and the stack of cards you are currently fondling."

"Did the cops come back or ask you any questions?"

Jocko took another slug of his coffee and shook his head. "It's gone. I could have extended the life of that cup of coffee if you had let me have my bottle of invigoration."

"Christ, Jocko. Hey, Margot." She jumped again. At least she wasn't pouring anything. "Could you bring half a cup of coffee over here for Jocko, please."

Jocko looked at me with a frown on his face that seemed to run down to his chin.

"What? Not enough room? And why do you keep calling

■ ● ■

them the two men?"

"Well, I don't think they were police."

"Why do you say that?"

"Years of experience."

Margot put a full cup of coffee in front of Jocko.

"How disappointing…she missed all of her elementary school classes on liquid measures."

I poured half of Jocko's coffee into my cup and slid the bottle of whiskey across the table.

Why don't you think they were cops?"

"Well…I don't think they asked many questions of Holly. I did hear the one who went out the back ask Holly if she knew where Lisa lived. Holly just said 'nope.' And then they never came back in to ask anyone, namely me, any questions."

"Maybe they thought you were a drunk."

Jocko looked hurt. He looked at me over his doctored cup of coffee which he held about six inches from his mouth.

"Nevertheless, my instincts tell me that neither of them were police officers. Especially when I found those identity cards and put them in my pocket…maybe it wasn't suicide."

I leaned back from the table. I had to admit, my curiosity was piqued. Jocko stood up and told me it was time to find more verbose company. I guessed the coffee had done its damage. I suggested he go home and sleep. He told me he didn't want to wear out his bed, plus he had to acknowledge his civic duty. I went to pay the check while I watched Jocko shuffle out of the diner on his way to some serious drinking. Margot told me the total. I looked at her.

"That's expensive coffee, Margot."

She stared at me.

"I never got the grilled cheese."

"You didn't?! Oh! I'm so sorry. I could bring it over to you."

■ ● ■

I smiled. "This is me leaving. How about we make it the tip."

When she smiled, Margot had a great smile. "That's very generous of you."

■ ● ■

Louie

"Put that shit down!"

"Christ, Louie, I didn't damage anything."

"You might'a fucked up the game. You don't play with my chess."

"I'm sorry. But I'm telling you, Louie, I don't think I should go back out there yet."

"And Bitch, I'm telling you that you need to get your ass back out on the street. We have expenses to meet."

"Well, maybe I should go over on the other side of town."

"Maisy, Patty and D'Sheba are over there and you are going to shake your ass back out there to where I tell you. Get it?!"

Louie slapped me so hard I thought I'd have a bruise on my face. I couldn't help it, but I started to cry.

"You didn't need to do that. Fuck, Louie. That fucking hurt."

Louie stepped toward me and I put up my arms to try to stop him from hitting me again. Instead he grabbed my arms and pulled me close to him. Then he put his arms around me and squeezed me.

"Come on. Don't cry. You know you're my favorite."

"Then why'd you hit me, Louie?"

■ ● ■

"Damn girl. Sometimes you make me so mad. You don't recognize the pressures I got on me. I thought you were supporting
me. And then you act like you don't care if I live or die. This is a
rough business and I gots to have your support. It's like you don't
care what happens to me."

"That's not true. I care what happens to you."

"But it's got to be all the time, baby. Can you do that for me?
Be my support all the time?"

I nodded my head on Louie's shoulder.

"All the time?"

"Yeah."

"Then we have to get the money right and I need you to go
out there and do some business, okay?"

"Yeah."

"Winch'll be out on the street tonight. If there's any problems,
he'll call me and I get it straightened out."

"I don't wanna spend any time in the tank tonight, Louie. I'm
not in a mind to handle that shit."

"Give me a kiss, baby. Winch'll be out there watching. Don't
worry about it."

Louie hugged me hard and I knew I was his favorite when I
kissed him. Then he wiped the tears on my face.

"Okay, baby?"

I nodded.

■ ● ■

Cards

I stepped out through the screeching screen door of the diner wondering where they kept the WD-40. I looked around at the night and watched a cab pull up to the curb in front of me. Three familiar faces climbed out. Andy, Elaine and lastly, Sharp.

"What are the three of you doing here? Something else bad happen while I was gone?"

Andy put both hands on his hips. "You're simply not glad to see us?"

"Only in a mild sort of way and where's fucking Mojica?"

It was Elaine's turn. "We were concerned about you after that fascist cop was standing on your neck and I suggested we give a copy of the tape to the T.V. stations. I know I almost had my arms broken on tape, but having some racist boy in blue standing on your neck is a lot different…obviously. If you don't want the T.V. stations to have the tape, we won't give it to them."

Andy crossed his arms. "How are you feeling?"

I smiled. "A little mixed right now. I haven't thought about what happened for the last half hour, if you can believe that. Actually I'm glad you're here. Let's go back inside."

We weren't even sitting when I heard Elaine say, "Margot?

■ ● ■

Margot, is that you?!"

And then there was such a high pitched squeal, I almost covered my ears with my shoulders. "Eeelaine! Oh my God!" Margot ran from behind the counter like she was flying out of the Ladies Room. They embraced in the center of the diner with Margot continuing to squeal like a bad fire alarm. I glanced at Andy, who sat down staring at the minor pandemonium with his eyebrows raised. I looked at Sharp who was wearing a crooked smile. He winked at me and murmured, "Babysitter."

I laughed. "Get the hell out'a here."

The squealing stopped and Margot exclaimed, "Elaine was my babysitter until I was like twelve!"

Elaine asked, "How long have you been here?"

"About two years. I'm workin' to work my way out west."

"West? Like California?"

"Uh-uh. Oregon. I heard Portland is really nice."

From the far end of the counter someone said, "Will I be able to get a cup of coffee tonight?"

"Oh. Elaine, I better get back to work. I'll give you my address and maybe we can catch up."

"Sure, Margot."

Elaine came over to the booth with a huge smile on her face. "Used to babysit for her. Five years. Haven't seen her in like eight. She must be 26...no, 27 now."

"So, guys...what do we do with the tapes?" Andy looked at each of us and then folded his hands on the booth table top.

Sharp spoke first. "Probably not good for running business if your face is on T.V. ten times in a week. On the other hand, something like this is bigger than our business."

Elaine jumped in like Sharp had said something wrong. "Yeah, it's fucking bigger than our business! We have to take a stand against this kind of bullshit and expose these bastards for

■ ● ■

the fascists that they are." Elaine looked right at me. "Plus your face is always sideways on the video. Nobody'll recognize you."

Margot appeared suddenly and put a plate in front of me with a grilled cheese sandwich on it. She said, "Sorry. I'm really sorry." She smiled at Elaine and walked away.

Sharp started laughing. "When did you order that? I didn't notice you order that."

"About a week ago. Look…I know a person can feel some humiliation when something like that happens. I guess that's what I was feeling a little. At the same time it can be a badge of honor if you survive…even though I didn't do anything but be black. A lot of people have gone through a lot worse than what I went through this afternoon." I glanced at Elaine. "If that cop hadn't been trying to hurt you with the cuffs I think I might have felt like I was alone. I'm not happy he was trying to hurt you, but I felt like we were resisting together. I was angry as hell and it is kind of humiliating to be on the ground with some bastard standing on your neck laughing at you because he temporarily has the power. I think maybe I was trying to deal with the humiliation part by leaving and walking over here. The anger part is still percolating somewhere. Let's send the tape to the T.V. stations. But don't kid yourself. The Black community will watch their sets with their heads at a right angle in every house north of Dorchester Road. They'll all want to know who it was the police were trying to abuse. What do you think, Andy?"

"If you feel comfortable with it, I think it's important for the entire city to see what happened. We should realize that once the stations play the tape…if they play the tape, we're not going to have many friends left on the police force."

Elaine said, "Do we have any right now?"

I shook my head slowly. "A few." Everyone now looked like the serious conversation was over. "Hey. Don't get comfortable.

■ ● ■

I want you guys to look at something. Jocko found these out in the alley. He thinks they were thrown there by a working girl named Lisa."

Sharp looked over the small pile and handed them to Andy. "This looks like somebody in some kinda' deep cover, with good connections and a lot of business to take care of."

"Jocko told me there was a suicide this afternoon down at the Dixon Hotel. Only, if this stuff is connected it might not be a suicide."

"Elaine. Do you think you can get your charge, Margot, to come over here and take an order? One cheese sandwich at our table that is now half gone is making me very hungry." Andy smiled at Elaine.

"You never been in a diner before, Andy? You could wave your arms or something."

"Y'all can't be more hungry than me, so try to be pleasant to each other. Elaine started to stand up. Sharp hollered, "Hey, Margot! Would you come over here, please!"

Elaine turned around and glared at Sharp. "What the hell did you do that for?! Scared the heck out of me.

"Hungry."

"I've never known you to be rude before."

"Never been this hungry before."

Andy started chuckling.

"That was a really good grilled cheese. Has my recommendation."

Elaine turned back toward the counter to find Margot's face about two inches away from hers. Elaine almost jumped onto the table.

"God damn, Margot. You haven't done that in a long time."

"Done what?"

We all laughed. Elaine glared at us and then broke into a

■ ● ■

smile, shaking her head. Elaine turned back and said, "We want to place an order, Margot. Okay?"

"Oh. Sure. Everyone?"

"Yes. Everyone."

"Okay."

Andy went first. "I'll have a cheeseburger with lettuce and tomato…and a coke…no fries."

I thought, 'This ought to be good. She isn't writing anything down.'

Sharp ordered next. "And ah will have an open face turkey sandwich with all the gravy you can afford. Mashed potatoes and corn. Peach pie that I see hiding on the counter. A black coffee."

"Are you from down South somewhere? You sound like a cowboy."

"Yes I am. Ah'm from Texas and ah'm hungry."

"Oh. Sorry. I'm sorry."

"Don't worry about it, Margot. These are trained adults and they know how to be patient. I'll have a Cobb salad and a diet Pepsi. Okay?"

"Sure."

Margot stared at me.

"Nothing for me."

"It's on the house anyway." Margot walked away and pushed the swinging door to the kitchen open. "Lester…we need a burned calf, milking and dragged through the garden. We also need a gobbler drowned with mashed and corn. And I need a Cobb."

I was slightly amazed. "Did I just hear that?"

Elaine chuckled. "That's a woman learning a trade."

"Well don't order a cheese sandwich if you want it tonight."

Elaine was looking at the cards. "Maybe we should try to find the woman who threw these away. If two guys came looking

■ ● ■

for her and they weren't cops, she might be in serious trouble. The work on these cards is real good."

Andy took the cards again. "You said Jocko knows who the woman is?"

"Yeah. He says she's Holly's sister. She's one of the daytime waitresses."

"And she's working for Louie Udo?"

"Yeah. That small time pimp who used to steal cars."

Sharp took the cards from Andy. "Just so we're clear. Nobody thinks us getting involved in this is a bad idea?"

Andy took the cards back from Sharp again, but it looked like Sharp held onto two. "Sharp, you have reservations?"

Sharp turned the two cards toward us. One said 'F.B.I.' and the other said 'University of Chicago.' They both had the same face in the I.D. photo. They both had different names. "Course I have reservations…look at these good. Apparently whoever this man was…he is now dead."

Andy stared at the table. "So you think we should stay out of this?"

"Hell no. This could be quite interestin'…and look at all'a that food comin' our way."

Andy looked up. Either of you two want to stay out of this? I shook my head.

Elaine said, "We don't even know what 'this' is…" Then she mimicked Sharp. "B'sahds, this could be quite interestin.'"

Sharp never looked up from his food, but I thought I saw him smile.

■ ● ■

Touch

"Lugo. There she is."

"You sure?"

"Yes."

The car pulled to the curb just a little past her. The driver got out and slowly closed his door. His eyes slid in two directions, scanning the sidewalk. He turned around and quickly ran his vision over the parked cars and the sidewalk on the other side of the street.

Lugo stepped out of his side of the car slowly and stretched his shoulders. Kelvin Leeds walked around the car to stand next to him.

"One fat man in front of the camera shop. Serious guy."

Without looking Lugo nodded his head. A smile, that might have been a grimace of anticipation, distorted Lugo's lips.

They both started walking toward her. At first she smiled at them. Then she thought, 'These are the cops that came after me today.' "Hey, Winch!"

Kelvin Leeds raised one hand and said, "Keep it down. We need to talk to you." He moved quickly and grabbed Lisa's arm as she tried to back away.

■ ● ■

Winch was a former boxer who now weighed 240 pounds, 26 pounds over his prime as he remembered it. He had lost sight in one eye in his last legal bout and when he was tense he tended to squint. Winch moved well for a man of his size. Quick, steady and confident. He was going to intervene to keep Lisa out of jail for the night. This was his block.

"Hey, fellas. I thought we had this all straightened out already. Just call overtown."

When Winch got close, Lugo grabbed his wrist. Winch tried to pull away and looked into Lugo's smile that suddenly turned into a snarl. Winch began to throw a punch but it never even got half-way to its target. Lugo hit him once in the stomach. Winch's one good eye got very large for half a second before he collapsed to the sidewalk. Lugo was stepping away before Winch's face slammed into the concrete.

Lisa looked past Kelvin Leeds to see Winch on the sidewalk with his knees tucked under his stomach. His head was slightly turned toward the street with his mouth wide open. His arms were lying flat on the sidewalk by his sides. His hands almost touching his feet.

Lugo calmly walked over to join Leeds and grabbed Lisa by the other arm.

"Let's go, K."

"You're not cops!"

Lugo laughed. "We're more than cops."

They walked toward the car, passing Winch who was crumpled in the grey light of a cheap dress window display. Leeds and Lugo never looked down. Lisa was now terrified in her silence.

Leeds opened the car's rear door while viewing the area. Lugo pushed Lisa into the back seat and then got in beside her. Leeds went to the driver's seat, adjusted the rear view mirror, buckled his seat belt and slowly pulled out into the light evening

■ ● ■

traffic.

Anyone who saw the pantomime thought two cops in suits had grabbed a working girl off the street and gave her pimp a warning.

"Where'd you put the cards and papers?"

"What papers?"

"Hold her up straighter, Kelvin."

Leeds grabbed Lisa by her hair and pulled her up so she was on the tips of her toes.

"Who'd you give the papers to?"

"I didn't give n…"

Lugo's left hand shot out at Lisa's face in an arc Lisa wasn't sure she saw. Lisa's head snapped and she heard something crack. Her tears ran involuntarily before the blood started.

Lugo smiled. "Look at that, Kelvin. Her nose is crooked."

Leeds twisted her head so he could see her face.

"Damn…that doesn't look good. See if you can straighten it out."

Leeds tightened his grip on Lisa's hair. Lugo's right arm swept toward Lisa's face until his fist hit her nose again. Lisa's knees buckled, but Kelvin Leeds held her up by a grip on one arm and her hair. Pain radiated through Lisa's head and she couldn't see through the tears.

"Ahn't kep ta pay pas."

Lugo smiled again. "What? What'd ya say, cunt?"

Leeds held her head steady and whispered in her ear. "What did you do with the papers?"

"Ah tos em."

A stream of blood ran down Lisa's lips to her chin. Mostly the blood ran from there down her neck and soaked a four inch

■ ● ■

tributary that ran down to her short skirt. The blood that didn't soak the front of her blouse pooled on the floor beneath her feet.

"So, bitch, where are the papers now?"

"Ah draw em in ta alley."

Lugo's right fist crashed into Lisa's jaw like a two-by-four. The snapping sound was unmistakable to Kelvin Leeds. Lugo had broken her jaw. Kelvin shook her, hoping to bring her back to consciousness with a simple violent shake. Leeds sighed, let go of her arm but held onto her hair. He lowered his arm and Lisa slumped like a doll in a child's hand. Her knees slid in the blood on the floor. Leeds reached into his jacket pocket and pulled out an ammonia capsule. With two fingers and his thumb he snapped the capsule and then waved it back and forth under Lisa's nose. Her head shook slowly at first and then she tried to turn away. A groan and whimper bubbled out of her mouth like she was trying to spit away her life .

"Get up, honey." Leeds pulled Lisa to her feet. She wobbled back and forth like she was stumbling down the street drunk, even though she was stuck in one spot with her feet slipping in the blood pooled under her shoes. Tears still streamed down her crooked face. Her jaw was broken and on one side the early swelling made her face look even more distorted.

"So who's got the papers now?"

"On't know. Lep em in ta alley." Lisa drew up her last bit of street-hardened courage and said, "Louie'll get ya fer dis."

Lugo smiled at Leeds. "We got a name." Lugo shrugged. "We can go visit Louie." Lugo's smile turned into a grin as he surveyed Lisa's body. His eyes went down to her ankles and up to her face twice. He took half a step toward Lisa and sent a vicious right hook to her ribs. Lisa gasped for air and started panting, her eyes barely slits.

"Did you hear that, Kelvin?"

■ ● ■

"Sounded like some of her ribs might of broke, but I wasn't sure."

"That's what I thought, but I'm not sure either."

Lisa wanted to spit at him, but she thought that would only make it worse.

"Listen close this time, K." Lugo stepped back, planted his back foot and sent a left hook to Lisa's ribs on the other side of her chest.

"I heard it that time. Definitely cracked some ribs. Lisa's body went completely limp again.

"You got her, Kelvin?"

"Yeah. Of course."

Lugo sent another left hook to Lisa's torso. Leeds held her up and Lisa's body swayed slightly with the impact. Lugo quickly threw a right to her chest and another right to her diaphragm.

"You lifted her off the ground, man. Like an inch."

"Really? Let me try that again."

Lugo stepped in toward Lisa and his right fist caught her in the stomach and she rose off the floor.

"How high do you think that was? Had to be four or five inches."

"Definitely. More like six probably."

"Well, let's finish this off."

"Go for it. I got her."

Leeds lifted Lisa's body by the hair so that her toes barely waded in the blood on the floor. Her arms dangled at her side. Blood trickled from the corner of her eyes. Blood still spilled from her mouth. Lisa's tears had stopped.

Lugo threw a right fist at Lisa's temple. Droplets of blood sped through the air. Leeds dropped her to the floor and began pulling away small wads of hair that stuck to his fingers.

"Damn, Luge. Bitch got blood all over the front of your

■ ● ■

shirt."

Lugo looked down at Lisa. "I've got a clean shirt in the car." He paused. "Look at that. No blood on my tie." He looked up at Kelvin. "Amazing, isn't it? Completely missed my tie."

■ ● ■

Searching

Andy knew Louie Udo, the pimp, who ran the woman we were curious about, named Lisa. Andy and I were going to talk to Louie if he was up. The way I was feeling, if he wasn't up I had it in mind to wake him, though that was probably a bad idea. But I was full of bad ideas this morning. Sharp was with us and he was part of the reason I was feeling unreasonable. He had insisted we walk instead of taking a car with an AC. I hadn't seen a cab we could hail in twenty minutes, so here we were, swimming to our respective meetings. Ours with a pimp, Sharp's with a client. Maybe our pimp had an AC. At the corner of Colombia and Douglaston we'd split up. Then, with Sharp gone, maybe some of my annoyance would dissipate.

It was only 10:30 and it was already muggy as hell. It was a grey, overcast morning that felt like someone was pushing against your head and shoulders as you walked. Traffic was heavy and noisy, making the feeling worse. I felt sticky and annoyed. I looked at Andy and his arm pits were already stained. I could feel sweat start to run down my left leg. I looked at Sharp and immediately my annoyance turned into unmitigated resentment. He looked as cool and crisp as a yellow refrigerated rose.

■ ● ■

His hair was tied back. His pants were neatly pressed. His shirt didn't have a wrinkle in it. His black cowboy boots were gleaming. I think he even polished his cane.

I was just about to say something about this when he pulled his sunglasses out of his shirt pocket and flipped them on in one smooth motion. Then he pushed the file folder he was carrying and his cane at me. "Hold these for a sec, partner." Out of his back pocket he pulled a black tie and put it around his neck. I watched him work it into a Windsor knot while all the time smiling at me.

"Warm morning, ain't it?"

"Fuck you, Sharp."

He started laughing and took the file and cane from me.

"Ah will see you two gentlemen back at the office this afternoon unless you get into some type of serious trouble. If you do, give me a ring so I can see if I want to get involved, too."

"I'm not going to have a dime I can spare, Tex." I don't think I was sarcastic enough because Sharp reached in his pocket to jingle some change.

"Want a loan?"

Andy grabbed my arm before Sharp and I started on our mothers. "Let's go. Maybe we can get to the pimp before he gets any blow up his nose. Sharp, we'll check you."

Andy and I left Sharp at the curb waiting for the light to change. I stepped into the street and Andy grabbed my arm again. Now I was annoyed with everyone. I turned to face him and aggressively said, "What?!"

Andy nodded toward Sharp. He was standing on the edge of the curb pounding his cane into the concrete like he was having arm spasms. We started moving closer to him and he turned toward us looking like he was lost. Andy was holding both hands out in front of him, palms toward the sky. "Sharp? What's up?"

■ ■ ■

He pointed with his cane at three men on the other side of the street who were walking in the opposite direction. "Who is that guy? Who is that guy?!" Then Sharp turned away from us and was moving up the sidewalk as fast as his bullet-riddled hip would allow.

Sharp started yelling. "Townley! Townley! Michael Townley!"

One of the men quickly turned his head for a short second and then all three of them started moving faster until they turned the corner, out of sight.

Andy had a puzzled look on his face. "Michael Townley?"

Sharp walked back toward us. "That was Michael Townley."

Andy put a hand on the back of his neck and started massaging it. "What the hell would Michael Townley be doing here?"

"What would Michael Townley be doing anywhere?"

"But this probably isn't a good town to start in for witness protection. At least not for him."

"Maybe they're just moving him."

"But why br…"

I couldn't help myself. "Who is Michael Townley?" Andy and Sharp both looked at me. For a second I thought one of them would try to make me feel stupid in my ignorance. But it was a quick second. I knew these guys better than that and the feeling just slipped by.

Andy spoke first. "Townley was a CIA asset who organized the bombing in Washington, D.C. that killed that Chilean diplomat and his assistant."

Sharp took his glasses off. "Michael Townley helped snuff people in South America that the CIA and the Chilean secret police didn't like. He was convicted in absentia in Italy for attempted murder. But all he did was cripple the man and paralyze the man's wife."

I remembered now. Townley had worked for the CIA and he

■ ● ■

had planted a bomb under Orlando Letelier's car. Letelier was a former member of Salvador Allende's government before he was assassinated. Townley's bomb ended up killing Letelier and a woman named Ronni Moffit. Raoul had said at the time that the CIA probably did it and that whoever got caught would just get dragged into a witness protection program. Guess he was right on both counts.

Andy crossed his arms and looked at Sharp. "You sure that was Townley?"

"Yep. I ran into him in Paraguay and again in Santiago. That was him. I'd like to run this past Raoul and see what he knows about it."

Andy stiffened. He still had a hard time with Raoul. He thought Raoul was reckless and that he couldn't be trusted. There were only three people I trusted more than Raoul and I worked with all of them. As far as I was concerned, we'd only had one bad experience when we worked with Raoul, but Andy couldn't let it go. I thought Raoul's intelligence experience and his networks of contacts were invaluable. Andy thought we could do without it. And then sometimes it was good to have a 6'6, 320 pound man with serious weapons expertise backing you up.

Andy's eyes narrowed and I knew something was percolating in his brain. "Let's talk about this back at the office this afternoon."

"Yeah. Let me get to this meeting before ah'm late and they get the idea we're a bunch of incompetents." Sharp turned and crossed the street. I wondered when he'd be able to get rid of the cane…or if he ever would.

Andy and I continued our sweatbox stroll down Colombia. The buildings were starting to be shorter and the more sky I could see, the more oppressive the heat seemed to be. After a few more blocks the buildings were pretty run down. The city

■ ● ■

didn't seem to be able to find a way to get the streets clean down here.

We finally came to 1174 Colombia. It was a grayish-yellow four story apartment building with a dry cleaner's next door that made the air taste like chemicals. We stepped up three stairs and went into a small lobby that was a lot cleaner than I expected it to be. A guy got up from a rickety wooden folding chair holding a newspaper in one hand.

"Where do you think you two are going?"

"You the doorman?" I watched him lift his shirt to let us see a pistol tucked in his belt.

"Yeah, I'm the doorman. Where the fuck do you think you're going?"

I turned to Andy. "Looks like Louie is diversifying his interests, doesn't it?" I was already annoyed and the doorman was just about to push me over the edge. Andy smiled, put his hand on my chest and said, "We're here to see Louie Udo. He's an old friend of mine."

"Oh yeah? Louie's an old friend of mine, too, and he don't want to see nobody today. So you and me are both out of luck."

I pushed Andy's hand away and walked toward the doorman.

He grinned, put his hand under his shirt and said, "I wish you would."

I put both hands up, palms forward, and walked past him, and the sneer he was wearing on his face. I grabbed his chair with two hands and swung it so hard that when it hit the doorman, two legs snapped off and flew toward Andy. He put both arms up in front of his face so he wouldn't get hit. The doorman fell sideways, unconscious, onto his shoulder.

"What the hell did you do that for?!"

"We should have driven down here. It's God damn hot and

■ ● ■

he had an attitude…"

"How're we going to find out where Udo lives now? There's twenty something apartments in this place. How many do you think we're going to have to knock on before someone will admit to knowing him. He'll get a warning call before we knock on the second door."

I started to leave the lobby. Andy hollered, "Where are you going? His name isn't listed by the buzzers."

"I noticed that, too, Andy."

I stepped outside and went into the dry cleaners.

"Excuse me, sir. Do you know what apartment Louie Udo lives in?"

Without looking at me he dismissively said, "Who wants to know?"

I stood there staring at this medium small guy with a bald head, graying hair, who was wearing a vest over a white dress shirt in a room that had to be 116 degrees. Now I was really pissed.

"Is everybody in this town tough today?! I just knocked out the door man next door and he's lying on the floor so he can't tell me where Louie Udo lives. That's who wants to know!"

The dry cleaner looked up at me from his shirt press. "That punk? My wife knock him out with my steam iron once. That ain't no big deal. Hit him right in the middle of his forehead. He fell on our floor in the middle of the shop like a wet rag. Customers had to step over him for twenty minutes…that punk. Like now I should care…and if you wanted to know where Mr. Udo lives, why in the heck did you knock him out?!"

I was staring at this man like I was five years old and he was the head of the July 4th circus parade. My head fell to my chest. I put both hands flat on his counter. I started to chuckle in frustration but stopped. It was so damn hot.

■ ● ■

Without looking up, I asked, "Mister…why are you wearing that vest?" Then I looked up. He pulled his press back down and steam filled the air around him.

"Appearances. It's business-like. Four D. He live in Four D."

I shook my head. "Thank you, sir."

I walked out to the sidewalk that felt like it had its own AC after being inside the dry cleaners. I went back into the lobby of 1174 wondering if the heat was driving everyone crazy. "Hey, Andy. If the doorman wasn't here, how the hell did you think we were going to find Louie's apartment?"

Andy grinned. "Knock on a few doors until someone told us where he lived."

This was not my morning, but it was going to be one of the memorable ones. "You bastard." I moved to the stairs without looking at Andy. "Four D."

When Four D opened I immediately recognized the ex-boxer named "Winch."

"Who let you up here?"

"The doorman. He said 'go right on up.'" I didn't need to tangle with this guy. He was almost as big as Raoul. I needed to keep this respectful. Plus, I could feel the AC was jacked up on high and I really wanted to be in some air conditioning.

"Who is it Wi…holy shit! Andrew! Come on in. Get the hell out'a the way, Winch." He stuck his right hand out to Andy and pushed Winch away from the door with his left. "You here for a game, Mr. Grandmaster?"

"I wish. Actually, we came up here to ask you about a woman named Lisa."

The air suddenly chilled about twenty degrees colder than the AC was blowing. I glanced at Winch and he seemed to tighten up. Louie's smile disappeared in a second. Nobody said anything for a good fifteen seconds until Louie said, "Da-veed."

■ ● ■

David or Da-veed came in from the hallway holding a Mac 10 at his waist. He looked like he'd been high since last month, so I was startled that someone would let him carry a gun around.

"Lisa one of my girls. Why you askin'?"

I noticed Louie's manner of speech had changed. Andy had a serious frown on his face.

"Don't go silly on me, Louie. Obviously something is wrong or you wouldn't be acting like this."

"I ain't actin' like nothin'. This is totally serious. Ain't no actin' involved here."

Andy studied Louie's face. I was trying to watch Winch and Da-veed at the same time. Under normal circumstances I figured Louie wouldn't want his apartment all shot up, but Da-veed here was so high I wasn't sure if he knew who Louie or Winch were. I couldn't see an available chair so I was getting a little nervous.

"One of your women didn't show up…"

Louie smiled again, "And…"

"And you know she didn't just split."

"Very good, Mr. Sherlock. So why are you asking about her?"

"Come on, Louie. Cut the shit. I think one of your employees was grabbed by two cops and you can't figure out why, which ones did it, or where the woman is."

"They weren't no cops."

Louie gave Winch a withering glare. Winch took a half step back. This guy was that intimidated by Louie? Maybe it was Da-veed that made Winch nervous.

"Okay, Sherlock. My man Winch got dropped on the concrete last night by two guys who grabbed my girl, Lisa. I got in touch with my boys over town and they don't know anything about it, or recognize the guys who did it. So what you got?"

"We have a drunk who was asked by Lisa to call somebody who works for you, to ask for help."

■ ● ■

"Yeah, we picked her up. She was going on and on about these two cops."

I heard Winch mutter under his breath, "They weren't cops."

Louie looked over at him. "What?"

Winch looked down at the floor. "Nothin.'"

Louie turned back to Andy. "What else?"

I had to cut in. "Hey! Can you send Da-veed back out to the kitchen to get high or something?" Da-veed was starting to sway back and forth and he was making me nervous.

Andy and Louie both looked at me. Louie turned around and took in the frown on Da-veed's face. He started laughing. "Da-veed, go out back and get a drink or something."

Da-veed's frown became more pronounced. "You sure?"

"I'm sure. This is my old chess friend, Andrew."

Da-veed blinked twice like he was coming out of a trance, then turned around and went back into the hallway.

Louie put one arm across his chest and one hand under his chin. "Andrew...you think you guys can find my girl? I been up all night and nobody knows nothin'. She's probably already on ice, but I don't care for the idea of two guys just grabbing one of my girls. So if you think you find somebody, I'll hire you. What do you think?"

Andy didn't even seem to think about it.

"We get paid for looking. We don't find her, we still get paid. We find the guys, we tell you where they are and that's it."

Louie put both hands in the pockets of his pants and pulled them out with a pack of Beecher's clove gum in one hand. He unwrapped a stick and popped it in his mouth. His eyes went from Andy, to me and back to Andy.

"I'm sorry. That's fuckin' rude. You want a stick, Andrew?" Andy shook his head. Louie looked at me. I shook my head. Louie's eyes went back to Andy.

■ ● ■

I said, "Does Winch want one?"

Louie started laughing. "Winch, you want one?"

"Sure, Louie."

"Then run your fat ass down to Colson's and get you a pack!"

"Hey, you know what? I changed my mind." I stepped toward Louie. "Let me have a stick." Louie's eyes narrowed. Andy was frowning at me when Louie handed me the gum. I stepped back toward Winch.

"Changed my mind again. I only chew Beech-nut. Here Winch, you take this." I turned to Louie. "Check."

Winch looked at me like I was crazy, but he took the gum. He unwrapped it real slow and then took four bites to get it in his mouth. Through the whole process he kept his eyes on Louie.

Louie started laughing. "So you're the crazy one. I heard one of you was up for anything. Must be you." He turned back to Andy.

"We have a deal? Let's talk some money. How much green you gonna' steal from me, Mr. GM?"

I looked at Winch who had a crooked smile on his face. He looked down at me from 6'4 or 6'5 with his one good eye. "That was cold, dude. Cold."

"Uh-huh. You know, I saw you fight a couple of times before I went in the service. I thought you had a lousy manager."

"I had a worse doctor."

"The fights I saw I thought you were overmatched. How old were you when you started?"

"Sixteen. Done by twenty."

"Damn, bro'."

"Only good thing about losing the eye, was kept me out of Vietnam. My brother, Joseph, went and he said it was good I didn't go. He said the officers didn't know what they were doing and the Viet Cong did."

■ ● ■

"Yeah. Well that sounds a little familiar."

Andy slapped my arm. "Let's get back to the office."

We left the apartment with Louie challenging Andy to a game of chess and Winch chewing like he had bone between his teeth. As we went down the stairs Andy asked me, "What the hell were you thinking with the gum routine?"

"I don't like clove gum."

"Next time you think it's a good time to get shot up over a pack of gum, remember that no time is a good time to get shot up over a pack of gum. Especially if I'm with you."

I reached in my pocket and pulled out a fresh pack of spear-mint. "Want a slice?"

Andy did a double-take. "You're the bastard, you son of a bitch!"

I started laughing. "Can we grab a cab back? And how do you know that guy?"

"Chess."

■ ● ■

Ice

When Andy and I strolled into the office, Sharp and Elaine were going over paperwork at her desk. I assumed it was related to the meeting Sharp had that morning at Collinsworth. Sharp nodded at us while Elaine continued to tap her keyboard. As we passed Mojica's office I could see him staring at his monitor. I wondered if he was looking at the surveillance tape we did last week at Seldon and Roberts. His eyes never left the screen.

Andy went left into his office and I went to the right, into mine. I intended to sit down and stare out my window at the sky for a few minutes, but when I did the chair tilted and I almost went over. I forgot that Blakeslee had shot off one of my casters. I bent over to look at the damage, wondering if I could find a book to fit under the leg.

As I was leaning over I noticed Sharp's boots and the bottom of his cane out of the corner of my eye. I raised my head to find Sharp smiling at me as he lowered himself onto one of my two chairs. I sat up straight, turned my head directly into the gleam of Mojica's Alfred E. Newman grin. Then I noticed Andy leaning in the doorway with a smirk on his face.

"What's up, guys?"

■ ● ■

Through his grin, Mojica said, "Andy thought we needed to talk some things over."

Why did meetings always end up in my office?

"Yeah, so what the hell are you grinning at?"

Mojica wagged his head. "You're thinking about finding a book or a piece of wood to fit under your chair so it won't rock."

I looked at his grin and knew that whatever I said next was going to be a lie. "Actually, I was thinking about getting a new chair."

Sharp apparently decided to team up with Mojica and his smile got larger. "That's a right nice chair you're sittin' in now. Why would you want a new one?"

"Why didn't you just saunter over to my office and say, 'Yo, Heeks. Can you fix my chair for me?' But you'd rather just stick one of Andy's books under it."

"What are you trying to be? A detective? I can put my own book under it."

"You don't own three books stacked on top of each other thick enough to balance that chair."

I couldn't help smiling. "I could go get one down at Lost In Print, jackass."

Sharp and Andy started laughing. Mojica just kept on grinning.

"What the hell are you laughing at?" I felt myself getting annoyed again like I did down at Udo's.

Elaine rolled her desk chair through the door and said, "So Sharp says he saw Michael Townley this morning."

Mojica's smile vanished. "Who's Michael Townley?"

"Former CIA, former Chilean secret police. I use the word 'former' tentatively. He blew up the former Chilean ambassador and his assistant in downtown Washington, D.C." Sharp's face looked like stone.

■ ● ■

"Okay. I remember that."

Andy began speaking as Elaine sat down. "I want to toss out a couple of ideas about that woman, Lisa, that Jocko said discarded all of that I.D. in the alley." Andy nodded toward me. "We went to speak with Louie Udo this morning and he hired us to find the woman. He said two guys snatched her off the street. They dropped Winch on the sidewalk when they grabbed her."

Mojica asked, "And who's Winch?"

"He's that ex-heavyweight that you might see over on Warton Street. He has one bad eye. He works for Udo now. When we talked to Louie we found out that the guys who took her were definitely not cops. They both wore suits. One guy is black; the other white."

"Sorry to interrupt. Apparently the woman we've been hired to find is being sought by the Police, too. There was a suicide at the Dixon Hotel and the cops think she was in the room when he jumped, or was pushed. The woman's name is Lisa Butler. Her sister is a waitress at Jackie's. Her name is Holly Mason." Elaine shuffled her papers like she was trying to find something else to say. She was always interrupting us, but she did it so politely it didn't seem to bother anyone except me. "Do you guys think it's a good idea for us to be looking for this woman if the Police are?"

Sharp chuckled. "Elaine, when was the last time we did anything around here that was a good idea?"

Elaine shrugged her shoulders.

Andy crossed his arms. "Maybe our favorite patron of Jackie's can get Lisa's address and find a couple of friends or contacts she has besides Udo." Andy raised his eyebrows while looking right at me.

I stared right back, and then said, "You really think Udo

■ ● ■

doesn't know where one of his women lives?"

"I don't see what advantage it gives to him not to tell us since we're going to find out anyway."

Andy kind of had a point, but Udo not knowing still didn't make sense to me.

Andy continued, "I want to bring up Sharp's sighting of Michael Townley this morning. I don't usually jump to conclusions, but I'm ready to jump right now. Sharp, you're still sure that was Townley?"

Sharp pushed some stray hair away from his eyes. "Yes I am. No doubt in my mind."

Andy looked down at the floor. "We have a pile of very good fake I.D.s issued to a man who is now dead. We have a woman whisked off the street by two suits who tried to track her down moments after someone goes through a sixth floor window. We just happen to have Michael Townley cruising through town. I can't believe these incidents are unconnected."

"Ah think we gotta add one more item in there."

This time I interrupted. "The dead Blakeslee laying on my office floor."

Sharp was nodding his head in agreement. Everyone was stone dead quiet, probably wondering what the hell we had fallen into. We were quiet for twenty or thirty seconds, which was amazing for our crew.

Then all of our heads turned toward the main office door when it opened, even though only Andy and I had an angle to see who had entered. A thin man in black, pressed pants and a white short sleeve shirt walked in. He held an envelope in his right hand.

Andy asked, "May we help you?"

The man said, "Yep," and then he walked across the waiting room to Andy.

■ ● ■

"I have an eviction notice for your business here. I'd like to give it to you."

Andy held his hand out.

"The landlord says your type of activities are bad for the other tenants in the building."

"Tell the landlord we promise to keep the music down if he'll just give us another chance." I whined 'another chance' and everyone broke up laughing except Andy. He opened the papers and stared at them.

"The landlord is afraid some more innocent people will get shot." He turned and walked out of the office.

I didn't have any quips for that one. The image of Ivars's face flashed in front of me. Who could be more innocent than a Finnish elevator operator.

Andy's voice made me jump. "Surprised the landlord waited this long. Elaine, could you get in touch with Daniels and let him know about this?"

"Sure, Andy."

Mojica was looking serious. "You know, Andy, we have seven more years on our lease. Daniels should be able to get us as much time as we want."

Andy nodded and then said, "I'm wondering if the landlord might not be right. Maybe we should look for a new location. We could improve our security."

I thought Andy had a point, but the idea of us being kicked out pissed me off.

Andy's eyes searched each of us. "I know we need a little time to really think this over, but do any of you, right off the bat, think it'd be a bad idea to look for new office space?"

It seemed like it took about five seconds for everyone to ponder the question and answer in the negative.

"So Elaine and I will start a search. If any of you guys see

■ ● ■

something promising, let's share. But let's get back to Ms. Butler for a second. We're being paid decent money to find her."

"Ah think we might want to talk to Raoul about the two guys who snagged the woman and the two suits escortin' Townley around the city."

Andy visibly stiffened and stood up straight. Just the mention of Raoul put Andy on edge.

"I think you're right, Sharp. Why don't you and Mojica make a plan to go over there. See what Raoul knows or can find out. Also see if he knows anything about Blakeslee."

My jaw almost hit the top of my desk. Elaine stared at me with raised eyebrows that slid into a deep frown. Sharp and Mojica were stoneface silent. From Andy's reaction I was guessing he thought we were about to wade through shoulder deep shit. If Raoul had any info we could use, Andy didn't want us to ignore it.

Mojica said, "I'll get in touch with Raoul as soon as I fix that chair over there. Watching him rock back and forth is making me seasick."

"You get seasick walking up stairs."

"Well, Capitan, could you at least just list in one direction?"

"Is that a thirty day notice?" Sharp had his cane between his knees, his hands on top of the cane and his chin resting on his hands. Andy moved from the doorway to hand the paper to Sharp.

I stood up and stretched my arms. "I'm heading for Jackie's. I will see you all later. Heeks! Don't touch my chair." I left my office with all of my partners still in it. But I trusted them.

I took the elevator down with one of the new operators. He was the silent type, whatever that type is. Basically it seemed he was good at conserving his vocal energy. If I said "Good morning," he said "Yep." When I said "See you later," it sounded like

■ ● ■

he said "uh-huh," but I was never sure. Now we were finally down to just nods. He opened the elevator doors. I nodded. He nodded back. That was the extent of our communication every day.

When I stepped off the elevator it struck me that if we moved the office, I wouldn't miss this lobby. Funny, I never had a nightmare about our little shootout, but my blood always ran cold as I walked through it to the lobby doors. I sometimes found myself staring at the morning newsman, half expecting him to pull out a weapon. I even had a tendency to break into a light sweat if I stopped for more than a few seconds. I definitely would not miss the lobby. I wondered how Sharp must feel every time he walked through.

Out on the sidewalk I was surprised by how much the temperature had dropped. It was welcome, but almost scarey. There was a gusty breeze working its way down the street that made me feel like I wanted to go over to the park for a little while and just sit.

On my way I tried to calculate how long it would be before the rain started. I could see some very dark clouds moving our way. What the hell, I'd been wet before.

I sat down on the third bench inside the park. Sometimes I felt very disappointed if someone was sitting there. I had no idea why I felt so proprietary about this bench. I guess it was the view. To my right the park was flat. But in front of 'my' bench there was a slope that ran down to some maple trees about fifty yards away. Over the trees I could see the hills and two farms. It was a very pleasing landscape for me. Today the third bench was empty. I leaned forward and put my forearms across my knees, staring out at the sky. Low, grey, heavy clouds directly ahead. I turned my head to the right and some imposing black clouds would soon be competing for control of the sky.

■ ● ■

Then there was crying. I sat up straight, folded my hands and slowly turned toward the sobs. A teenage girl was sitting at the other end of the bench. She twisted her hands together like she was trying to break her fingers. I looked around to see if anyone else was close.

"What's up? You okay?"

She nodded. I looked around again.

"You break up with your boyfriend?"

She turned her head toward me and then stared down at the ground. "I wish."

"You want to break up with your boyfriend?"

"Leave me alone." She wiped her face with both hands, then started doing battle with them again in her lap.

"If you didn't want someone to talk to, why'd you sit on this bench?"

She kept wrenching her hands. They were turning red. She looked to be about fourteen or fifteen. I thought maybe I could be funny.

"You want to call off the marriage and he doesn't."

For some reason that caught her attention, but clearly she didn't think I was funny. Her head twisted toward me so fast I thought her spine might snap. Her mouth fell open and her eyes were huge. "Oh God!" Tremors shook her body and she wept like her mother had died.

Then it struck me. I felt as dumb as a dime-store detective's sidekick. Stupid, stupid, stupid. She's pregnant. Now I'm sitting, staring out at a darkening sky and suddenly realize I'm rubbing my hands together like my left is attacking the right and the right is defending itself. I looked at her quickly, grabbed the edge of the bench with both hands and start rocking a little. How could I be so stupid?

"How do you know that? Do you know him?"

■ ● ■

"What?!"

"How did you know about the marriage?"

I looked at her more confused than I had ever been in my entire adult life.

"Marriage? Aren't you a little young for that?"

Now she was rocking back and forth, so I stopped.

"My parents don't think so."

"Your parents want you to get married? I'm not trying to be nosey, but are you pregnant? That's why they want you to get married?"

In between sobs she managed to say "no."

"Then why would your parents want you to get married? You seem pretty young."

She clamped both hands on her face and tilted her head back. "I'm fifteen."

"Fifteen? You can't get married at fifteen."

"I'll be sixteen in a few months. That's when they want me to get married."

I was feeling cold. Something was really wrong here, or this kid was a really good psycho liar.

"Look, if you want to tell me what's going on, I'll listen. I'm a pretty good listener. And I have some friends who might be able to help you."

"No one can help me."

"You'd be surprised. So why don't you tell me what's up?"

"My father'll beat me...beat me bad if he sees anyone getting on my side." She paused, took a blue handkerchief out of her back pocket and blew her nose. I was impressed that she didn't just use her shirt sleeve.

"My parents want me to marry this scum ball named Larry. He's really old. He's going to give my parents two thousand dollars to marry me."

■ ● ■

"What?! That's not legal." What the hell was wrong with me today? Mr. Naïve.

"It's not?"

"Not really. Tell me the rest of the story and what does Larry do?"

"That is the story."

"Your parents get $2,000 when you marry Larry."

She nodded.

"I could take you to a social service agency, I…"

"Uh-uh! He'll find me and beat me with the hose. I can't do that. He'd find me. He finds me every time."

"Who'll find you? Larry?"

"No! My father!"

Panic was beginning to choke her. The first drops of rain fell on my arms. Something stung my face. Sleet. The girl jumped up running. It felt like a rock hit me in the head. "Wait!" I put my arms over my head. Hail was coming down the size of marbles. I looked around and ran for the old oak tree, hoping for a little shelter. The girl was gone. I hoped she found some cover.

I pressed my back against the trunk of the oak as the park turned quickly from green to glassy white. The grass was getting buried under silver pearls of ice. Every now and then I'd get hit by something even though I was under the tree. Leaves, and pieces of them, were falling, stripped off by the ice pellets. Every once in a while, one about the size of a golf ball would bounce off the ground.

It was the sound that got to me. The storm reminded me of that patrol boat when Andy and I were in the Mekong. The rain was coming down harder than I had ever seen it rain. It fell so thick on the water it was like the river was crackling. It was beautiful and it was eerie. And then two sailors pulled an air force captain out of the water with hooks. When his body

■ ● ■

flopped on the deck I couldn't even hear the sound it should have made. Andy turned to me and screamed, "Let's get to work." I said, "Fuck that. I don't want to drown. Let's wait for the rain to let up." He ignored me and slid over to the body. I tried to light up a Chesterfield, but my pack was soaked. About five seconds later the rain just stopped. Everyone on deck stood still, listening to the silence. No birds. No engines. No one spoke. The slight sound of water lapping at the boat. Andy and I stared at each other. The sailors were all looking at the sky. Then Andy whispered, "Let's get this done." And now the hail stopped. I felt a little chilly and was having one of my 'amazed at nature' moments. Ice everywhere.

Time to catch a cab and get over to Jackie's.

The streets were quiet and looked slippery. Except for the leaves on the trees, you might have thought it was December. When the cab stopped at the front of the diner, Lester, the cook, was out front with a shovel, pushing the sleet into the gutter.

"Do you believe this bullshit?"

"Quite a storm, wasn't it?"

"Fucking bullshit. I'm the cook!"

"Hey, is Holly here today?"

"Her ass should be out here shovelin' this crap."

"So she's on."

"Unless she went out the back door. You placin' an order?"

"Just coffee."

The door screeched as I went in and I saw Holly immediately.

"Hey. Don't you guys have any WD-40 around?"

"Not unless Henry buys some, the cheap bastard."

I moved all the way inside and took a seat at the counter. Holly stalked over to me like I was in the wrong place. "Just a coffee."

■ ● ■

"Where the hell you been? Haven't seen you in here in two, three days."

"Oh, I've been visiting at nights mostly. Keeping Margot company."

"Margot…does she even notice? Sometimes I wonder if she knows where she works…on the other hand, she shows up every day on time. Got to give her that."

Holly grabbed a pot of coffee and started to pour.

"Where does your sister live?"

Holly stopped pouring and stared at my cup that was only half full.

"Don't know. Don't care." She started pouring again. "I have nothing to do with my sister. Once in a while I see her pass through. I usually just turn my back. She comes in here, I don't know her."

"You know any of her friends?"

"Friends? Who the hell are you kidding?"

"Well, do you?"

Holly walked away to the other end of the counter. I took a ten dollar bill out of my pocket, put it on the counter with my hand partially over it and asked Holly to come back over. She made her way over to me, a wicked waitress of the west frown on her face.

"What?!"

"How are tips today?" She looked at the ten and then looked at me.

"That's not going to get you much."

"Don't need much. Where does Lisa live…give me a couple of names besides Louie Udo."

Holly looked confused. "Who's Louie Udo?"

"Never mind. Address. Couple of names." I took my hand off the ten. Holly snatched it up like she was playing jacks. She put

■ ● ■

her hand and the ten in her uniform pocket. She kept her hand there.

"She used to have an apartment over at Franklin and Pierce. I can't remember for sure, but maybe 116 Franklin."

"What floor?"

She shrugged.

"Chris Whitfield, Angela Cox, Marty Felter."

"Know where any of them live?"

She sneered at me. "I don't even know if any of them are alive."

I started on my coffee while Holly hovered over me.

"Why are you looking for my sister? What'd she do?"

"I need some information about a couple of guys that were looking for her."

"You mean those two cops that were in here for her?"

"Yeah. But I don't think they're cops."

"What makes you say that?"

"Jocko, for one."

"Jocko?!"

"Jocko said they didn't appear to be cops."

"Are you kidding me? Jocko doesn't think he appears to be a drunk."

I smiled. "Good point. Look, if your sister does show up would you give her my card?"

"No."

"No?"

"That's right. No. As in I won't do that. I want nothing to do with my sister."

I started to pull my wallet out again, but thought better of it. I paid the forty-five cents for my coffee and went outside. Lester was done with the sidewalk and was leaning on his shovel. An unlit cigarette was wedged in the corner of his mouth.

■ ● ■

"Hey, Lester. Two guys were in here looking for Lisa yesterday and…"

"You wanna know about them?"

I nodded.

"Yeah. White guy and a Black guy. The white guy was about 6'2 and the Black guy was 6 or 6'1. The white guy reminded me of an animal. The Black I wouldn't trust to spit. Bad people. Very bad. The white guy had short blond hair. He probably went 230. The Black, his eyes wouldn't stop shifting. He looked like somebody tried to put a telephone on his face but got cut off before he could complete the call, if you know what I mean. I didn't see the Black guy too good, so I can't tell ya' how big he was. They both seemed very athletic."

I found myself staring and shook my head a little. He remembered all that? I should have started with Lester in the first place. Trying to be funny, I said, "Did you notice what color socks they had on?"

Lester looked at me like I had just won asshole-of –the-day honors. Then his expression changed.

"The white guy had brown socks on. I didn't see what the black guy was hoofin'. They both were wearing kind of grey, loose suits. Nothin' flashy, but not cheap. No jewelry. Both had ties."

"Are you always like this?"

Lester frowned. "Like what?"

"Nothing. I…uh…I'll be back for a sandwich later, I think."

"Take your time, Mr. G. Cheese." He picked up his shovel and opened the screen door so it could scream again.

"Hey! Any chance you know where Lisa lives?"

He stopped in the doorway, smiling as he stared down the street. "Nah."

Through the diner's big front window, I watched him walk

back to the kitchen. How come I never knew this guy had a photo memory. I wondered if I asked him the right questions. After noticing that the temperature seemed to be rising again, I walked back into the diner to see if I could ask Lester one more question. Holly was holding a coffee pot.

"You getting something?"

"I want to talk to Lester. I'll just pop back and be right out."

"No you won't. Henry doesn't want anybody back there."

"Henry? He's not here is he?"

"No."

"Well, just out of curiosity, when the hell is Henry here anymore?"

"Sometimes. Henry is here sometimes." Holly went to the back. Lester came through the swinging doors a few seconds later holding a spatula.

"You want that grilled cheese now?"

"Lester, those two guys…"The front door screeched like fingernails on a chalk board. My shoulders raised up to my ears. Lester got a big smile on his face. "Do you know where they were from?"

"Sure." He stared at me like the conversation was over.

"Would you mind telling me?"

He shook his head. "The military."

"I meant what city or something."

"How would I know that?"

"Accent or something."

"Accent?! What the hell you expectin' from me. I told ya' everything I noticed. I also noticed you gave Holly ten dollars for nothin'." I pulled my wallet out and handed Lester a ten dollar bill and sighed.

"Now, do you want that grilled cheese or not?"

"Yeah. Let me have a grilled cheese and a coffee."

■ ● ■

Lester looked at me like I smelled bad. "So tell Holly. I'm the cook!"

I sat down at the counter again and gave Holly my order. I pulled the paper over. The Cubs won a game. The White Sox lost. Like me.

■ ● ■

Cheike

"I'll have a cheeseburger, well done, with lettuce and tomato and a cherry pop."

The voice was like low thunder. Velvet thunder. I turned my head to see where the most outrageous female voice I had ever heard was coming from, because it gave me shivers. It was the kind of voice that could turn a roomful of very good men, bad. She had a black portfolio between her knees and the counter. She was wearing silver bracelets on her left wrist that jangled a little when she moved her arm. Her hair was long and very black and completely hid her face.

I felt like I had to say something and I knew it would be stupid, so I turned away from her and looked at the paper, which I quickly realized I was now holding upside down. I put it down on the counter and cringed when I heard her ask if I was done with it. I swiveled quickly on my stool and said, "Yes. You can have it," with the clearest diction I could muster, while holding the paper out toward her.

She turned her head toward me and I realized she was asking another guy at the counter if she could get his sugar. Holly looked at me with a condescending smile, grabbed the sugar that

■ ● ■

was an arm's length away from me and put it in front of the woman. How could I be so stupid, so many times in one day?

"Are you from upstate New York?"

She didn't even look at me. "Why?"

"Just curious. How you asked for the soda."

She turned her head and pulled her hair behind her ear.

"Rochester." I thought I saw a slight smile dash across her face.

Holly put the burger and the cherry coke in front of her and moved to the other end of the counter.

"Do you ever eat them?"

"Eat what?"

"That grilled cheese you seem to be ignoring."

I looked down at my grilled cheese just off to the right of my coffee. I wondered during which two seconds it was, where I missed Holly putting it in front of me. I tried to think of something witty to say, but 'witty' didn't seem obtainable today. Instead I evaluated my grilled cheese. Batting .900 on the stupidity chart, through a mouth full of cheese and burned, greasy white bread I managed to say, "Are you an artist?"

"Are you the police?"

"Naw. I'm a private detective."

"Well I'm a nuclear fission engineer and these are the plans for a neutron accelerator."

Her voice was killing me. It was rich and deep with something else in it. All I could think of was fresh ground cinnamon. This was stupid. You can't fall for a voice.

I took a slug of tepid coffee. "So what kind of art do you do?"

She looked over at me with a real smile that almost completely hid the fact that she was chewing part of a hamburger. She turned her head again so that her face was completely hidden by her hair. "I draw nuclear reactors. Where do you detect?

■ ● ■

Over at the supermarket?"

I got up quickly, walked two tables away and sat down directly behind her. I hadn't done this since high school. I watched her
look toward where I had been sitting, and then swivel around a
little more, but she didn't see me. She turned back to her food,
shrugged and went on eating.

Margot walked in, gave me a stiff wave that never got higher
than her belt and walked to the kitchen. She came out a few
seconds later, gave Holly the same belt-high wave, spoke to her,
then watched Holly grab her purse and leave.

Margot looked directly at me. "Did you have the grilled
cheese?"

"Yes I did."

The woman with the voice turned on her stool. I held up a
business card at eye level with a smile.

"You're ridiculous. Is that how it's done over at the supermarket?"

"Is there anything wrong with working at the supermarket?"

She gave me a full face smile before she said, "Not a damn
thing. It's hard work though." She got up, walked to my table,
took the card, read it and then sat down.

"So now you know my name. Do you have a card so I can
know yours?"

She looked over at me with squinty eyes. "No. And I think if
this card is real, you should be able to find that out without my
help."

"At least give me a first name."

"That would be cheating."

"Cheating? How's that?"

"I have an unusual name for this part of the country." She
stared at me like she was making a decision. She looked at the
card again with a smile. "Cheike."

■ ● ■

I laughed. "C-h-e-i-k-e?" She nodded with a smile. "So is that name like really common in Rochester?"

She laughed. "How did you really know I'm from upstate New York?"

"I took a wild guess. 'Pop.' You ordered a 'pop' and not a 'soda.' In that area of New York you folks have a tendency to say 'pop' instead of 'soda.'"

"Seriously? Is that the extent of your detection skill? Identifying personal origins through regional dietary preferences?"

I smiled again. "When you're not drawing nuclear containment chambers, what kind of art do you do, and in what medium?"

Her face took on a serious pallor that made me feel uncomfortable, like I had been stupid for the fortieth time today. I was hoping I hadn't blown this.

"I do portraiture for extra income. I work mostly in acrylics in what I call abstracted representationalism…" I nodded my head. "…and you don't know art at all, do you?"

"Correct. How did you guess that?"

"It was when your eyes glazed over for a moment or two. But you think you know what you like."

"Not really…when do you draw nuclear reactors?"

She looked past me toward the sidewalk. "When I'm having nightmares."

It looked like she was going to stand up. I went into panic mode.

"How long have you been in town?"

"About two weeks. Long enough to find a place to live."

"Are you going to have a studio here?"

"Actually, I'm living in my studio."

"So where's that?"

"Mr. Detective, are you cheating?"

■ ● ■

I smiled. She really was going to make me track her down.

"Have you been around enough to see anything exciting around the city?"

"Not really. I've wanted to get back into my work routine."

She gave me a smile that I thought was saying, "What's next?" But I've never been real good with languages. She started to get up.

"Hey! The moon will be rising soon. I know a great spot on the river where we could watch it come up."

She looked at me like I was insane. "I'm not…"

"Margot will vouch for me. You have my business card."

"You're fucking cra…who's Margot?"

"She's the waitress standing over there filling the sugar."

Cheike turned her head to look at Margot. "I don't know." She looked back at me and kind of scrunched half of her face. "Maybe." She walked over to Margot and showed her the business card. Margot nodded in an exaggerated way. They whispered for a few seconds. Margot looked at me over Cheike's shoulder and then went back to whispering. Cheike glided over to her portfolio, picked it up with both hands, looked over at me and said, "Okay. Let's go."

As I moved to the counter to pay my bill I heard Margot mumbling, "…very respectable…very respectable…I think… maybe." Cheike was standing next to the register smiling at me.

"Margot gives a hell of an endorsement, doesn't she? Still in?"

"I guess so. Do we have to drive?" I nodded. "Let's take my car. It's down the street a little. I might have to make an emergency get away."

I went through the diner's door slowly hoping to keep the screech to a minimum. Cheike followed, just pushing the door closed. She grimaced. "Couldn't they just put a bell over the

■ ● ■

door? That metallic scream is ridiculous. This is ridiculous, too."
She looked at my business card, then held it up to the streetlight,
that wasn't on yet, to examine it more. "Looks legit." She half-
smiled, winked at me, nodded her head to the right and said,
"This way."

I thought for a second that my knees would buckle. Her
voice made me think of Ulysses tied to the mast of his ship. She
was right. This was ridiculous and I wasn't tied to anything.

We walked past the alley, the cab garage, the electronics fix-it
shop, down to the corner. We made a right and crossed the street
to a black Audi.

"Nice car."

"It's okay. I'm not big on cars. I just want one that starts and
goes when I need it to."

"Never been big on cars myself."

She put her portfolio on the back seat. We both slipped in
and I started giving directions out of town.

"How long will it take to get there?"

"About twenty minutes."

"Yeah. This is ridiculous."

We made it half-way across town before we hit a red light.

"What nationality are you?"

"What kind of question is that to ask someone you don't
know on the first date?"

"First date?"

"That's what this is, isn't it? You asked me to go somewhere
with you at night and I said 'okay.' You know, boy-girl thing.
Date."

"I was just being friendly. You being new in town."

"Right. A date. My mother was Cherokee and my father is
Iranian. How about you?"

"Your mother's gone?"

■ ● ■

"She's dead. What about you?"

"My mother and father are both dead."

"Sorry…what about you?"

"What about me? Oh…my mother was Black. She was from Cow Pens, North Carolina. My father was white, originally from Queens."

"You visit either place much?"

"My mother never wanted to go back to Cow Pens. And she used to emphasize 'never.' Relatives would come to visit, but we never went down there. I heard an aunt once say, it was probably better if Meggie didn't come back home. But I never found out why that was. We went to New York a few times. More after my mother died. After my grandmother died, never. My father was killed on the job. A floor collapse in a building he was working on. Where's your father?"

"He lives in London."

"Are you close?"

"I suppose I should say "yes,' but I don't get to see him more than once a year."

With my inattentive street directions, what should have taken twenty minutes, ended in more like thirty-five. But with the extra road time we began to talk about Vietnam and she talked about the Wounded Knee occupation. Then she mentioned she had to be home from 'her date' by twelve. She had a meeting in the morning.

When we parked by the side of old Route 47 I began to tell her about the son of the farmer who owned this land. "The farmer was alright about people coming out here. He usually just ignored us. His son is a creep, though. And creepy. Twice he came down here and ran us off with his shotgun. Took us an hour to circle back to our cars. They say the son shot this kid named Whitney Teller, but I never found out if that was really

■ ● ■

true."

Cheike stopped dead in her tracks. "This doesn't sound like such a great idea."

"It's okay. The son was committed to a mental hospital a few years ago. We don't have to worry about him. Just letting you know the lore of the land."

Cheike looked around and then started following me down a well-worn path until we came to a large clearing that was surrounded by trees and brush. She passed me looking up at the sky.

"Damn...look at those stars."

"Yep. But look over there."

The moon was just breaking the ridge, shining through the trees. Cheike walked over to the edge of the short cliff. Moonlight was doing a two-step on the creek that ran about seventy yards toward the moon and then curved away to the left. I could see Cheike look to her left where the creek disappeared into the little used farm.

"Oh my...this is definitely the spot."

A wave of something like satisfaction started rising up from my chest to my head. For a couple of seconds it felt like I was drunk. What an insane day. I hadn't said anything really stupid since we got in the car. That was a definite improvement over the way the day had gone.

"Can you swim here?"

"Sure. It's usually eight to ten feet deep." I sat down in the grass and leaned back to look at the stars.

Cheike walked back to me and pulled her shirt over her head. Then she took off her bra.

"What are you doing?"

"You expect me to swim in my clothes?"

"Oh." Stupid number one.

"Well...come on. What the hell are you afraid of?"

■●■

She pulled her jeans down. Apparently she didn't believe in panties. I stood up and watched her walk over to the edge of the cliff while taking my shirts off.

"How do you get down there?" She sounded like an excited little kid with a stolen baritone voice.

"Hold up. I'll show you the path."

I kicked off my shoes, pulled off my pants and boxers and whispered, "Shit! Cheike, come over here!"

"Why?"

"Shhhsh. Come over here." She walked back toward me with a look in the fading twilight I took to be confusion.

"Did you hear that?"

She looked around. "Hear what?"

"Keep your voice down."

She whispered, "What are we listening for?"

I stooped over and then stood still. Cheike froze.

"It's him! The farmer's son with a gun! Run for the water!"

I grabbed her arm and ran toward the cliff, pulling her with me. She almost screamed when we went over. It was more like a roar. I noticed her legs kicking as we sailed through the air. When we hit the water it occurred to me that I had done stupid number two.

When I came up on the surface I could see Cheike's eyes scanning the ledge. Her nose was barely out of the water.

"What're you doing?

She raised her head a little and whispered, "How will we get our clothes?"

"We'll walk up the bank path over there."

'Astonishment' was the only word I could think of as I looked at her face. Suddenly it was like she rose three feet out of the water to yell, "You son of a bitch! There's nobody up there with a gun!"

■ ● ■

"No? You're probably right."

In what sounded like it came in three different keys, she screamed, "YOU SON OF A BITCH!!" She started splashing so much water at me I thought I was going to drown. I had my back to her as much as possible, but it was like a fire hose had been turned on me. Then it just stopped. I turned toward her slowly thinking it was a ruse to get more water down into my lungs in a surprise attack. Instead I saw her calmly gazing up the stream. The moon had just risen over the tree line and the entire creek was a gleaming yellow.

"This is unbelievable. It was totally ridiculous for me to come out here with you…but I'm so glad I do ridiculous every once in a while…this is just unbelievable. Do you still have your socks on?"

I chuckled. "Yeah. I thought it would add a little bit of realism to our escape from the farmer's son."

Cheike laughed. She lay back, floating in a small circle.

"Those stars…I'll bet you've brought dozens of women here, haven't you?"

"I would have to say you're the first."

"Get out."

"In high school I'd come with a gang of kids, but this is the first time I ever came here with a woman."

"Well, well, well, well, well…I'm honored, Mister Detective."

She went into a back crawl and as she went by, she flicked water at me with her fingers. I looked at the moon and then its glow on the creek. The thought ran through my head that this could be the beginning of the best part of my life.

■ ● ■

Morning

Elaine was already working at her computer when I walked in. I smiled, said "Hi," and went to my office. I started to sit down slowly thinking I had to find something to put under my chair. But when I sat, it didn't rock. I bent over and saw a copy of "Finnegan's Wake" where the caster had been. Fucking Mojica. I pushed back a little by accident and the chair rolled. I bent over again. I looked closer at the book. It wasn't a book. It was a box with the cover of "Finnegan's Wake" glued onto it. The box had a hole in the center and it looked like the chair was resting on a book. I tilted the chair to see a brand new caster underneath Mojica's box deception. Fucking Mojica.

I put the chair down and stood at my window thinking about the night before. I had woken once during the night thinking I had heard Cheike's voice. I woke up again at four a.m. and thought about her through six cups of coffee, all the way to the office.

I sat down and looked at a copy of the report Sharp had written after his meeting at Collinsworth's. I stood back up having read fifty words of nothing. I clearly couldn't concentrate. I started chuckling at almost drowning in the creek during the

■ ● ■

water fight. Then my skin chilled thinking about Cheike's body gliding past me in the water. I sat back down.

"What's up with you?"

I looked up at Elaine standing in the doorway. She had a concerned look on her face.

"Nothing. I'm fine. Just anxious to talk to Andy about our approach to finding Lisa Butler. And the shooter here in the office. And curious about why the Police won't give us any info on the victim. Especially since he was draped dead over one of my good chairs."

"Uh-huh…If I didn't know better, I would have guessed you owed someone a hell of a lot of money, or you found out the world was going to end…or let me make another guess… you met a woman."

I couldn't hold Elaine's stare, so I picked up Sharp's report. I glanced up at her and then dropped my eyes back down to the report.

"So how'd you find out the world was going to end and when the hell were you going to tell the rest of us?"

"Don't you have anything else you could do?"

"Nope. Not right now."

Elaine tapped a pencil against a pad. Elaine shifted her stance so she could lean on the other side of the door jam. I waited. Elaine waited.

"So how'd you meet her?"

"Jesus Christ. We went swimming. Had a nice conversation. That's it. Okay?"

"That's it, huh?"

"That's right. That's it."

"Looks like a lot of 'that's it' is on your face right now."

I looked up at Elaine who was now sporting a glowing grin.

"Screw off, Elaine."

■●■

Elaine started walking away sideways, looking over her shoulder, sharing a grin with me that I didn't want to see. Andy passed her and said "Hi," as she went back to her desk.

"Hey, man. How are you feeling this fine day?"

I put Sharp's report down. "Pretty decent considering the felt grey cloud cover. You know, I've been thinking about me running down Lisa's friends. I think it's a waste of time. If we want to find her, we have to find the two guys who grabbed her."

"I know you're probably right. But look, if she's been lucky, she might be holed up with an old friend. She might not go back to Udo because she's afraid he'll put her back out on the street."

I stared hard into Andy's eyes. "Then why in the hell are we looking for her?!"

"Because we're being paid to find her."

"If she's afraid of Udo, pimp money is not a good enough reason to find her and turn her back over to him."

"There's also a, 'maybe we can find her before she turns up dead' idea."

My back stiffened. In my world, and Andy's, that was reason enough to follow up leads that weren't really leads. Maybe we both suffered from 'Damsel in Distress Syndrome.'

Andy sighed. "Until Heeks and Sharp talk with Raoul, we probably won't get any idea about the two men who snatched her. But maybe we can eliminate some other possibilities around this situation."

I nodded my head. "Okay. Maybe you're right."

So, as I drove across town, I kept seeing Cheike glide past me on her back, lit up by moonlight and flicking water at me with her fingers. I wondered what her hands felt like. What would it be like to hold them. I raised my eyebrows, took a deep breath,

■ ● ■

shook my head and muttered to myself, "Moron."

One Sixteen Franklin Place was boarded up. It looked like it had been boarded up for some time. It seemed like the two buildings on either side of it should have been condemned before that. One Fourteen looked like it was going to fall into the street. One Eighteen needed a sign that said, "if you can afford a beer, you can afford a room in here.' How much money had to slide under the table to keep places like this open?

I got out of the car with less than a flicker of hope something good would happen. In the fifteen minutes I spent flashing her photo, the two people who showed the most interest asked me if she was dead. I said I didn't think so and they lost interest immediately. Most of the people who even paused when I asked them to look at the photo, had only moved to the neighborhood about five minutes before I turned off the car engine. Half of them gave me the impression they were going to try to find a new place to live sometime before lunch tomorrow.

I crossed the street back to the car thinking my next stop would be wherever Chris Whitfield supposedly lived. If I wasn't in such a fog and annoyed at Elaine, I would have checked out addresses before I left the office. Instead I just told Elaine to give me the keys to one of our agency junks. When she tossed them to me she asked if I knew where I was going.

I gave her a look like, "what the hell do you think?"

I drove away from One Sixteen ready to embarrass myself with Elaine by calling her to get Chris Whitfield's address, if one was listed in the phone book. After about five blocks I saw a phone booth. I pulled over and when I walked up to it I felt like I was in the Twilight Zone. It had a phone book. Old and wrinkled inside the black plastic binder hanging from a chain, but it was for the most part, intact. I half expected Rod Serling to start talking behind me. "This man is about to enter a phone

■●■

booth and find that he has no change. The door will close and he will never go swimming again." Yeah... I ran my finger over the wrinkled pages and found an address for my next stop, while I wondered how a phone book survived in this neighborhood.

Chris Whitfield lived over a storefront church. The building was run down but reasonably clean. There was no answer at his door so I thought I'd drop into the church to see if anyone knew Chris. If I was real lucky, maybe someone noticed Lisa wandering around. How'd I get from 'no chance' to 'if I was lucky?'

Inside the church breakfast was being served. Half-filled picnic benches were lined up beyond the serving area. There was a line of about twenty men and one woman stretching back toward storefront windows that were partially covered over with brown kraft paper. As I approached the line two of the men glared at me. The shorter one hooked his thumb over his shoulder.

"End of the line's back there."

I glanced in the direction of his thumb. "I'm looking for Chris Whitfield. You ever heard of him?" I almost started laughing when this guy's face transformed from a threatening stare to a 'curious, who's asking' expression.

"Who're you?"

"I need to ask him about an old friend. Do you know him?"

"Chrissy? Sure. He's up there serving breakfast."

I turned toward the serving table and the bigger guy snarled, "End of the line's back there."

Three or four more men were giving me the evil eye now. I didn't think it would help if I started a riot in the church before these men had their coffee and bacon, so I drifted back toward the front windows. As I sat down in a wooden chair I noticed the two men who gave me directions had followed my progress all the way back here. I gave them a friendly wave and they turned back toward the serving area.

■ ● ■

For a second I thought I heard Cheike's voice, but it was only sound mixed in with an echo of the night before. It was still strong enough to give me a shiver through the shoulder blades. This was ridiculous. I was definitely going to have something to talk with my shrink about this week. How one man became infatuated with a woman's voice and slipped into the abyss. Except it's not just her voice. Her walk. Her hair. Her damn jewelry. Her...

As I turned my head I saw the 'thumber' talking to the guy serving the eggs and bacon. He stood up straight to stare at me for second. I assumed that was Chris Whitfield. I crossed my arms as he bent back over the eggs. Fifteen minutes later Whitfield was standing in front of me.

"Can I help you?"

I stood up. "I hope so. I'm looking for a woman named Lisa Butler. Maybe you've seen her recently."

Whitfield's body seemed to contract everywhere for just a couple of seconds.

"So she's still alive?"

"Well I hope so."

"Gosh, I haven't seen her in years."

"Sorry to have bothered you." I turned to leave.

"Wait." He grabbed my arm. "What's she doing now?"

He looked sincerely curious.

"She spends a lot of time over by the Dixon Hotel. You know it?" He let go of my arm and put his hands in his pants pockets.

"Yeah. I know it." He looked like he going to cry and then he snapped out of it. "I always hoped she'd find something she was good at that wasn't self-destructive."

Now I was curious.

"How'd you know her?"

He lowered his eyes and pushed his hands deeper into his

■●■

pockets. His head snapped up suddenly and he crossed his arms over his chest.

"We were both about as close to each other as two junkies could be. We were so pitiful together we were even sharing needles. Funny…we both woke up at the same time. When we did, neither of us liked how the other one looked. I ended up here. The last time I saw Lisa she was doing tricks down by Rockland."

"The high school?!"

He nodded while looking away from me.

"By any chance would you know Angela Cox?"

"Angela was in our circle. She didn't make it. She's been dead about three years. O.D."

"How about Marty Felter?"

Whitfield sucked his lips into his mouth. "Oh boy. You're running down the whole gang." He shook his head. "You'll probably find Marty over on Marion Street by the overpass. I think he lives underneath it."

So that I wouldn't have to pull out the city map, I said, "Where the hell is Marion Street?"

The directions were very precise. I was there in fifteen minutes. I sat in the car watching two kids about 10 or 12 playing catch. Watching them told me I shouldn't even get out of the car. They were playing catch with a dead rat. One kid would pick it up by the tail and wing it through the air toward the other kid, who would try to grab it by the tail before it hit the ground. A few men shuffled past them like it was just a tryout for the White Sox.

I decided I wanted to talk to Winch without Udo around. Feeling like a city street pinball, I drove toward downtown. I parked about half a block past Udo's on the opposite side of the street. The dry cleaner's windows were completely fogged over.

■ ● ■

A white van with a big, pink peace sign pulled in behind me about ten yards back. I leaned over to my right to get an angle. A candy store-magazine shop with huge windows was three steps up. I thought about getting a soda, but who knew how long it would be before Winch came out, if he came out. Then I'd have to convince the candy store owner to let me use his toilet.

I sat there about twenty minutes before the driver of the white van reappeared and hopped in behind the wheel. I finally decided to chance it and buy a soda. I crossed the sidewalk, and as I climbed the stairs I noticed the grey Impala sitting behind the van. As the van pulled away I could see a white guy and a black guy in the front seat looking at Udo's.

I quickly picked up a copy of the Sporting News, grabbed a Hires, paid and took up a position at the front window where I could see the gray car. I couldn't have been at the window two minutes when Winch came out, took a left and disappeared around the corner. I almost put the paper under my arm to go after him, which made no sense since I wanted the two in the grey car. No sooner had my thoughts rambled away, than I heard car doors slamming. They both were out of their car and going into Udo's building.

I left the store, jogged up the street toward the Impala, looking over my shoulder for Winch. I took down the license plate number. The inside of the car was empty of anything useful in identifying someone. There was a sky blue Van Heusen shirt, still in its wrapper, lying on the back seat. I tried to see if I could get lucky and pop the trunk, but I didn't get lucky.

I ran back to my car to park it around the next corner so I could pull out and tail my two new friends. There was no reasonable place to park if I wanted to get out quick, so I double-parked with the engine running. Funny. I never checked to see how much gas I had.

■ ● ■

I walked back to the corner, stood behind a white Valiant station wagon, and waited to see if my new friends would come out. I didn't have long to wait. They came flying out of the building with their suit tails looking like kites in the wind. I ran back to my car and pulled it up close to the corner in case they did a U-turn. They didn't. They rolled right past my street but the driver seemed to look me right in the eye as he went past. Damn. He made me that fast?! Nah.

I waited a few seconds to let another car go by and pulled out to follow the Impala, from what I thought was a safe distance.

I hadn't thought of Cheike, now, for at least an hour. Probably would be good if I wasn't thinking of her now. The car ahead of me stopped for a red light. I pounded the steering wheel twice when I saw the Impala make a right turn one block further down. I stepped on the gas, swung around the car in front of me, cut off a car with right of way and gassed it down the block parallel to the Impala's. I skidded to the stop sign fish-tailing just in time to see the tail end of the Impala passing through the intersection to my left.

I laid some rubber trying to beat the Impala to the next corner. I heard someone scream, "Slow it down!" They were right and I was wrong, so I gave it more gas. I slammed on the brakes at the corner. A woman pulling a shopping cart glared at me.

The Impala turned left and so did I. We drove for ten or fifteen minutes, with me laying a block and a half or two blocks back. Then they pulled up to a corner and stopped. If I went past they'd get a good look at me and run my plates. Or I could just pull up and wait, since I was now certain they knew they were being followed.

I reached under the seat thinking, 'People must think I'm crazy and goddamn it, I can't let them down.' I squealed the tires, ran up to the Impala, slightly sideswiped it when I hemmed

■ ● ■

them in and jumped out with a crowbar. I hopped up on the hood of my car and smashed the Impala's windshield three times. The white guy was getting out of their car quicker than I expected, but I slid down from the hood, jumped in my car and left the guy in the intersection after he tried to jump in front of me.

I figured they'd have to call a tow truck. They certainly couldn't see out the windshield very easily. I raced back to Evanston Avenue looking for a phone booth. When I found one I called the office. Elaine picked up.

"Elaine, are any of the guys there?"

"No. What's up?"

"Close the office. I need you to bring another car for a tail job. I think it's the two guys who grabbed the prostitute."

"I can't clo…hold on a sec."

For some reason she put me on hold. What the hell was she doing?

"Where are you?

I told her the cross streets. She put me on hold again. What the hell?

"Someone will be there in seven to ten minutes."

"Someone?! Who Someone?"

She hung up, leaving me wondering who was going to show up. It'd have to be Andy, Heeks, Sharp or Elaine. If it was Elaine we'd argue about who was going to drive, but she didn't give me the feeling she was going to be coming. I leaned against my car wondering about 'Someone.' This was bullshit. I dialed the number for our office again and I heard Elaine's voice just as the car pulled up.

"Get in."

I bent down to make sure it was who I thought it was.

"Elaine, Helen just got here. You shouldn't have sent her."

■ ● ■

"She was the most available driver and clearly the best."

I couldn't argue with 'best,' but Heeks was going to be pissed when he found out.

"Elaine, listen…run this license plate for me." I gave her the numbers. "Gotta go."

I slipped into Helen's Ford Fairlaine.

"Where?"

I gave her directions and we ended up parked three blocks from the tow truck that was pulling the damaged car up onto its bed. My two quarries were standing on the sidewalk looking around. Just when their car was being jacked up, another car arrived and they both got in. Their new car went one block and took a left. I almost said, "Helen, speed up. You're going to lose them." Helen took her first left with a smile on her face. She made it to the corner so fast I needed to catch my breath when she made the turn. There they were. Helen closed to within two blocks.

"I thought you were at Med school."

"I have a couple of days break. As soon as I walked into the office Elaine said, 'Hi! Are you up for tailing someone?' I nodded. She gave me the address."

"Heeks is going to be pissed at her for sending you out on a job."

"I doubt it…and if he knows what's good for him he better say, 'How'd it go, honey?' Isn't that Pomeroy up there?"

"Yeah?"

Helen took a left.

"What're you doing?"

We're disappearing for a little while. There are no right turns off Pomeroy because of the reservoir. We're going to come out just a little ahead of them or we'll see them if they take a left."

Helen pushed on the gas enough for me to hope some ran-

■ ● ■

dom patrol car didn't pass by, even if I knew Helen could lose them. I just didn't want to lose Huey and Duey.

After five blocks Helen made a right and pulled half-way in toward the block behind a parked truck. I was blind to the street ahead.

In a sing-song voice I said, "I can't see anything."

In a voice one octave higher than mine, Helen sang back, "You will sur-vi-ive. So tell me 'bout the woo-man you met and it's about ti-ime."

I stared at her. "I thought you didn't talk to Elaine. You walked in the office. She gave you directions…"

"Hold that thought. They should be coming by any moment now."

"Or we lost them."

"Fuck that." Helen's eyes were totally focused ahead. Her right index finger tapped the steering wheel. "There they are." We were off again, behind them a block and a half.

"So tell me."

"Okay. That was really good. I could never have done that. Satisfied?"

"Huh?" Helen glanced at me. Then she started laughing. "Not this. The woman. Tell me about the woman you went out with."

"What the fuck?! We went swimming. Had a nice conversation in Stendahl's. That's it."

"You mean 'Jackie's?'"

"Yes, I mean 'Jackie's.'"

"So when are you seeing her again?"

"Maybe I won't. I'll have to find her."

"What do you mean?"

"I think it's a game thing. She knows I'm a detective, so she wants to see if the P.I. can use the clues she dropped to find her."

■ ● ■

"You can use an entire detective agency. That shouldn't be hard. On top…here we go."

Their car pulled into a circular drive in front of the Zilmont Cloisters, a rather expensive building to live in. We went past and Helen coasted to the curb. In my side view mirror I watched both of them enter the building. Helen and I got out of the car. We started walking toward the building. Helen grabbed my arm with one hand and slipped the other one around it.

"Is this Heeks' training, or did you just dream this up?"

She squeezed my arm. "Since you're one of my favorite people, showing affection every once in while can't hurt, can it?"

"Depends upon how close Mr. Mojica is to a knife…which means I might be in serious trouble."

As we approached the entrance the doorman moved over in front of us, very stylishly.

"Can I help you with something?"

"We were curious about the building. It seems like it might be a nice place to live. But we didn't want to move somewhere with a high tenancy turnover."

The doorman smiled with the bottom half of his face. "Well, I think you would have a difficult time finding an apartment here."

"Oh. I had the impression that the man who just went in may have lived here."

The doorman looked over his shoulder. "No. He's just going to see someone."

Helen pulled on my arm. "Let's go. I don't think I'd want to live here."

We turned around. I went down on one knee and began tying my already tied shoe as three policemen in civies walked by. I looked behind me in time to see the doorman nod to all three.

When I stood up Helen whispered, "It's not even two o'clock yet."

■●■

Andy

When I walked into the lobby at Udo's building, I stopped, looked down the first floor hallway, looked behind me out the front door and then walked slowly to the doorman. He was lying on his back with a gash in his forehead and bullet hole in his knee. I squatted down to see if he was still alive.

The lobby door opened behind me and I went into a spin on the floor.

"What the hell?! You had to fuck him up like this?! Chair wasn't good enough?!"

"Winch…" I took a deep breath. "I don't know what happened. I just got here. We need to make a tourniquet for his leg. He's bleeding pretty steady."

Winch stared from behind a deep frown. "Maybe there's something in the utility closet." I followed Winch into the first floor hall. He opened the closet door, flicked on the light and I was taken aback by how much of everything I didn't want was in here in one place. There wasn't even a broom I could break the handle off of.

"Can you cut off a piece of this rope? About four feet. Grab that wrench for me."

■ ● ■

We went back to the doorman, who was just regaining the ability to moan loudly in pain. I wound the rope around his thigh and twisted the wrench inside the rope.

"Winch, hold this tight like this until the blood barely oozes. I'll call for an ambulance and see what's going on upstairs."

"Maybe I should go with you."

"No. Stay here. We don't want him bleeding to death for no good reason."

I climbed the stairs trying to see if there was any movement ahead of me, hoping there wouldn't be since I wasn't armed. I slid down the hallway against the wall to Louie's apartment. It was partially open with bullet holes scattered in the door. I thought Louie would have had a heavier door. I heard voices inside and I pushed a little on the knob.

"Louie?"

Automatic weapon fire tore through the metal and made plaster splatter all over the hallway. I jumped back with my shoulder and arm curled toward my chest and my head lowered like a turtle's. Louie started screaming.

"Da-veed! What the hell are you doing?"

"Louie. It's me. Andy."

Louie screamed again. "Go in the fucking kitchen, damn it! I'm okay."

A door a little way down the hall opened and a woman's head with half closed eyes peered out. "Who the fuck keeps pounding on the wall? We's all trying to sleep goddam it! Quit fucking pounding on the fucking wall!" She slammed the door shut.

Louie appeared in the doorway with what looked like a mini uzi in his left hand. "Come on in, Andrew."

I followed Louie into his living room, noticing the bandage wrapped around his upper right arm. "Louie, you need to call an ambulance."

■ ● ■

"I don't need no ambulance."

"They shot up your doorman downstairs, too."

"Watchya mean, 'too?' They didn't shoot me. Da-Veed shot me. Didn't you Da-Veed?! He came from the porch out the kitchen and shot up everything. And me too!" Louie lowered his voice. "I'm a have to get rid of Da-Veed somehow. He's loyal, but he's gonna kill somebody I don't want dead and then where the hell we be? You know, GM?"

"Louie, call an ambulance."

"I don't want no ambulance over here. I got it under control. My doctor will be here in five minutes. How bad is Willy?"

"He'll probably be okay. Winch is down there with him."

Louie turned toward me totally indignant. "Winch? Winch set me up didn't he? He leaves. They break in. I deal with him, you better know that!"

"Louie, who broke in?"

"A big white cocksucker and some black son of a bitch. I thought I heard somebody at the door. Then they just came in with their pieces out. White boy pushed me on the couch. That black fuck put his pistol right on my nuts screaming at me about, 'where the documents?' Then Da-Veed came in shooting everything that wasn't moving except me. The two assholes ran out the door. I think Da-Veed missed both of them." Louie looked around the room. "How can one man do this much damage, shoot me and miss the two men he trying to shoot with the kind of weapon I got for him?" Louie shook his head in disbelief and then stared at me. "How? Da-Veed started to chase them, but I grabbed him. You know they were out there waiting. Had to be." Louie started shaking his head, doing a four step pace back and forth, like he was trying to work himself up to something. "Goddam Winch left the door unlocked for them. Motherfucker!"

"Louie, I don't think Winch did that. These are the guys who

■ ● ■

grabbed Lisa."

"Winch didn't go down from no one punch, ya know."

"I have a feeling he did. I have a feeling the two who came in here are very dangerous. I'll bet you one of them picked the lock."

"My lock?!"

"That's not all that much door, Louie."

Louie was looking at me with his mouth half opened. "You think they that bad…"

"Yeah. I do. When does Da-Veed go outside?"

"He don't. He goes out on the back porch sometime."

"That's what I thought. That's why they came in like they did. They had no idea you had a man up here with you. Winch left and they thought you were alone."

Louie looked around his living room. "Damn."

"Are you calling this in?"

"Hell no! I'm a deal with this myself. I don't want no cops in on this. You find the girl and those two motherfuckers and I double you money, GM. Hell, forget the girl. You get me a location on those two, I double you money period."

Winch came through the door like a bull. "Louie, you okay?"

"Yeah."

"What the hell happened?"

"Gimme a second and I fill you in."

Louie turned on me with his head tilted like something wasn't right. "Why you here, Andrew?"

"You had Winch out there with Lisa the night she was kidnapped. Do you have protection out there in the daytime, too?"

"Why you askin' that, GM? You think I fucked up? I ain't never had no daytime problems."

"Well, what do you do if someone doesn't want to pay some afternoon? How do your women find their customers in the

■ ● ■

daytime?"

Louie looked down at the floor and then up at me and I could see he already understood.

"The girls look for the older dudes. The professionals who want to take the afternoon off instead of going back to the office. They always pay. The stupids don't come out until after the sun goes down…or my girls got the sense to ignore them til then."

"So where was Lisa supposed to be?"

"She did pretty good over by Simpson, by that electronics building."

"Louie, is anybody else from your company missing?"

Louie's smile slit from ear to ear. "My company, huh? I like that. You think I put somebody on ice, Andrew?"

"No, Louie. I was wondering if somebody took off or someone else got hurt."

"Winch! Call over to Marquez and…"

The doctor came walking in. "I don't have time for all of this today, Mr. Udo. That man downstairs needs to go to the hospital. Who bandaged your arm? Let me see that."

Louie pulled his arm away. "You go sit your medical ass down over on one of those chairs 'til I finish my conversation, which you interrupted, and you will devote as much time as necessary to today's problems. That is why you are on retainer. And ain't nobody goin' to no hospital today. Somebody over there see a bullet hole in somebody and they just got to call the police. No fucking police."

"That man's kneecap is shattered. The bullet is still in there. There's only so much I can do outside of the hospital. He'll never be right if we can't get him in a surgery."

"So then he'll have to learn how to limp."

Louie turned back to me totally exasperated by the ignorance of his doctor.

■ ● ■

"You see what I gotta put up with? Look, man…find me those two bastards and I double you money like I said. Where's that crazy guy you work with? Winch, call Penelope and see if there's any problems over there."

"Like what?"

"Like what?! Like any! You know the word 'any?'"

"I have to go down in the street then to make the calls."

"Why?!"

"Da-Veed shot the telephones."

"Go next door to Elizabeth's and use hers."

"All of the girls probably still be sleepin'."

"And they probably sleep right through your phone calls."

Winch left the apartment shaking his head.

"Okay, Louie. I'm leaving."

"What's the hurry, Andrew?"

I just want to be out of here before the infection sets in on your arm and it falls off. By the way, can you shoot with your left hand? And how the heck did you get one of those? That's a new model, isn't it?"

Louie held up his brand new mini uzi. "What? I got my people. And shit…with this all I have to do is point in somebody's general direction and squeeze the trigger. It not like I gotta sight somebody down, you know?"

■ ● ■

Distortion

Andy was pacing. "Nice fucking detective work, Sherlock. Is that the only way you could shadow them? Break out their windshield? Didn't we do this one before? Why the…"

"I was going to lose them, Andy. They made me before I could get in my car. I couldn't think of anything else I could do."

"Well, why'd you two get Helen involved? She shouldn't be involved."

Elaine leaned back in her chair. "Look, Andy, Helen walked into the office. I asked if she wanted to help. Her eyes got big. She nodded 'yes,' so I gave her the location. The Collinsworth reps were already on their way here. Besides, she's our best driver."

Andy's head snapped up. "She's not our driver! She's a medical student. Mojica will probably be furious when he finds out we sent her out chasing around after some gangsters."

I heard the elevator door open, close and then Helen and Heeks came strolling into the office. Helen was describing how we tailed our two boys and Heeks' eyes glowed at her like she was giving him a lifetime supply of Bazooka bubble gum.

"Tony, I'm sorry we let Helen get involved in this. It'll never happen again."

■ ● ■

Helen looked stunned. "What'd I do wrong?"

"You didn't do anything wrong, but we…"

"Why are you talking crazy Andy?" Mojica looked one part confused and two parts perturbed. "Besides seeing me, that's probably the most exciting thing Helen will be able to do while she's here." Helen pushed him in the shoulder with both hands. Mojica fought off a smile. "Helen's driven for us before. Why are you making a big deal out of it? Helen and Mon Capitan found our boys and a lot more. You need to stop looking at Reader's Digest so much, Andy. It's affecting your sensibilities and personality. By the way, guys, all of our cars should have the phones in by Saturday."

Andy looked embarrassed. The phones? I don't know why I was surprised. "How much will that cost?"

Elaine crossed her arms and swung her chair toward me. "If you came to meetings instead of going swimming all the time, you'd probably know."

"Fuck you and your dog's afterlife." I noticed Helen smiling a very evil smile. I was on the verge of being outnumbered.

The elevator doors opened again and I could hear Sharp coming toward the office. Andy finally sat down. Mojica went to his office and came out with two padded folding chairs I had never seen before. Sharp closed the outer office door.

When everyone was seated it occurred to me that we were about to have a meeting, but for the first time it wasn't going to be in my office space. I felt slightly offended.

Sharp did a slow take of all of us; then he started recapping the meeting he and Heeks had with Raoul. "Amazingly, Raoul doesn't know who the two kidnappers are. He's pulling some strings in Washington, but so far he's come up empty. When the rumors about some white guy putting Winch down with one body shot got back to Raoul, he became curious. There are

■ ● ■

a number of new faces around town and it seems most of them hover around a newly arrived lunatic named Alex DeFord. DeFord is a very wealthy person who seems to laugh out loud frequently at things other people can't see. He is also connected to the Commission and apparently the kidnappers. Raoul has no idea of why he's here. It's possible that DeFord has a good number of friends in the police department. He is also in the process of buying a farm out on Castor Hill Road."

That was pretty far out. I remembered going to a high school graduation party out there. Way out there. It was underneath some blinking red T.V. broadcasting antennas.

"Sharp, where is this guy from?"

Sharp looked at Andy. "As far as Raoul can tell, Rhodesia by way of Montgomery, Alabama. When it became obvious to him that the white minority government was going to fall to ZANU, he packed up his plantation and went to Alabama."

"Is he British?"

"Nope. American."

Mojica joined in. "Raoul says there are five or six cops who visit the apartments DeFord has rented."

Andy looked surprised. "How does he know that? We've only known where the kidnappers were located for about five minutes."

"Raoul was curious about the cops. He's had a few White Lightning boys checking out the hotel for a week now."

"How'd he get the Irish to agree to do that?"

"He gave them a car." Mojica shrugged. "On top of that, Raoul found out that Blakeslee's I.D. was fake."

I winced, wondering if I had screwed up again.

Andy gave his report next. "Our two kidnappers visited Udo this morning. They knee-capped the doorman on the way in. During the fracas upstairs, Udo was shot by his own man."

■●■

Andy turned his head toward me. "You must have seen them just after Da-Veed shot up the apartment. Udo told me he would double his payment to us for the location of the kidnappers."

"Ah guess we could hand over an address on a piece of paper and let Udo have his little war. But I'm a little curious about what happened to the woman. We signed on to find the woman and that's what I'm in for. Ah'm of the opinion that we will have to pay a visit to Mr. DeFord and his friends if we want to find out. Our client wanted to know what happened to Lisa Butler. We're not going to find out without speaking to the two men who snatched her."

"I think Sharp's right, but I think a couple of us need to stay in the background."

Andy was looking at the floor when he started speaking. "I have a feeling there is no 'background' here, Elaine. These guys are connected to the Commission. We can't believe they haven't been checking us out since our incident down in the lobby. Whoever they are, they probably know just about everything there is to know about us …and Helen, now, too. How do we protect Helen in Chicago if we have to?"

Everyone was quiet for an extraordinary five seconds.

Sharp broke the silence. "If they know all about us, Andy, they knew about Helen before today. Ah think we can talk to Raoul and get some coverage up in Chicago." Mojica was nodding his agreement.

Elaine crossed her hands in her lap and said, "We haven't been looking very long, but doesn't it seem like something's missing?"

"Of course something's missing. A fat ton of information about what's going on." How is it that Elaine could irritate me by asking a simple question. Was it because she was a woman and I still had male hang-ups, or was it because Elaine asked

■ ● ■

questions I wanted to ask about half a second before I did.

"No. What I mean is, a guy goes out a window. The woman with him takes off with his stuff. Two guys go after her to get the stuff back. They assumed that the flyer had the stuff with him."

"Yeah, so?"

"C'mon Capitan, let the woman speak."

"The stuff that Jocko picked up. We missed something. Or Jocko missed something. Something that should have been there, wasn't. Or we haven't seen something that is there."

Sharp got up and went into his office. He came back out with an envelope containing the I.D. Jocko found in the alley next to Jackie's Diner. He dumped it on Elaine's desk and everyone, but me, stood up. They started picking up pieces of identification randomly and looking at them. Mojica kept holding pieces up to the light. I was convinced we didn't miss anything in the cards.

Suddenly Helen spoke up. "What if it's still back in the alley?"

Everyone stopped moving and started staring at Helen. "And you call yourselves detectives?"

"Wait until you botch your first open heart surgery, Doc."

"Just hope it's not on you, Tex."

Sharp started laughing.

I felt like I needed to move. "Maybe Elaine and I can go back over to see if we can find something Jocko didn't notice."

Elaine turned her chair toward me again. "Why me?" She was borrowing the same evil smile I saw on Helen's face a couple of seconds ago.

Elaine and I took the elevator down and crossed the lobby. The newspaper hawker was loading up his cart. A few people passed us on the way to the elevators. When we made it to the sidewalk Elaine tugged at my sleeve. "Still bothers you, doesn't it?"

■ ● ■

"Always will. I get a chill every time I go through there."

"It's probably good we're moving then. Well, in the meantime just don't pop the newsman. He's innocent."

We made a right to go get one of the agency cars. As we approached the corner there was a low rumble of words, like distant thunder.

"Hey! P.I. guy!"

I was stunned and momentarily paralyzed. It was Cheike leaning against a mailbox with a very sly grin on her face.

"I thought you would have found me by now. Pretty busy doing detective things?"

I started to speak but my throat felt tight. I noticed Elaine's eyes shifting from me to Cheike and back.

"Uh, this is Elaine. Elaine, Cheike. Elaine is one of my partners in our agency."

Cheike raised her hand to shake Elaine's, while her wrist jewelry sounded like a wind chime.

"So he really is a detective."

"Did he tell you that? He tells everyone that." Elaine stopped with her sing-song whiny voice and glanced at me with a grin. I frowned. "Actually, he's a very good detective. I'd say that he's my mentor." The frown slipped off my face and I couldn't seem to get it back on. When I looked back at Cheike she was sporting the same grin Elaine had just owned. I felt like half an idiot.

"Where are you heading for? Anyone for lunch?"

"Elaine and I are heading for an alley over by the diner where we met. We have to look for something, but if you could give us an hour or so we could meet you in the diner…if you can take the food."

"The food is actually decent, I think. Okay. Deal. I have to go get my car. So I'll meet you two over there in an hour, give or take."

∎●∎

Cheike walked away with her jewelry tinkling out a song I could almost remember.

"Damn…was that your swimming partner? She's got a voice like Lauren Bacall squared and some kinda' walk."

"Yeah. She's my swimming partner."

"She's enough to make me consider swinging the other way."

"Hey. That's not funny."

"Yes it is. I can see you got nervous with me just suggesting there might be some competition."

"This is not a competition. What's up with you? I just met the woman."

Elaine was quiet until we opened the car doors.

"I'm happy you met someone. It seems you haven't run into anyone you've been really interested in for a very long time. I'm glad for you."

"Uh huh. Well I just met her and I'm not interested in having this conversation across the top of the car roof."

A postman walked by, did half a salute accompanied by an, "Afternoon."

When I sat down behind the steering wheel I turned to Elaine as she slid in. "Why the hell aren't you driving?"

She looked at me like I had burped in her face. "You want me to drive? Okay. Get out."

"Forget it."

"No, really. Get out."

"No, really. Forget it."

"No, no, nonono, no. Get the fuck out of the car."

We both got out and walked to opposite sides of the car. I glared at her for a second before I got back in. She snorted.

"I don't know what happened to you. You used to be so cool. Now it's like you're practicing to be an irritating old man."

"Why did you say I was your mentor?"

■ ● ■

Elaine looked at me like her feelings were hurt. "Because you are."

"Shit, Elaine. You do as much around the business as any of us. I'm not your mentor. You're my equal partner."

"Well how the hell was, 'he's my equal partner' supposed to help impress Cheike?"

"I don't need your help."

Elaine started the car and pulled out into traffic. "The way you're acting…the hell you don't."

I knew there was probably something Jocko missed in the alley. It was eight feet wide and one hundred feet deep. Since Jocko had picked up Lisa's papers there had been a storm and now there were new pieces of paper trash scattered around. The weeds in the corner were annoying. All types of paper seemed to find the growth a great place to rest and decompose. On top of it all, seeds kept sticking to my jeans, and the goddam weeds kept scratching my hands.

We were walking up and down the alley for the fourth time when I heard Cheike say, "Can I help? Is this what detectives do?"

I looked up smiling. "We're almost done here. Would you be offended if I asked you to put in an order for us?"

"Yes, but I'll do it anyway."

"You could order me a grilled cheese and a cherry coke. How about you, Elaine?"

"Could you order me a bowl of chili and a sel…hold the phone, as Sharp would say."

Elaine bent over and pulled part of a piece of paper from under a sock it was sticking to. She unfolded part of a sheet. "How'd we miss this?"

■ ● ■

Elaine studied the piece of paper holding it at the edges between her forefinger and thumb. "Looks like a formula." I looked over Elaine's shoulder and it did look like part of a formula.

Cheike held her hand out. "Can I see that?"

Elaine didn't even hesitate. I almost said 'what the hell are you doing?" Fortunately I kept my mouth shut.

Cheike stared at the paper like she thought she was going to figure out what it was. And she did. "Obviously it's not complete, but I'd guess this was a water flow formula. But I can't tell what this part is, or the number sequence down at the bottom. I mean the rest of it must be out here in this alley. Don't you think?"

Elaine put her hand out. Cheike gave the paper back. Now Elaine stared at the paper. "This could be a volume equation."

Cheike took the paper back to take her turn staring at the writing. "Damn, I think you're right." Cheike stepped past us into the alley. "We should try to find the other pieces of the page."

"Maybe we should get something to eat first." The two women moved back up the alley with their heads down. My contribution to the discussion being ignored, I put my head down and joined them.

An hour and a half later we agreed that what we were looking for was no longer in the alley. Cheike looked very disappointed. Elaine and I headed toward the diner door. Cheike seemed to hesitate.

"I have to make a phone call. I'll meet you inside."

■ ● ■

Found

Fifteen minutes later Helen walked into the diner just as our food arrived. Elaine beat me to an introduction of Cheike and the four of us squeezed comfortably into a booth by the window.

"Tony said he'd meet me at 2:30. I was wondering if you were still going to be around when I got here."

Elaine passed the piece of paper to Helen. We think it might be an equation for water flow, but we can't figure out if the part on top is related to the volume quotient." Cheike put her finger on a fraction and explained it. Elaine added something else I didn't understand. Then Helen stared at both of them.

"I think this stuff at the top is a formula for a toxin."

I was definitely on the outside of this conversation looking in. The three women were totally engaged with each other. I was close to feeling completely half-ass ignorant. Kind of like a base-ball card with no stats on the back.

Elaine turned the paper toward Helen. "I can't get a grip on this sequence of numbers at the bottom of the page. They're not multiples of anything and they're not sequential."

Cheike said, "Maybe they're page references."

■●■

Helen nodded her head slowly. "That could be. But in reality they might be just about anything."

"Route numbers."

The women all looked at me. Helen looked back at the paper with a frown and squinty eyes.

Elaine shook her head slightly. "What?!"

"Route numbers. Directions that start someplace near Haley." I looked down at the paper and lifted my eyebrows. "Too bad all of the directions weren't there." When I looked up Cheike's eyes were slits and she had this odd smile on her face. It made me feel like she was thinking, 'Maybe this guy does know something.' I noticed my back was wet from perspiration. Apparently I didn't realize how much the previous conversation made me feel not only dumb, but nervous. Elaine was right and I was hating her for it. I used to be cool or something like it, and now Cheike was completely breaking down my front.

I picked up my grilled cheese, took a glorious bite and listened to Helen say, "Anybody want to take a ride?"

Cheike sat up straight. "I'm game. Where are we going?"

I swallowed and tried to spit out, "Good question," without choking.

Helen looked at me like she couldn't understand why I'd say that. "Somewhere out near these roads. The ones at the bottom of this paper."

"May I point out, Ms. Kildare, that we don't have the all of the route numbers. We may drive out to the middle of no place near somewhere next to nothing. What if we're going northeast and we're supposed to go southeast. There's a lot of road out there."

"Mmm hmm…I'm for driving out there anyway."

"You'll drive anywhere if you can drive fast."

"Is your name really 'Kildare'?"

■ ● ■

Helen turned toward Chieke with a smile. "No. If it was I would have changed it by now. He's just being jerky."

Cheike put her elbow on the table, rested her hand against the side of her head and mouthed a silent, "Why?"

I shrugged while taking another bite. She smiled. I felt better, but still a little stupid.

Elaine pushed out of the booth. "I'll be right back."

"Seriously Helen, we can't…"

"Okay. I get the picture." Helen picked up her tuna salad. She looked at it with intent. She looked at me and bit down on it so hard I said, "Ow!"

Cheike started laughing.

Elaine ran back in and sat down out of breath. She pushed her Cobb salad to the middle of the table and then plopped down a 1981 state road atlas. She started flipping to the index to find County Route 7.

"What are you doing, Elaine?" I took another bite of my sandwich and sucked down a good part of my cola.

"We have route numbers to somewhere from somewhere. We're all guessing they have something to do with water…"

"I haven't guessed that yet."

"You've got to be kidding." The three of them were glaring at me.

I stuck out my chin. "Okay, let's pretend the route numbers have something to do with water."

Elaine turned on her evil smile. She grabbed the paper and began tracing the route in the atlas with a pencil. Then she started shading in the areas on both sides of the routes. Finally she put both of her hands on the map with her fingers spread out. "We probably want to be looking for bodies of water in these areas."

All three of them were looking at me again, but now I felt

∎ ● ∎

like maybe I was supposed to be the voice of reason. I took the last bite of a great grilled cheese. "That's a lot of driving. We won't even know what body of water we're looking for unless there's something spectacular or crazy odd going on when we see it."

Cheike murmured, "Something singular."

I couldn't help smiling.

I heard Helen say, "We have roads, water and poison."

"Yeah. Maybe we have weed killer."

"It's not weed killer. I'm sure of that."

Then it was Elaine's turn. "What if these people were going to assassinate someone?"

Everyone got quiet. The front door screeched and I considered buying some WD-40 and bestowing it on the diner. Funny I didn't notice the screen door today until now though.

"You know what, Elaine? Let's go talk this over with our other partners, because off-hand I think trying to kill someone by poisoning their well is very inefficient. I think if poison and water go together it's got to be something other than knocking someone off at their kitchen sink." And then a chill ran down my spine followed by a deep shudder.

Cheike asked me if I was okay. I nodded yes, but I had a scarey thought creeping around in my mind.

The food slowly disappeared with the three women trying to find lakes and ponds they thought we should check out. Elaine would circle them and one of the three would ask me what I thought. I kept saying "possibly" while I wondered why Cheike knew about water flow. Of course I also wondered how much Elaine knew about water volumes. Helen could be explained. She had medical training and she was probably a genius.

"Hey, guys! You planning a day trip?"

Three voices suddenly took turns explaining what was on

■ ● ■

the paper while Mojica alternately frowned and smiled. When they had finished Heeks looked at Cheike with eyebrows raised. "Obviously you belong here, but uh, who are you?"

Elaine spoke before I could get the straw out of my mouth. This is Cheike. She's an artist, new to town and likes to swim."

Cheike laughed while trying to stand up to shake hands. "So you're one of the partners."

"Yep. And I'm her partner." Heeks reached down for Helen's hand. When he found it she pulled him down until he was kissable. After Helen was done planting pecks on his cheeks, Mojica grinned and looked around.

"Damn girl…you're going to embarrass the staff."

Helen smiled up at him like I wished someone would smile at me some day. I glanced at Cheike and my wish seemed to be coming true. Or else it was the best illusion of my entire life. Right now I was taking either one.

Mojica's voice broke through my short daydream. "We just can't go out riding around looking for something that even if we did see it we may not know it's what we're looking for. Did that make sense what I just said? There's maybe three or four hundred square miles of area you're talking about. We don't know if we'd be looking for a well, a stream, a lake, a water tower or what. What we have here is a piece of paper that Elaine found covered by a sock that could have been dropped by some college student."

Cheike spoke up in her bass baritone. "Doubt it." I thought I could feel the vibrations in the table top.

Then Helen jumped in. "Antonio, you know damn well no college student dropped this out in the alley. A student studying toxicology and water movement? C'mon…"

"I was just trying to emphasize the fact that we don't really know what we have."

■ ● ■

It looked like euphoria was drifting toward the rusted tin ceiling and the air vents.

Mojica did an extended shoulder shrug and said, "Maybe we should go back to the office and talk this over with Andy and Sharp."

I wanted to appear as even-keeled as possible. "Yeah. I think we should. Cheike, if you want to come, I'd say you're welcome."

"You know, I don't think I should. Now that I think about it, I need to get back to my studio and get some work done."

Everyone got up while I figured out the tip and tried to put a face on my deflation. When I started to slide out of the booth I noticed Cheike seemed to be looking me over.

"Doing anything later? Maybe you could show me more of the town."

I think a grin exploded out of my face. "That could be arranged. How about eight o'clock?"

"I'll be waiting."

"I still…"

She suddenly gave me this cold, glassy look that froze me. "Uh huh." I still hadn't taken the time to find out where her studio was and her eyes told me the challenge was still there.

Out on the sidewalk everyone was giving Cheike a lost old friend found 'good-by' hug. When it was Mojica's turn he quipped, "Who are you again?" Helen slapped his shoulder and called him an "ass."

Cheike walked off down the sidewalk with her jewelry jingling. I heard her say "eight," without turning around. When she turned the corner I said, "You guys have to do me a favor. Heeks, take the keys. I need you guys to follow her and find out where she lives."

Helen shook her head 'no.' Elaine grabbed Helen's arm when she asked, "Are we serious here?"

■ ● ■

"Yes we are. It's for a good cause."

I whispered a "Thank you, Elaine."

"It's for the virgin over there."

Then I whispered a "Fuck you, Elaine."

Heeks ran off laughing, while I watched Elaine drag Helen toward her car.

I shook my fist. "Gotcha!" I felt good. It was nice to have sly and evil friends. I slipped into the alley between the taxi garage and the diner, waiting for Cheike's Audi to turn the corner. A few seconds after she did, Mojica turned out of the next side street to follow. A moment later Elaine slid past with Helen at the wheel.

I was about fifteen minutes into my walk back to the office when I saw her. She was going in the opposite direction across the street from me.

"Hey! Hey! Slow up!" She kept on going. I ran across the street dodging a Volkswagen that honked at me rudely. "Hey. Aren't we friends anymore? I'm the guy from the park. She stopped, but she didn't turn around.

When I got close enough to see her face I was shocked at how red her eyes were. "Okay. What's going on with the marriage?" The tears started coming by the bucket. She charged me and wrapped her arms around me while she sobbed. I didn't know what to do with my hands so I held them about a foot away from our bodies. A woman with a package walked by, glancing at me twice while I tried to communicate that I was baffled by my situation. After about a minute the sobbing slowed down. I patted her back very gingerly and suggested we find some place to talk. We made it to a deserted bus stop and sat down.

"Larry said I wasn't going to be doing school. He said I'd be

■ ● ■

busy with some business."

"Did you tell your parents what he said?"

"No. Larry did."

It was hard to believe what I was hearing. "Look, before we go any further, I don't even know your name."

She looked at me like a puppy dog. "Marty…it's short for Martha."

"Martha's a nice name."

"I like Marty better. I chose it."

"Okay, Marty…I really think you need to at least talk to one of my friends at Social Services. We don't even have to tell her your name or anything. Just talk about Larry and your parents. They might have a really good suggestion about how to get out of this situation."

Marty started shaking her head. "I don't want to do that."

"Well, what do you want to do?"

"You could marry me. You're a really nice guy and you can't be married to two people. I looked it up."

"You can't marry me."

She looked at me like she was going sob and melt. "I should have known. You're already married, aren't you?"

I started to speak, but fortunately held my tongue so that my brain could catch up with the situation. I was contemplating doing something stupid.

"No. I'm not married, but I need time to think this through. I have two good friends of mine I want to talk to about this and I'd like you to be there to add anything I might have missed. It's not Social Services, so I'd like you to go back to my office with me. Okay?"

A bus came along, slowing down. I stood up and waved it on past.

"Come with me, okay? This is a big decision."

■ ● ■

She looked up at me, definitely uncertain. "You have an office?" I nodded. "What do you do?"

"I'm a detective."

"For the police?"

"No. We're private detectives."

She frowned, staring at the street. Suddenly she stood up and said, "Okay."

When we walked into the office Mojica was bent over Elaine's desk speaking with her. Helen was sitting on the couch. I could see Andy at his desk. Sharp's cane was resting in the doorway so I knew he and Andy were talking. I turned around to find Marty standing shyly in the office doorway.

"Marty, come on in. I want to introduce you to my friends."

She took a step toward me, bent over slightly at the waist and whispered, "Are these all detectives?"

I smiled and whispered back. "They're supposed to be. Except that one over on the couch. She's a doctor."

I turned back to find Antonio's smile beaming at me like a laser.

"The guy who looks like a Cheshire cat is called fu…uhh… Antonio. You can call him 'Heeks.' The woman at the computer is Elaine. The doctor's name is Helen. Guys, this is Marty. We came up here to get some serious advice about marriage." I heard Sharp chuckle. The guy who's coming at us with that stick in his hand is called Sharp. The man behind him is Andy."

An hour later Elaine and Helen had Marty in a very deep conversation. At one point I started to walk toward Elaine's desk, but Elaine frowned at me and waved me away with the back of her hand. I did a 180 back to my office. I looked out the window for a few seconds. When I started to sit down I noticed

■●■

three of my partners were in the room.

Andy rubbed the back of his head. "We need to figure out what we're going to do about Lisa Butler. Sharp thinks we're going to have to confront DeFord about the men that visit him or work for him. I don't really see how we can get around it."

Sharp sat down on one of my two chairs. "By the way, Raoul called. The Irish lads were rousted by that scout, or whatever he is, and a couple of cops."

I laughed. "That didn't last too long."

"Ah get the impression that boy is pretty good."

Mojica moved over toward my window. "Are we ready for that kind of confrontation? You know it's not going to be a one shot deal."

"If we want to find the woman I don't see how we can avoid it. We have to get somebody moving. The two kidnappers aren't going to say anything."

"Which is my point, Andy. If she's dead nobody's gonna move anyway."

I looked at them while rocking in my chair. "Then we give Louie Udo the address, get paid and let nature take it's course."

"That's cold bro...but that's a way to go ah suppose." Sharp took a toothpick from his front pocket and slid it into the side of his mouth.

Andy looked at the floor. "Basically we're all agreed. We need to go face to face with DeFord and maybe the two kidnappers."

Mojica moved over by my desk and peeked out of my office door. "Think we should get Elaine in here to see what she says?"

I looked up at Mojica. "Elaine was the first one who said we needed to go over there." I stopped rocking, sat up and looked out my office door toward Elaine's desk. "They're still talking?"

Andy leaned in the doorway. "That's a serious conversation they're having, man." On cue all three women burst out laugh-

■ ● ■

ing. Andy frowned. "There can be serious in humour, right?"

"Boy, how'd you meet that little girl again? That story is just raw." Sharp's toothpick rolled from side to side, even when he talked.

"In the park…and I wouldn't mind meeting that Larry character somewhere."

Mojica chuckled. "By the way Capitan, I think Cheike expected someone to follow her. But we got her address. When she parked she went into 795 Sherman Place."

"Aren't there a couple of large empty factory buildings over there?"

"Not so empty now. There are some people redoing the interiors for studios and big lofts. But anyway, Cheike went into 795. In fact, your brother detective, me, determined that her place is in 798 up on the third floor."

A big smile was creeping across my face. I wondered if it was as big as Mojica's.

"Do you think it's okay for me to leave?"

Andy put his back to the door jamb and crossed his arms. "You should probably ask them."

"I don't want Marty to think I don't care."

"She's in pretty good hands and glad of it."

"So the wedding is off?"

"Drop dead, Mojica."

"Dude, you better get moving or you're gonna screw up your first date since like what, 1968?"

"Why does Helen put up with you?"

"A mystery you'll never discover, Capitan." He winked at me.

"That does it!" I pulled out the drawer, hit the button and let the Colt fall into my hand. I shifted it to my left hand, reached down further into the drawer, stood up and threw a handful of tootsie rolls at him. I put the gun back and sat down.

■ ● ■

My three partners started laughing.

Heeks walked around my desk picking up the tootsie rolls. "Where'd you get these?"

"From your office under the porno magazines."

"Hey! What the hell you doing in my office?!"

Sharp had to jump in. "Lookin' at your porno."

Andy put his hand up. "We do have a child out there."

"We have one in here, too." Mojica punched me in the arm.

I walked out to Elaine's desk. The three of them stopped talking to look at me. "Marty, I have an appointment. Do you feel comfortable with Elaine and Helen?"

"Sure. I'll see you later, maybe."

"Of course you will." The wedding was definitely off.

Elaine smiled at me. "We're good. We're working on a plan."

"Okay. Good. Fill me in later."

I made my way to the elevators. Marty suddenly appeared at my side. "You tricked me."

"I guess I did. Was that bad?"

"No, I guess not. It was kind of stupid for me to think you could marry me. You're kind of old and I'm a kid. It was kind of stupid."

"That was kind of like desperation and nobody should have to be that desperate to have to marry a kind of old guy like me."

Marty took a step away from me and scrunched up her nose. "You're not really that old. Just compared to me. And you're still kind of cute."

"Oh."

"Really you're kind of handsome."

"Thanks for the compliment. It might do me some good later."

"I'm sorry I caused you so much trouble."

"You didn't cause me any trouble so far. What do you think of Elaine and Helen?"

■ ● ■

"They're great." Marty rushed me and gave me a teenager's hug. "Thanks." Then she turned around and I watched her walk back through the office door.

I started wondering what was up with the elevator when the door slid open. I stepped in and nodded at my silent operator. I wasn't sure, but I thought he might have nodded back.

■ ● ■

Questions

She was walking down the stairs in her building holding the handrail. I started down after her from the floor up above. Her jewelry tinkled and echoed up the stairwell. When she reached the first floor I saw her look at her watch. She strolled up to the front door with her weight shifting back and forth from foot to foot like she was playing a game. She surveyed the street in both directions while glancing at her watch.

I tip-toed up behind her. I bent my head close to her ear.

I whispered, "Do you think he'll make it on time?"

She didn't move. She whispered back, "Son of a bitch."

"I thought you'd at least jump a little."

She still didn't move. "After that night in the diner and our episode with the farmer's son, I expect deception, illusion, misdirection and some clumsy sleight of hand."

I was about two inches from her ear. She still hadn't moved. If there had been anyone walking by, I'm sure we would have appeared odd. Somebody had to move.

"Does dinner sound good?"

"At the diner?"

"Hell, no! I know a Cajun place just outside of the city."

■ ● ■

"Who's driving?"

"I brought a car. I know the way."

Cheike finally grabbed the door and pulled it open. "After you, sir."

I went out first, hopping down the stairs doing a poor imitation of a 6'2 rabbit. At the bottom I turned and smiled and wondered why I had done something so ridiculous. Cheike glared at me and then began to slide down the stairs in slow motion. Each foot had to be firmly planted on the next step before the other one could move. Before the last step she placed the back of her hand on her forehead and tilted her head back. When she eventually hit the sidewalk she put on a crooked grin. I started to say "the car is over this way." Before I could do that she reached up, put her hand behind my neck, pulled my head towards her and placed a very light kiss on my lips. Then she said, "Which way, hemlock?" The words disappeared but they kept breathing around me like something crazy was going to happen.

My throat felt so tight that the best thing I could do was point. We started across the street and half-way she slid her arm inside mine. I glanced at her wondering if she'd go swimming with me again.

The restaurant wasn't full when we arrived. Before we were even seated I could feel Cheike checking out the place like she worked for Fodor's.

"I approve. Nice ambience."

"It's one of my favorite places to eat."

"I suppose you bring a lot of women here." She looked around with a smirk on her face.

I laughed. "I've brought more women here than the swimming hole. I think a grand total of two. You would make three."

■ ● ■

Cheike's eyebrow's raised. Her mouth opened in mock surprise. "You mean this week?!"

I looked down at the table and then I locked on her eyes. "No. Since I've been back. Like 1976."

"In five years you've brought two women to one of your favorite places to eat."

My head kind of slipped to the side. "Why don't we order, get some drinks and then you can continue your embarrassing interrogation about my private life."

"Do I detect a chink in the armor, Mr. Detective?"

"Nope. More like massive gaping holes."

She started laughing and it became infectious. I was laughing, but felt uneasy because I wasn't sure of what I was laughing about.

"You're intelligent, handsome, fun so far and that makes me curious."

I looked at her waiting for the next line. She seemed embarrassed for a second.

"And you're right. We should order and I should ply you with alcohol so that I can get the answers to all of my curiosities. And if we need a lot of the truth serum, I have more than enough taxi cab money."

"Uh huh. So I will have a gumbo and a beer."

The food seemed exceptionally fine. At first I thought it had to be the company, but Cheike kept complimenting the food so maybe it was really good tonight.

"So how did you meet Andy?"

"We met in the service. Somehow we both ended up in C.I.D. Actually, I knew who Andy was before the Army. Andy was the city chess champion two years in a row before college. So I kind of knew who he was from the newspapers. The first time he saw me he told me he knew who I was from football and basketball and he hated me for making his school lose all the time. Anyway, we

■ ● ■

went through some bizarre stuff in Vietnam and got real close. I'd say he's the best friend I've ever had. We talked about setting up an agency when we got back home…I think we saw the Humphrey Bogart movies too many times. I had considered applying for the CIA, but I saw the spooks do so many outrageous things, I didn't want to be associated with them in any way."

"What about Elaine?"

"I knew Elaine in high school. I think she had a severe mental problem back then."

"Seriously?"

I grew a smile.

Cheike giggled the way I thought Walter Cronkite would giggle if I ever heard him do it.

"Oooooo…that's so rot-ten. You never said that to her did you?"

"Only a few dozen times. Then she went off to Princeton and managed to get her ass expelled. Don't you dare repeat this to her, but I think she's great."

"Is she one of the two women you brought here?"

It was my turn. I felt like I had spent two days answering questions about my partners.

"How do you know about water flow formulas?"

She shook her head. "You need that stuff when you draw nuclear reactors."

"Come on. Seriously."

"School. I took a lot of geology and physics…"

"And seriously."

"School."

"And why aren't you married?"

"What makes you think I'm not."

"You don't seem to have a curfew and no shadow of a ring."

"So Elaine is one of the women you brought here."

■ ● ■

"Nope. I've taken Elaine out on stakeouts, to diners, but never out to dinner and I could have sworn you were going to tell me why you haven't been married."

"And what makes you think I haven't been?"

"Detective's intuition and now, the way you're acting, I think maybe you have been."

"Is 'detective's intuition' quantifiable?"

"I thought you were an artist?"

"I was married for one year." She looked around like she didn't want anyone to hear her. "He didn't like my jewelry. So for our first anniversary we agreed to file for a divorce."

"Ever see him again?"

"No. The last I knew he was out on the West Coast."

"What brought you two together?"

She shrugged. "I was a sucker for engineers."

"You thought…" A familiar face suddenly appeared outside Cheike's glow. I pondered for a second how long he had been there.

Cheike turned her head and then asked, "You okay?"

"Yeah. I was just thinking…I know an Italian café with great desserts. Want to give it a try?"

Cheike turned around again. She turned back with a frown on her face. "There's good Italian pastries in this city? Yeah. Let's do the pastry thing. You've been doing alright so far, so lead on."

I dropped money on the table and glanced at the solitary man over in the corner who was about half way through his dinner.

"So who is that guy?"

"To tell you the truth, I have no idea."

I parked a couple of blocks away from the café. It was a nice area to stroll in and I could scan the street very easily. I point-

■ ● ■

ed out a couple of shops that had interesting window displays. Cheike was giving me her opinion of the Shetland wool sweaters in one window. It was then that I noticed that when Cheike whispered, her voice sounded like waves coming in gently at the beach during low tide. For a second I wondered 'how did this happen?' From somewhere the reply came immediately, 'nothing has really happened yet, has it, stupid?'

We were looking in the window of a collectibles shop where a six car, Elgin freight train was going around in a figure eight for probably the ten thousandth time of the day. All of the lights in the store were off except for the one illuminating the train set with its warehouse, miniature trees and a lonely station attendant waiting for the train to pull up at his tiny ticket booth. I raised my eyes and saw dark Cheike's reflection smiling at me in the window.

I heard Cheike whisper, "Look at me." I felt like I had no choice but to turn my head toward her. Her jewelry was suddenly singing in my ear and her other hand slid around the back of my head. This time it was not a light kiss. My arms wrapped her up so tight I think I worried I would hurt her. It felt like her breath was inside me. And then the train stopped. We both looked in the window at the same time. The display lights went out and we could make out the figure of an older man who gave us a wave, then turned around walking toward the back of the store. We started laughing at the same time. Her hands lingered on my shoulders and ended up wrapped around my left arm.

"Let's find your café before they turn the lights out."

"So will Sharp ever recover?"

"The doctors say he will in time. He's a lot better than the first two months he was out of the hospital. I think he was still in

■ ● ■

pain but he pretended not to be. Now it's the cane and balance mostly. He says some parts of his legs feel numb but they're getting better. He might be lying to us…or himself, but he moves a whole lot better than he used to."

"Did you know him from here?"

"No. Andy and I met him in Vietnam, but that's a longer story than I want to get into right now."

"Okay." She spun her spoon in her espresso and looked up at me with a sliver of a smile. "Want to come back to my place?"

I wasn't dumbstruck but for a few seconds I was frozen. She looked back down at her empty espresso cup.

"There is probably nothing I would rather do than…"

"I'm sorry. I didn't mean to get so fast…yes I did…I thought we were, you know, I…"

I reached for her hand even though it was me who was probably more shaken by this sudden insecurity.

"Cheike…hey…could you look at me for a second? Please."

Her eyes locked on mine like a wolf's. I squeezed her hand in part to see if she was still there, or if I was with a different woman.

"There's probably nothing I would rather do tonight than go back to your studio and see where you live and see where you do what you do. My partners and I are going to have an early morning meeting with some crazy men and I can't be late. If I go home with you I will definitely be late…or useless. So if you're not leaving town tomorrow, I was hoping we could do something a couple of nights from now…or even tomorrow. Is it a date?"

She was back. Her eyes changed and she put on her best sneer. "You betcha."

"Good. There's a Popeye cartoon festival at the Emporium and…"

■ ● ■

"I'm not going to go watch four hours of Popeye, unless someone drags me there."

"I was only kidding."

"Damn it! I was hoping we could sit in the back row and make out until an usher shines a light on us and tells us to get a room."

This, was bad. This, was very, very bad.

■ ● ■

Sneer

In the morning I managed to get to the office before everyone except Elaine. I nodded as I walked past her desk. She immediately got up and followed me.

"We're going to try to get Marty away from her parents and see what we can do about getting custody."

I looked at Elaine like I didn't know her name or where she came from. "What?
Custody? Custody with who?"

"Me, I think. Helen knows a lawyer who specializes in cases that involve children. She's going to call him as soon as the sun comes up."

"She may want to wait until nine o'clock, just to stay on his good side. And what in the hell are you thinking that you want to take her in? You just met her yesterday."

"I know…I don't know what came over me, but she's really sweet and we need to help her."

"Like social services needs to help her."

"That might take too long. Helen and I think…"

"Hold on. Helen is in med school, one of the most time demanding occupations someone can force themselves into. So

■ ● ■

let's not pretend this is you and Helen. It's just you."

"And you, sideshow. You're the one who started this, so let's not pretend you're going to abandon her now. I know you better than that."

"But I'm not her parent or her guardian. I'm a concerned bystander."

"You're more than that. You're…Morning, Andy."

"Hey, Andy. What? No coffee?!" I dragged my fingernails across the top of my desk making them screech.

"Calm down. I saw Heeks in the coffee shop getting a tray." Andy turned around. "Sharp's not here? Hey, how did the date go?"

"Fine. We had a really nice time."

"That's cool."

Elaine was giving me the eye.

"What?"

"So what'd you guys do?"

"We had dinner."

"Uh huh."

I picked up a pad and then sat down behind my desk.

"Then what?"

"Had dessert."

"Did you show her your place?"

"We went for a walk."

"Where?"

"Some place nice."

"Did she show you her place?"

"This is really a crass form of porno voyeurism, Elaine."

"I know that!"

From his office I could hear Andy laughing. The elevator doors opened and I recognized Sharp's walk. He was coming with someone else. He was coming with someone with coffee.

■ ● ■

Sharp came in first. "Howdy, partners…and I mean that in the contractual sense."

Mojica trailed in with five large coffees balanced on a four hole tray. "Hey, guys. So, capitan, how did the date go last night?"

"He doesn't want to talk about it apparently."

"Fine. We went to Duchamp's."

"Cajun, huh?"

"The gumbo was outstanding. We walked for a while over on Cherry Street. Looked in a few windows. Then we had dessert over at Torino's Café. Nice evening."

Elaine was looking at me like I destroyed her computer. I smiled. She gave me the finger. I grinned. Sharp laughed.

"What happened with that little girl?"

"She's with Helen until this afternoon. I'll fill you in later."

Andy was standing in the doorway. "Should we get down to business? Heeks, can you get us in clean?"

"The back door is not a problem. No cameras. Lock is a cinch. He's up on the eighth floor."

Sharp put his coffee on my desk. "Based on…"

"Based on standing on the fourth floor for fifteen minutes and watching all the elevator traffic to eight. We just follow the traffic."

Andy crossed his arms on his chest. "If we get inside I do all of the talking. You two try to gauge the other people in the room. I'll talk about the kidnappers and the woman. Heeks, you don't let anyone behind you. You put your ass in the wall if necessary. We need to see if anyone has a reaction we might be able to exploit."

Elaine tapped her finger on the wall. "What if they only let one of you in the apartment?"

Sharp pointed his finger at us. "Then no one goes in, right? We'll have made our point anyway. Someone will move."

■ ● ■

Andy was nodding. "Sharp will be one block away if something happens to our car. Did I leave anything out?"

I was holding my coffee cup with both hands. "No weapons on the way in. If we need weapons Sharp will bring them in."

Andy nodded again. "Right. Sorry, I should have said that. If we need weapons Mojica will contact Sharp through his transistor radio. Anything else?" Andy paused. "We get in. I do the talking. We get out."

Everyone was quiet.

"Finish the coffee and go?"

Andy, Mojica and I were at the back door of the apartment building by 9:05. We had parked two blocks away. Mojica led us through a wooded area that separated the Zilmont Cloisters apartments from any homes of the less wealthy. I was surprised there was no security in back other than a lock that Mojica had open in all of 15 seconds.

We left the service area emerging into one of the main halls. The carpets were maroon and gold and thick. Heeks took us up the stairwell to the second floor and then went out into the next hallway.

Andy was starting up to the third floor, but turned around. "Heeks. Where are you going?"

Mojica held the door, looking slightly miffed. "What do you mean, Andy? I'm going to the elevators. I'm not walking all the way up there. It's not like we're really trying to surprise anyone. We just didn't want to be stopped at the front door, right?"

I slid past Mojica to walk to the elevators.

When I turned back Mojica had his 'do you believe this guy' smile on. Andy pulled up next to us. "Okay. I'm dumb…should'a had more coffee." Andy looked up and down the hall. "How'd

■ ● ■

your date really go? That woman has some voice."

"It was fine. I'm pretty sure we'll do it again." The elevator doors slid open like a knife cutting through soft butter. "I need to talk to you guys about last night's dinner though."

"You don't need to worry about which fork to use first when you're doing Cajun."

"You know what, Mojica? Fuck you."

The doors opened on the eighth floor. When we stepped out we immediately saw which door we needed to knock on. A guard turned toward us with his feet planted about two feet apart with his hands crossed behind his back. He was wearing a dark grey, double breasted suit with a white shirt and black tie. His black shoes had a brilliant, useless shine on them. As we got closer I could see the tassels on one. He had a crew cut I guessed he learned to take in the Marines. We kept about ten feet away from him. I wondered what kind of weapon he had behind his back.

"We would like to talk to Mr. DeFord for a short moment."

Our Marine stared at Andy for a couple of seconds, opened the door and spoke to someone inside. Then there was laughter. It was one man laughing, kind of out of control, but I could hear him say "Yes, Yes. Oh yes." He continued laughing as we were waved into the apartment. While the door was closing behind us the laugher was trying to contain his giggles. Everyone else in the room was glaring at us. The two kidnappers were on the other side of the room by a big picture window. Two cops I recognized were on a couch in the corner in their civvies. Another Marine in a single-breasted, dark blue suit was off to our right. I felt Mojica pull away from us, but I didn't look back. Suddenly another man and a youngish looking kid of about twenty, entered through a door at our far left.

"I'm Mr. DeFord," the laugher said. He was sitting in a high-

■ ● ■

back chair that gave the impression of being a throne. The man who came into the room with the kid walked right up to us.

"You won't mind if we take some precautions." DeFord smiled while we were frisked. When the man finished with me he went over to Mojica. I turned slightly so I could watch. He took Mojica's blue-green transitor radio out of Mojica's pocket. He looked at it for a second then smashed it against the wall and let the pieces fall on the floor. DeFord was almost hysterical with laughter.

"That cost me $2.95 twelve years ago."

DeFord arched his back laughing, but I noticed he pulled out his wallet. He handed his man a ten dollar bill and nodded at Mojica. The man shoved the ten in Mojica's front shirt pocket.

"So where's the gimp and the Princeton tramp?"

Andy started to speak. "We want…" I cut him off. My brain went from calm to boil.

"We have the girl. Her jaw's wired but when the swelling goes down she'll be able to speak and fatso and pepper over there will get to do some time."

DeFord was laughing again. "You, my friend, are full of ex-crement." He shook his head with his lips pouted like he was being coquettish. "Just full of it."

I could feel Andy staring at me. He turned his head toward DeFord. "She won't be walking any time soon, but our doctor says she'll be able to talk. You need to hire some people who really know how to clean up."

"You too, Mr. Chess player? You, too?"

DeFord was apoplectic with laughter. Over by the window the black kidnapper looked calm with his arms folded across his chest. His white partner was clenching and unclenching his right fist. He slid both hands into his pockets glaring at me from far, far away. The kid had made his way to a desk just to the right

■ ● ■

of the picture window and was doing a slow, four foot pace like a clock pendulum.

DeFord slammed his hand down on the arm of his chair. "You two…no, no…you three are great. You are all so full of shit. You have nothing. At least in poker you would be holding cards. Here…you come in here…you're holding nothing. You can leave now." DeFord was laughing again. My skin was crawling. I wanted to smash his face in. He stuck his lower lip out. "Maybe you can double you money."

"7…18…22…"

DeFord stopped laughing. Now he just wore a lunatic's smile. He let a lazy "what?" drool out of his mouth.

As calmly as I could, over-emphasizing my pronunciation, I repeated, "7…18…22…"

The smile disappeared. "You don't…"

"28…You're right. It is time for us to leave." As soon as I said that I heard paper being torn behind me. Andy and I turned just as Mojica let the fragments of a ten dollar bill flutter to the floor. The marine had a sneer on his face. Mojica made a face at him I could see he didn't like. I noticed the two cops in the corner were now on the edge of the sofa looking like they were wondering what they had just seen.

As we went out the door I glanced back at DeFord. He was staring at the floor with a severe frown on his face. His head suddenly snapped up. He started laughing like a hyena. When the door closed I could still hear his laughter.

Mojica had jumped behind the wheel with me in front. He was pulling away from the curb when Andy said, "Heeks, head for Udo's?"

"Andy, you don't think we should try to hook up with Sharp?"

■ ● ■

"Didn't you hear the arrogant son-of-a-bitch say 'double you money?'"

Mojica looked at me with his eyebrows raised. "Oh shit! I'll drop you guys at the pimp's and come right back with some equipment."

I turned sideways in my seat. "When do you think they bugged the place?"

"Does it matter? But if I had to guess I'd say they did it when our kidnappers broke into Louie's before his lunatic shot the place up. And you know what? I thought I was going to do all of the talking."

"I'm sorry, Andy, but when he called Elaine the Princeton tramp, I wanted to beat the hell out of the guy."

"Yeah, well, the next time we have a plan let's stick to it. And what the hell made you say the woman was still alive?"

"I don't know. I had this feeling that the blond likes to beat people."

"Well, if they put a bullet in her head your bluff was just that."

"Your improvisation was good, though."

"I didn't want to improvise!"

"It turned out okay."

"Did it? I don't know that."

"What do you think, Heeks?"

"What Andy said. Did you guys notice the kid? I think he was the most dangerous person in the room and we sure as shit better watch out for him."

I was fairly surprised. "You mean the pacer? I thought some-one would tell him to stand still."

"I don't think anyone tells him anything. If you two weren't doing the Bob and Ray routine you might have noticed that the kid had about an inch of knuckle callouses. He also had two

■ ● ■

knives strapped to his legs. He had a weapon in his belt and he had a crossbow built into the lamp on that desk he kept strolling up to. I think we just left a room where half of the people in it were certifiable."

"Guys…Two things. Heeks, the transistor ra…"

Heeks glanced at me like I was the dumbest kid in class. "Backup in the toe of my shoe. You think I'm just going in there with something so obvious as a Sears-Roebuck transistor radio? C'mon…damn, bro, c'mon…"

I felt like a complete idiot but I had to drop this on my partners. "I hate to bring this up at apparently the wrong time, but…"

"Dude! You gettin' married after all?! At least this one is around your age and legal."

I'll say this for Mojica, he never stayed annoyed at someone for very long. Mojica had a grin that let me see all of his molars. "You jackass. Remember when we snagged Barthelme and that one guy just kept eating and watching through the whole thing?" Mojica nodded. "He was in the restaurant last night about four tables away."

"Did he seem interested? You sure it was the same guy?"

"One hundred percent sure, Andy."

"But we haven't seen this guy in almost two years, right? Maybe he just likes to eat."

"Yeah, but what are the odds, if that's the case, that we only see him once every year in a city this size?"

Andy looked out the window. Mojica had a frown on his face. He shrugged his shoulders like they were stiff.

"Do you guys ever feel like we have too much going on at one time?"

■ ● ■

There were two doormen at Udo's now. They called upstairs, then let us pass. Andy stood off to the side of Udo's door and knocked. I was looking at the bullet pocked wall on the other side of the hall when I heard Winch yell, "Who is it?!"

Andy spoke through the door until it opened. Inside there were two new men with mac 10's. Da-veed stood behind them, swaying slightly with bug-eyes. Someone really needed to put him down to sleep for about three days.

"What's up, GM?"

"We found the woman."

"What?! You found my girl? Where is she?"

"She's with our doctor. We can take you there. She can't talk yet, but the doc says she'll be able to in a week or so."

"How far away is she?"

Andy said about forty-five minutes. Louie cocked his head to the side. I could see a question mixed with disbelief forming on his face. I raised my index finger to my lips while I shook my head. Louie opened his mouth and then closed it.

Andy looked at me and then back at Udo. "Do you want to go over there right now? We can drive."

"I can drive, Andrew. I can drive right behind you."

Louie was now sharing a 'what the fuck is going on look' with me and Andy.

"Louie, you should bring a man with you to help do some guard duty. We can't do it all." I smiled.

"I bring two men."

"Just one will do. Check out the set-up first...and someone you can trust." I nodded at Winch. Louie eyed Winch. "Monroe. We takin' a little ride. Go pull the car up."

It was obvious that Udo still didn't trust Winch. Back in the corner of the room Da-veed was swaying even more to some tune no one else could hear. I wanted to say 'somebody get that

■ ● ■

boy some drugs before he starts shooting everyone.' I really wanted to get out of this apartment.

"Okay. Let's go. I wanna see how my bitch be doin'."

When we stepped out on the sidewalk Andy asked Louie to have his man move away a little. "Your place is bugged, Louie. Those two guys who broke in on you must have planted it."

"You serious? They weren't in there that long before Da-veed went off."

"These people are good, Louie."

Louie stared at Andy and then at me. He looked back at Andy. "Where's the girl?"

"She's probably dead."

"So that whole monologue upstairs was you sending a message. Kind of a Queen's Gambit."

"Yeah, Louie. We're playing for position."

"You got the address for these guys? I wanna straighten their asses the fuck outa' town."

"We've got the address, but we want them to make a move for Lisa."

"Gimme the address and I give ya' yer green."

"Hold on, Louie." Louie looked at me like I spit on him twice.

"You must be crazy you interruptin' me when I'm conversing with my man, Andrew. You…"

"You're not that big, Louie. Just because you're moving guns now don't make you something big. Second, we get the money before the address because you might not be here long enough to pay us if we give you the address first."

Louie stepped toward me and his man was drifting back toward us. Andy put his hand on Louie's chest. "Slow down, Louie. This is check."

"Check my ass!"

■ ● ■

"We can find the woman and give you their address, but let us make our move first."

"You don't put your hand on me, GM. You never put your hand on me."

"Sorry, Louie." Andy pulled his hand away. "But we think something big is going on with these assholes and we really need to get the whole story."

Louie lifted his chin. It seemed like he gazed right through Andy's head. "Okay, Andy. I give you two days. I pay you. You give me the address." Then he lowered his chin to his chest and locked his eyes with mine. "You remember this…you may be crazy, but I ain't no pussy. I fuck you up."

"I'll remember that. I just want to get paid before your ass gets blown up."

Louie raised his head a little and turned back to Andy. "This motherfucker really is crazy, ain't he."

Andy looked down and nodded. "Yeah. He actually is."

Louie looked me up and down and chuckled.

■ ● ■

Casualties

Udo had just finished talking to his doormen in the lobby when Heeks pulled up. Andy and I watched the pimp, and now gun runner, drive off for a ride with Monroe at the wheel. Heeks got out of our car with a three foot long black box.

"Sharp called. He said our kidnappers came out of the Cloisters like somebody's tail was on fire."

Andy and I looked at each other, then back at Heeks.

Heeks just said, "Right?"

Something was wrong.

Andy took the keys from Mojica. "Where's Sharp now?"

"He's outside a restaurant on DeVries. When I find it, do you think I should get rid of it or move it?

Andy shrugged, looked at me and raised his eyebrows. "Move it if you can. Kitchen?"

Mojica nodded and walked into Udo's building.

Andy started the car and pulled us out into the street. "Do you know a restaurant on DeVries?"

"Yeah. The only one. Kind of swanky." I looked out the window at four kids riding spider bikes on the sidewalk. I smiled thinking about my old black Rollfast. "You know there's some-

∎●∎

thing so wrong about this. It has to be a heavy-duty set up in the making."

Andy started to speak but then paused. "What's that you always say when something stupid might be happening…'exciting, isn't it?'" Andy turned to me with a short grin on his face.

"Not this time, Andy. These guys are a little scary."

"Serious, brother. Serious. A whole lot of scary."

We found Sharp parked across the street from a restaurant that was perched magnificently at the top of a slight rise. We drove past him and went around the block. Andy parked at the corner so that we could see the back of Sharp's car, but we were blind to the restaurant.

"Let's get Sharp on the horn."

I picked up the phone and shook it for no apparent reason. "If Sharp picks up the phone do you think they'll make him?"

Andy looked at me like I was crazy. "If they're as good as they seem to be, they made Sharp about half an hour ago."

"Right. My turn to be stupid."

Sharp filled me in. Our kidnappers had gone inside. There hadn't been any other activity except for staff going in for their shift. The restaurant was opening for lunch in fifteen minutes.

"They're setting something up."

Andy stared at me and sighed. "Give me the phone."

In twenty seconds I was as stunned as I would ever be.

"Raoul, this is Andy…no it's not Mojica fooling around!... We need a favor."

Sharp's tail lights came on. We watched his car pull away from the curb. Just before we pulled out a car sailed past us tailgating Sharp.

■ ● ■

"Looks like they're late for ballet class."

I laughed and opened the glove compartment to pull out a pair of binoculars. Andy swung around the corner to follow behind the two cars at some distance.

"Andy, do you really think it's smart to go in unarmed?"

"By avoiding a shootout we might stay alive a little longer."

"Unless these guys just decide to shoot us on sight."

We pulled up short at a red light. The mother turned right, squealing her tires. "Ballet class must be that a way." Andy looked around, then ran the red to catch up with Sharp.

"They're not making a very big effort to lose anybody."

"Let's get Sharp off them and then see what happens."

Our kidnappers went left. Sharp went straight. We stayed back a very good distance. Our targets suddenly made another left into the parking lot of an abandoned factory. I remembered they used to do something with rubber out there when I was a kid. But I could never figure it out just by looking in the windows. Andy drove past the parking lot while I watched them drive the 150 yards across the dirt and gravel to a huge, grey multi-story building. Andy pulled the car over close to a parked truck. Through the glasses I watched our kidnappers go into the building.

Andy picked up the phone and told Sharp where we were. A few minutes later Sharp parked across the street from the truck. When he sat down in our car Sharp asked, "Anybody think that's where they did the deed?"

I answered first with a simple, "Nope." Then I heard Andy's echo.

"So, shall we take the bait and go on in?"

Neither of us answered, so that passed as "yes."

We walked into the building like we were stockholders. Someone was humming 'Stairway to Heaven,' so we followed

■ ● ■

the humming down a dark hallway. Blondie was leaning sideways against a wall in a musty room with concrete walls and one
broken out window. He had a vicious looking grin on his face
that I didn't think he needed to practice.

I looked around the room. "This isn't where you brought her.
This room is too big. You want a space about a quarter of this size
because you're not quick enough to catch a girl if she tried to run
away."

"Doesn't matter now, does it?"

I turned around and Blondie's Black companion was holding
two .45s on us.

"So you're going to do all three of us here and you think
you're going to get away with that?"

"Hell no. When the box truck gets here you will get in back.
Then we're going to drive you to a place where we will leave your
sorry asses with a couple of holes in your head."

I turned to look at Blondie's partner again, who hadn't said
anything yet. "Ya know, why the fuck do you Tom for DeFord,
'Pepper'?" I could see that didn't bother him but a slight smile
appeared.

"We are employed by Mr. DeFord at an extremely healthy
rate of pay."

I wondered where 'Pepper' went to college. At least I got him
talking. "So we are, what…gay?" Like you and Blondie are lov-
ers? That didn't bother him either, but my neck snapped, a couple of stars exploded and I found myself lying in a half inch of
industrial dust. I shook my head, stretched my neck and quickly
rolled away from Blondie. I sprang to my feet in time to see half
a smile on Blondie's face just before one of his fists smacked me
in the mouth. I crouched down a little before I threw my first
punch. I missed, but he didn't. He hit me on the ear as I tried
to slip his overhand right. I staggered back a little to try to get

■ ● ■

my bearings, when Sharp grabbed my shoulder and yanked me away.

Sharp stood in between us. He tossed his cane to Andy. Blondie's smile got huge, like this was as much fun as he'd had since his mother's funeral.

"Sharp, let me back…" I took a step toward Sharp, but Andy grabbed my arm. I looked at Andy who was barely shaking his head. 'Pepper' had a self-satisfied smile on his face like he was watching his younger brother. One gun was now tucked in his waistband. He shifted over behind me to watch the fight, which started with two quick jabs to Sharp's mouth. Blondie's smile turned into a grin. His eyes widened like he didn't want to miss anything. He threw a jab and a hook which Sharp blocked. Then two more jabs put Sharp on a knee. He wiped the blood from his mouth and started to get up. I didn't like seeing Sharp take this kind of punishment.

"You should'a stayed down gimp."

Blondie threw a round house right that Sharp took on his shoulder and he staggered back on me. I fell backwards as hard and fast as I could. 'Pepper' tried to push me away but Andy was on him like lightning. We all fell on the floor. Andy had one hand on 'Pepper's' arm. His other hand was at 'Pepper's' waist. I pinned 'Pepper's' gun arm to the floor and then the other gun went off. 'Pepper's' grip on his .45 loosened. I was able to pull it away and turned to see Sharp wrestling Blondie on the floor. I pushed myself up and put my gun to the back of Blondie's head. He immediately stopped struggling. He looked up at me from the corners of his eyes. Then he squatted on his knees and put both hands on his thighs.

"You alright, Kelvin?"

Kelvin just nodded. Andy had Kelvin up on his feet. The bullet had apparently just creased the inside of his thigh down

■ ● ■

toward his knee. He had to be in some pain, but his face didn't show it.

"Gee Kelvin, you don't remember that trick? We used to do that in grade school. Remember? One guy confronting his mortal enemy. His best pal goes down on his knees behind the enemy and the enemy gets pushed over on his ass. Everybody standing around laughs. You don't remember that grade school bullshit? I mean we just did grade school on you, Kelvin." That got to him. His eyes burned like white hot coals. He did not like being thought a fool.

"Just simpleton stuff, really."

He took a step toward me. Andy slapped him hard on the side of his head. He stopped and turned all of his attention on Andy. I could see in his face that being slapped with an open hand was a bigger insult than being pistol whipped. This man had a serious mental problem.

We heard a truck pull up outside. Blondie started to grin. The fire in Kelvin's eyes stoked from simple rage to vibrant cunning. If these two were smiling, the truck must be carrying enough men and weaponry to deal with us.

Andy slid over to cover the door. I moved away from Blondie so I could have a good angle on both of the kidnappers.

Then nothing happened. We waited. Andy looked at me and nodded. Sharp was bent over massaging his leg. Blondie and Pepper stared at the doorway. And we waited.

Finally we could hear some shuffling and steps.

"Andy?!"

"In here." It was Raoul.

Through the door came three white men in suits. Right behind them came two young black men in T shirts and jeans carrying sawed off shotguns. One of them was Marcus Williams. It was two years since I had seen him in Raoul's office.

■ ● ■

"Get over against the wall."

"Which one?" One of the suits asked the question like their two escorts would be too stupid to figure it out.

"Straight across, motherfucker. If you can make it." The mouthy prisoner glanced over his shoulder and hunched forward like he thought something was about to happen to him.

Then Raoul came through the door. He was holding a man up by his neck who was staggering half blind, with a face so swollen one eye was just a slit. Raoul looked like a giant holding up a puppet. He looked to his right and nodded at Andy.

"You boys got this whole situation on lockdown. Y'all didn't even need me and my associates." Ray started laughing. I looked down at Blondie. He was huffing and puffing like he was going to do something. Sharp stood up straight and waved Blondie over.

"Let's go."

Blondie looked around the room. The corners of his mouth almost curled down to his chin. He looked at Sharp like he was seeing a disgusting pile of human shit. He stood up with some spring in his legs, while Sharp raised his fists.

Raoul yelled across the room. "Turn those men around. Sit their asses on the floor. Let them watch."

Blondie approached Sharp, who was still favoring his right leg. Blondie threw two punches. The first one glanced off Sharp's forehead. The second one landed at the corner of Sharp's mouth.

One of the three against the wall yelled, "Fuck him up!" Then a second guy chimed in with, "Get him. Knock his fucking head off, Lugo!"

Kelvin's head spun around so fast he must have dislocated a shoulder. "Shut up!" Now we had two names. I looked over at Raoul. He had half a smile going. Blondie was grinning again. Another jab landed on Sharp's mouth. Blondie looked totally confident.

■ ● ■

And then Sharp threw a double left hook. One punch hit Blondie's arm. The other one hit his hip. A look of concern replaced Blondie's grin. It struck me that Blondie had never been hit that hard before. Blondie tried to circle away from Sharp's hook. Sharp cut him off, faked with his left and put a right cross on Blondie's neck. His eyes squeezed shut in pain and then Sharp went to work. He hooked to the body. He threw an overhand right to the chest. Hooked again to the ribs and drove Blondie against the wall. Blondie had both arms in front of his face. Sharp was taking his time now. He'd shoot out a jab and there'd be a 'crack' when Sharp's fist landed on Blondie's face.

"So is this how you beat that little girl to death?" Crack.

"Where'd you take her?" Crack.

"Where'd you take her, punk?" Crack.

"Is this what you think fun is?" Crack.

Finally Raoul moved over and put his hand on Sharp's shoulder. "You don't want him dead do you?"

Sharp took a step back. "Ah'm not sure we don't." Sharp turned around to Andy. "What do you think, Andy?"

"Let him go, Sharp."

Sharp turned to me for a second opinion. "We need to keep them alive, bro."

"Really?" Sharp turned back to face Blondie, who had lowered his arms thinking he had been given a reprieve. Sharp's left flashed out, connecting with Blondie's nose. The snap made me wince. I heard Blondie cry a quiet "Oh," and then he fell to the floor.

"Ah need to find a comfortable place to sit down. Mah leg is startin' to put a bother on my brain. Let me have my cane, Andy."

"How you gonna work this, Andy? Those three and this one just drove a truck. However they do have some weapons in their truck that are probably illegal."

■ ● ■

Andy looked up at Raoul. "Uh-huh…well on tape it's probably pretty clear they had expectations of taking three men to their
executions. Got it all here on tape." Andy lifted his shirt to show
off one of Mojica's little recorders.

As I smiled at my man, Kelvin, it suddenly occurred to me
where they had taken Lisa. "Andy, I think you should call your
police friend and have him check that building over by the train
tracks. That old signal tower. The one Mojica scouted when Raoul
was having trouble with Baron and Ickey." I kept my eyes on Kelvin while I spoke and I thought I saw him flinch a little. Why
would we re-check a building we had already driven them out of?

"Well, if you're going to have the police involved, it doesn't do
me and my associates to be in here with these sawed offs."

Raoul looked around the room. He walked across to Kelvin and stared him in the eyes. "You're on the wrong side, man.
The wrong side." Raoul turned back to Andy. "You have enough
weapons?"

"Yeah. I think we've got it covered…Raoul?"

"Yeah?"

"We appreciate your help."

I almost passed out. Then I looked at Kelvin again. His eyes
were blazing.

Raoul started toward the door. "You know, you inflicted some
casualties on the other side. You should expect some retaliation
in the next couple of days." Raoul's associates walked past him
out into the hallway. Raoul started to follow and then he paused.
"Sharp. My man Sharp. It was good seeing your work again. You
comin' back, man. You comin' back. And you, tough guy, you got
beat by a one-legged man." Blondie spit blood. "And you as dumb
as the dirt you got put down in, aren't you?" Raoul winked at me
and turned to leave. "Yep. It was good to see your work again,
Sharp. Yes, indeed."

■ ● ■

Safe

I walked into the office and did a double-take in the direction of Elaine's desk. Cheike was sitting there with a smile on her face that almost made me stumble. She pushed her hair away from her eyes, her jewelry tinkling, and stood up. She was wearing a black dress that reached half-way between her knees and her black ankle boots. The sleeves went half-way between her elbows and her wrists. The neck line was loose but rose a little up her neck. The chest was cut away, kind of like a tear drop. She looked magnificent.

"Seeing you in that dress makes me feel like there's not enough of me."

She moved toward me slowly with her smile growing larger the closer she came. When she was within arm's reach she grabbed my belt with both hands and pulled us together. She kissed me, ending it with a bite of my lip. "Oh I think there's more than enough of you to go around."

"Around where?"

"I think that translates as, 'you will do in a pinch.'"

"I think I liked 'more than enough of me' better."

She kissed my chin. "So where are you taking me for a good

■ ● ■

time?"

"Not hungry, huh?"

"I'm all set for dinner but I just want to make clear I'm not going to watch Popeye tonight unless it's at your place with the sound turned down."

"There's a new Indian place I've only been to once over…"

"I can't eat Indian."

"Oh? Garcia's has the best Mexican food in…"

"Can't eat Mex."

"Really? How about Ukranian?"

"Nope. Don't you guys have any Lithuanian food in this town?"

I looked at my watch. "You have time to drive to Chicago?"

She laughed and shook me by my belt. "Indian's fine. I was joking."

"Oh yeah? Well you almost drove me to reserve a booth down to Carl's Pizza."

"That would have been cool. Sharp said Carl makes a really fine pie."

"Sharp was here? I know where Elaine is, but do you know where my other partners are?"

"Yes."

"Yes?"

"Yes. I took notes."

"You took notes."

She walked back over to Elaine's desk and read off the destination of each of my friends. I looked down at the floor. This was kind of nuts.

"Okay. Let's get dinner." I started to step away. "Is Elaine's computer on?" I walked over to it and turned it off. "Funny. Elaine usually turns it off when she leaves."

Cheike smiled and we left for dinner.

■ ● ■

Madras Cuisine was apparently right up Chieke's alley. She knew all of the breads. Made suggestions for the main course and turned me onto a drink called a 'mango lassi.'

The conversation was so thick and enjoyable I wasn't sure how good the food actually was. The drive back to my place seemed to take thirty seconds. I could hardly remember being in the elevator. It was like we were in an embrace from the time we finished our tea in the restaurant until I unlocked my apartment door.

I never got to the lights. We were locked together in my living room moving in a slow circle. Somehow she flipped off her shoes.

"Unzip me."

Her dress fell to the floor. No bra. No panties. Detective skills not necessary.

"Is it this way?" She pulled me by the hand into my bedroom and I began losing my clothes through no effort of my own. She pushed me back on my bed and straddled my hips. She reached over and turned on the lamp next to my bed.

"I'd like to see what's gotten into me…or will get into me."

"Don't get too crude. I might like it."

"Oh, you'll like it." She frowned a little through her smile. "What's this scar from?"

"Um…a bullet."

"From the war?"

"No."

She didn't smile. She ran her fingers across my shoulder. She stared in my eyes. "And this one?"

"Another bullet."

"This one, too?"

I nodded. "None of them were deep. I guess I'm lucky."

Cheike had both hands on my chest. "Wait."

■ ● ■

She left the bedroom. I thought she was going to the bath-room. I heard a door close. It definitely didn't sound like the bathroom door. I swung myself off the bed. I moved into the living room and turned on a light.

"Cheike?" I scanned the living room twice, like there was someplace she could hide. I walked past the kitchen to stand by the bathroom even though it was obvious she had left.

I moved to the center of the living room. I stood there for a while, naked, turned off the light and sat down on my sofa. I stood up to go get dressed. I would go over to her apartment and find out what had just happened. I turned on a table lamp. I looked at the clock on the kitchen wall. It wasn't even twelve yet. I turned off the light and sat back down. I watched the light from the streetlights crash into the room. I was in a very bad black and white B movie, but I couldn't remember the title. I had that sick, can't latch on to anything good feeling in my stomach. My brain felt like it was buzzing. I wanted the credits to roll and just see "FIN."

I got back up, walked over to a window and stared down into the street. I raised the window and screamed, "FUCK!"

Maybe I should take a walk. Nope. A hot steaming bath. Nope. A scalding hot steaming bath. Yep.

I watched the water rise higher than I should have let it, just mesmerized by the gurgle sound of the tap. I turned the water off. The squeeking sound from the knobs seemed to echo in my head. Water splashed over the side as I stepped in. I slid down to my neck. I wished I had turned out the light before I'd gotten in.

It didn't take long to realize the water wasn't going to do anything for me. I should have taken that walk.

I always thought that somehow my death would be related to water. When I was fourteen out at the lake, that little girl's green, inflated beach ball had gotten away from her. I dove in

∎ ● ∎

to retrieve it and the wind toyed with it and me until I was ex-
hausted and too far away from anything to save me from drowning except for that damn ball. Panic set in and I barely made it to
the ball. Then there was the time I got caught in the river current
and almost went over the dam. And then swimming out to a
sand bar in the ocean that was there in the morning and gone in
the evening. I was so far out I really thought I was done. Body
surfing in the ocean and the waves…what the fuck was that?

I climbed out of the tub trying to listen through the water
sloshing back and forth. I grabbed a towel. Maybe Cheike had
come back, but I was sure I had locked the apartment door. I
slowly opened the bathroom door to peek out. I thought I saw
movement by the kitchen.

I heard the laugh. De Ford's laugh and I realized they were
all around me. I started to slide back toward the bathroom but a
very large hand grabbed my shoulder. The lamp turned on by the
couch. De Ford was straight across from me giggling. There were
six others. The crazy pacer kid was one of them. He was wearing
a khaki army jacket and had both of his hands in his pockets like
he was fondling something.

"Let's get some clothes on this man so that we can get going.
The big guy pushed me toward the bedroom. One of the other
men went in before me.

"Get dressed."

The first guy had a snub nose .38 in his right hand. He
nodded at the clothes on the floor. I picked up my pants and
straightened the pockets before I stepped into them. When I
buckled up I scratched my ass a little.

The big guy said, "Don't get funny."

"Pin worms."

"Finish getting dressed."

We walked out to the living room and all of the men stood

■ ● ■

up. As we moved out into the hall I realized all of them wore poly gloves.

"Turn off the lights, Peter. No sense in running up the electric bill." De Ford started laughing again. Just as my door closed I heard another one opening. Mrs. Culletti stepped out into the hallway with a garbage bag. She looked very surprised. I hoped she wouldn't say anything that would get her hurt. She stared at us like she was outraged.

"It's about time the police did something about his carrying on at all hours. It took you long enough to put a stop to his shenanigans, though." She started walking toward the garbage chute muttering, "About time. It's about time. Maybe I can get a full night's sleep now."

De Ford was laughing again. "You don't have a very good reputation in this building, do you? Finally the Police are cleaning up the neighborhood." A few of his men joined in with De Ford's laughter.

We drove out into the country for half an hour before I realized where we were going. Our cars pulled up and parked in front of an abandoned condominium complex. At one time it was going to be an exclusive, upscale, out in the country but not, condominium community. Until the developers ran out of money.

It seemed like everyone but me and De Ford had a flashlight. We started up a stairwell that smelled of mold. Closer to the city this place would have smelled like piss. I scratched my ass again.

"What's with you and your finger up your ass, asshole?" The big guy pushed my shoulder.

"Pin worms."

I heard De Ford chuckle up front. "Pin worms? You should

have pineapple juice in your refrigerator. I didn't see any. That's the cure for pinworms. Pineapple juice. Of course, I didn't see much in your refrigerator at all."

He was quiet again and then suddenly he burst out laughing. One of the men close to him did a sidestep away, but he tried to act like nothing out of the ordinary just happened. De Ford looked at him and chuckled. He started laughing again and everybody just proceeded up the stairs, happy to be part of the crowd.

Except for me. I was hoping to come up with a nifty escape plan. But unless four of these guys had heart attacks at the same time, I couldn't imagine anything that would work. Another real sick feeling swept through me. I was getting light-headed.

I did manage to count the flights and when we hit the sixth floor we all went into one of the apartments. I guessed they were going to see if I could learn how to fly before I hit the ground. The flashlights were moving around randomly like lights at a movie star event. I noticed a big sheet of plywood and a couple of power drills over by one wall.

De Ford looked at me with a smile. "Take your clothes off."

I looked at him like he was kidding. I glanced at some of the other men. No one except De Ford was smiling.

"Take your clothes off." He was emphatic this time. I thought they were just going to throw me out a window, but two men picked up the power drills. If they intended to torture me I thought I could get out the window before they started. That was like no chance of survival from six floors up, but I wasn't going to let them drill my knees or my skull. That was the line. Torture by drill meant out the window before they could start.

"You take off your clothes, or we just toss you out."

I glanced around again. When I pulled my pants off De Ford walked toward the window. "Notice how small a pecker can be

■●■

when you think you're about to die?"

De Ford leaned over the ledge. "Oooo...this is hiiiigh...This ledge is wide though, don't you think? Originally the developers thought plants would be nice out here so the women could think they were farming out here in the country. Bring him over to the ledge."

The big guy grabbed my neck from behind. Two guys snagged my arms. I began to push away from the window, but my feet just slid through the dust. When they had me almost to the ledge I put one foot up against the wall and pushed back. The big guy's grip loosened and I got an arm free. I threw a punch at the guy holding my other arm. My shins exploded in pain. The kid had some kind of telescoping black rod that he laid on me like an expert. I fell on the floor and looked up. As he put his toy away De Ford in a completely calm voice said, "Thank You, Alan." De Ford began laughing again. "Get him up on the ledge."

I was pushed up on the ledge and then the plywood was coming at me. The sheet completely covered the window. The power drills started up. Even through the noise of the drills I could hear De Ford cracking up. The drills went all the way around the board. I kept staring down the side of the building looking for anything that would help me get down to the next floor. I couldn't see anything in the dark. Then the drills stopped. Someone started knocking in the center of the board.

"Anyone home?" De Ford's laughter. "Well, when you get ready, you know the way down." I could hear some of his men laugh. "You wanted to get mixed up in my business? You really shouldn't have. We really don't appreciate that. By now I suppose you don't either. Have a wonderful flight." All of them were laughing now. "I think you know the way down." Silence. "Nothing to say? And I thought you were the talkative one."

■ ● ■

I turned very slowly until I was sitting on the ledge squeezed in between a sheet of plywood and the open air of a seventy-five foot drop to the ground. I put my hands on the welts rising on my shins. They felt sticky. I winced.

I thought I should get to work before I got messy. I stuck my finger in my ass and found the paper. After a few minutes and a lot of cursing I pulled the twenty dollar bill out. I hoped it was somewhat clean. If I was lucky someone would actually come by whose attention I might be able to hold for a few seconds.

I looked up at the stars. At least it wasn't cold. The sun would be up in a few hours. Maybe then I'd be able to see a way down, or up. De Ford never should have left me alive. I was going to kill him.

■ ● ■

Black

When the sun started to come up I could see that the building had sheer exterior walls except for the window ledges. The ledges themselves were staggered down the façade, so there'd be no chance of climbing down by them. The ceilings in these apartments seemed unusually high, so there'd be no way to swing into another one. Nothing to grab. Nothing to climb. No way to jump unless it was the end of the show.

Eventually I could see that there'd been about a seventy or one hundred yard field around my side of the building. Now it was all brush and saplings, with a few maple trees scattered around. It looked like there was a path that weaved through the bush out toward the woods. Probably a deer trail.

The sun was coming up on the other side of the building and I realized that at about one o'clock it was going to be very hot where I was sitting. If someone didn't find me I was probably going to get some really ugly burned skin.

When I first decided to yell I was tickled that there was an echo. After a few hours of occasionally yelling the echoes became pretty depressing. I was hoping there would be a squatter somewhere who might hear me, but eventually I felt like I was

■●■

naked in a raft out on the ocean. At least here I wasn't surround-ed by sharks and the current wasn't very strong.

When it was time to piss, I wanted to make sure that I pissed without getting anything on my leg. I was marvelous. I only put two drops on the ledge.

And then the sun was on my side of the building. I knew I was in trouble. I was sweating, but one half of my body was on fire. If I wasn't found soon my skin would burn wickedly. If I was real unlucky my skin would probably blister. I didn't think I'd be around for anything worse than that.

I put my head between my knees, concentrating on not fall-ing asleep and accidentally dreaming myself to a crash landing seventy feet below.

For a few minutes I wished I had one glass of water. I knew I had to think of something else and food popped into my mind. That was like thinking about water, so I had to find something I could focus on. So I thought about De Ford and that I was going to kill him. I was going to kill him for putting me out here and because I was now certain of what he was planning to do.

By the time the sun started to go down I was extremely un-comfortable. My ass was ridiculously sore. My back was aching. At least I could stretch my legs., but that only helped a little.

I pushed on the plywood once out of frustration and lost my balance. I almost went over. That panicked my heart for quite a few minutes. When my pulse was back to normal I started laughing. 'What are you laughing at? This is not funny.' My in-terior voice. Listen to my interior voice. I had always wanted my interior voice to sound like the guy who did the voice-overs for the NFL. Instead my interior voice sounded like the sing song guy from 'Industry on Parade.'

In the twilight I saw a small herd of deer coming from the woods at a very leisurely pace. I decided to start yelling for help

■ ● ■

again just to see if the deer would run. They did and I chuckled when two of them ran into each other like Keystone cops.

Wood Thrush cries seemed to be all around me. Then the crickets started. Eventually stars began to get my attention. It suddenly struck me that I had not even noticed the sunset.

Tomorrow I would be in serious trouble. Like wasn't I right now? I had been sweating all afternoon. I had pissed three times. I wondered how long I could hold out without water. Two days? Three days? Not likely.

For the first time my thoughts drifted to Cheike. She left without saying anything. She ran her fingers over a couple of my scars and that was it. She was gone. I wondered what the scars meant for her. Maybe that eventually my luck would run out? But she could have at least said, "Good-bye. I can't be with a man whose luck will eventually run out." It started to get as dark as my thoughts. Maybe something else was going on. What if she set me up for De Ford? That I could think of that possibility actually scared me. It just couldn't be.

I stared out into the black and the sounds of the night. Somewhere out there an owl was hooting. Every once in a while I heard a fluttering sound swish by. I assumed it was a bat. Occasionally the trees would murmur from a slight breeze. If I wasn't up here on this ledge it would have been a beautiful evening.

I wondered if the other guys were okay. I hoped none of them were in the same situation I was in, or worse. Because if they were, who in the hell was going to rescue me?

I had started thinking about my bank account and I knew I was in trouble. Whenever I had trouble sleeping at home, I'd think about my bank balance and how would I pay a certain bill. Most people, that keeps them awake. Me? I lie in bed, shrug beneath the covers and I find myself asleep. I wondered if my electric bill was paid. I tried to remember how much money I had in my banking account, since this was probably the first time since elementary school I actually had some real cash in there.

I began pinching myself to stop my slide toward dozing. That didn't work so I began to bang my head against the plywood. That seemed to work, but I was afraid I'd knock myself unconscious.

I tried to remember the storyline from Sartre's "The Wall." I wondered how Sartre would piss if he were up here. Under the leg, like me, I suppose. The sun rose with me pondering the social significance of Abbot and Costello meeting Frankenstein.

About noon I was replaying a high school basketball game where I scored thirty-two points. I shook my head a little and then tried screaming. Four teens were walking away from the building on the deer path. At first they kept looking around, obviously confused, without looking up. Then one of them pointed at me. They started coming closer. I could hear them start to laugh.

One of them yelled, "Hey, faggot! What are you doing up there queer boy?"

"I need your help. I'll pay you. I have money." I waved the twenty dollar bill.

"What'd you say, gay boy?"

I was having trouble hollering down to them because my throat was so dry. I balled up the twenty and threw it down.

The biggest one of them walked through the bushes and started looking for it. The other three were all yelling at me at the same time.

"Yo! Butt boy!"

"They coming back for you, faggot?!"

"Jump, femmie. C'mon, jump!"

"Hey! Check this out! Gay boy tossed me a twenty!" He said something else and the other three laughed.

■ ● ■

I tried to holler down again, but my voice was so weak I couldn't penetrate their taunts. I watched them follow the deer trail out to the woods and then they were gone. At least I had some hope that someone else would come by.

I was getting dizzy now. My skin felt like someone was putting a blow torch to it. The worst spot was my neck. I kept trying to keep my hand over it but I was so tired, I'd drop my hand and wonder if I should try to cover my neck again while it burned.

Every once in a while I'd yell at a person walking on the path that turned out to be a bird. Once I think I saw a black and white mutt going down the path. I tried to say, "Go get help, Lassie. Go get help." My voice didn't seem to travel very far, so I was surprised when the dog jumped and started trotting down the path. By the time it got to the tree line it was walking and pissing, marking its territory.

A little while later the dry heaves started. I was dizzy, nauseous and retching. I was terrified I was going to lose my balance. When the heaves stopped I held my breath and wiped my eyes. I saw colors. Orange and green. Little explosions of color like you'd see when you were a little kid and pressed on your eyes with the lids closed.

I was starting to feel real panic. "I have to keep my shit together." Did I say that out loud? "What for, stupid?" It was the man from "Industry on Parade" answering me. I straightened out a little when I heard Andy say, "We've been in worse situations than this." No we fucking haven't.

The sun was gone and the orchestra started up again. I had a free ticket to the performance. All reed instruments, imitating birds. It was the most beautiful avant garde piece I had ever heard. It attacked and swayed. It grabbed and pulled out memories of someone's childhood. I think they should have titled it, "The Heart of Life Before Death." The sounds were swirling all

■ ● ■

around me and it was magnificent.

"Why had you never fallen in love, Mr. Detective?" I never had the chance. But I guess that's a lie. I would have fallen in love with Cheike. "No. That's just bullshit, isn't it?" Yeah, I suppose so. "You were already in love with her, weren't you? Admit it. Admit it." Okay. So? So?! Are you listening to me? So?!

Half of my body was freezing. The other half was just cold. I was still dizzy I thought, but now it was hard to tell how bad in the darkness.

The first one went overhead so fast I wasn't sure I saw it. Then another one streamed by in a brilliant flash. I was fascinated. Two more flew past, one right after the other. Just like life-long friends. Another.

"Do you mind if I sit here with you? I'll keep you company."

I didn't even flinch.

"Sure. I haven't had anyone to talk to in a couple of days."

It was weird. It was completely dark, but I could see its black smile. She was completely black. A black so deep I didn't think I'd be able to remember it.

Another one streaked across the sky.

"That was my sister."

"Are you an angel? What are you doing here?"

"Keeping you company."

I saw the angel staring at the sky. I slowly started to stare up along with her.

"Are those angels, too?"

"Yes. Aren't they beautiful?"

I nodded. "What are you doing? Why are you all doing this?"

"We are abandoning heaven. It's time. Our pain and frustration has become inconsolable."

I looked at the angel through the dark. Her eyes were obsidian. Her tears were beautiful. She was crying black, shimmering,

■●■

glassy tears.

"Can you get me down from here?"

The angel's tears were streaming now. "No. I can't. It is his will. We cannot cross it. But we can ignore it. That is why we are leaving. He will be alone. There is no reason for us to be complicit in his indifference to the pain and evil of the universe. We have decided to share the life of those below and leave him to himself. Maybe he will fade away forever and the memories of millions may eventually understand."

The angel raised her hands to her face. "We have come here to die. Death is permanent. You must take this life and embrace it just as we will. Now we have no choice. Do you?"

I stared at the sobbing angel and wondered why she was telling me things I already knew.

"I just want you to be sure of your thoughts."

"Will I get down from here? Will my friends find me?"

"Don't you have faith in their friendship?"

I felt sick. I had cramps in my stomach. I couldn't help it. I felt like I was exploding. The stench was making me worse. I was ashamed of having diarrhea like the stench of Satan in front of an angel.

"Oh! I must leave."

"Of course you must. Why would you want to sit here with me and smell this? Do angels smell? Hey! Hey! Did the White Sox win?" She was gone. She and her sisters and brothers were falling from heaven and the ones that made it here would walk among us until they perished. How long would angels on earth live? How would God feel when all of his angels had abandoned him? Would God ponder his solitude or ignore it with indifference? How alone would God be once he watched me fall from this height? It was so black here.

■ ● ■

Sharp

He was missing for two days now. A Mrs. Culletti had given us our only lead. The police seemed indifferent for the most part. The Animal Control guys showed more curiosity than the police. It seemed like we were making up for their indifference by not sleeping.

Elaine was splitting her time between Marty, the courthouse and county property records. Every few hours she'd drop some new files on my desk of recent real estate purchases. Bundled in the hope that one of them would lead us to a De Ford property where our partner was being held. Seemed like a long shot, but we didn't have much else to grab on to. I kept playing that Bogie line. "When something happens to your partner you're supposed to do something about it."

Andy had been on the phone for a day and a half. He had given Udo De Ford's address at the Cloisters the day before. The apartment was bare, but apparently Udo and his boys put some serious hurt on the wise-ass doorman to find out where De Ford might have gone. They drove out to De Ford's new farm but there wasn't any activity to speak of out there. Udo wanted to burn the place down, thinking that would get De Ford's ass back

■●■

to his farm. I heard Andy say, "The only thing you would get out of that is the volunteer fire department."

And then here came Elaine with more tears streaming down her face than were shed in all the Hollywood movies ever made. She stopped in front of my desk and shifted a stack of documents to her left arm and tried to wipe her face with the sleeve of her right. She shifted the paper back to her right arm and wiped her face with her left while half of the stack of papers slid down randomly onto my desk.

"Put the rest of those papers down, Elaine."

"They took her."

"Who took who?" Like I didn't know who we were talking about.

"The Police took Marty. The damn judge just kept saying 'a child belongs with his parents. It was like we were trapped in the 1950s with a sclerotic judge. He kept calling Marty 'he,' like he couldn't tell she was a girl. I got home and the Police were already taking her away. She looked petrified and she wouldn't look at me when I said we'd fix this. Child Services doesn't seem to be doing a thing. Our lawyer is trying to get them to move their ass."

Elaine tilted her head back like she was beseeching someone for guidance. "I've made a mess of everything. Her father is probably going to beat her silly. I just fucked everything up."

"You didn't make a mess of anything. You're doing the best you can in a difficult situation and…"

"We have to find him before something happens."

"Something already may have happened."

"What? What?! But you said he always gets out! He always gets out!"

Elaine's eyes were about as big as baseballs. She was leaning over my desk yelling for truth, and I needed her to sit down.

■ ● ■

"Elaine, we don't know what's happened." She stood there staring through me. Even though I knew that besides the tears, Elaine was a hard woman, I wondered if she was on the verge of a nervous breakdown.

"What's with the hollering? Do we have some new information?"

"I'm sorry, Andy. I'm having the worst day of my life."

Andy frowned and was just about to say something.

"And I stopped by Cheike's and I got the impression she was packing."

That made me sit up straight. Andy moved from the doorway all the way into my office.

"That's curious, don't y'all think so, Andy?"

Andy nodded. "What did she say to you?" Andy kept edging around Elaine so he could look at her straight on.

"She didn't say much. She asked if there was any news. She really wasn't talkative so I left. There's just too much to do."

Andy and I exchanged glances. "You think there could be anything up with that?"

Andy shrugged. "If there is, following her around isn't going to help us find him."

"But maybe we should talk to her just the same, if ya'll know what I mean."

"Guys, come on. I think that maybe she's just leaving."

We both stared at Elaine who finally sat down. Looking down at the floor she mumbled, "She might just be leaving."

I shook my arms. "Look here. I'm going to order some food."

"I can't eat."

"I can't eat either."

"We got us an echo in here. Y'all can't survive on that coffee from downstairs. I'm orderin' some real food."

I watched Andy shrug and shuffle off toward the rest room.

■ ● ■

Elaine shrugged. "Get what you want for yourself." Then she got up with the stack of papers that didn't fall on my desk, and trudged over to her own.

"Uh-huh."

I ordered food for six people. When it was delivered I went to the men's room to wash my hands. When I got back I was afraid they only left me some pickles to nibble on. I stood there with my eyes like slits staring down at the pickles and a tiny cup of cole slaw.

I glanced at both of them, shook my head and then picked up a pickle. "You know, I wasn't gone that long, was I?"

Andy started laughing and Elaine started choking, so I had to pat her on the back. Then Andy left and came back from his office with a card board tray of what was left. "You are no good, Andrew. You have always been no good as far as my recollection takes me." I picked up a Bratwurst in a roll while I laughed. "You no good, too, Elaine. Make a man panic like that at a time like this." I should have left off the 'time like this' part. Both of their faces seemed to go pale at the same time.

I looked at my watch. "Hey. Y'all come with me for fifteen minutes." Elaine started to open her mouth. "No arguments, please."

I led the two of them to the elevators. Amazingly they both followed me to the tenth floor. Quietly we climbed the stairs to the roof.

Then Elaine started. "We don't have time for this, Sharp. We need to get back downstairs."

"Ah asked for fifteen minutes and ah got twelve more comin'."

Andy walked over to the edge. "City looks deceiving, doesn't it?"

"Look up, Andy."

■ ● ■

Another meteor trailed across the sky.

I could hear Elaine whisper. "Oh, God..."

Andy put his hands on his hips with his eyes on the sky. Another one flew across the sky and burned up.

"Did we lose already?"

I looked at Elaine. Half of her face was covered in shadow. "No. Not yet. The boy always makes it out. Didn't we say that?" Ten minutes later Andy walked past me and slapped me on the arm. We all took the stairs back down to our offices. Andy went into my office and came out with a BLT. None of us were speaking. In the middle of our uncomfortable silence, the phone rang.

Elaine picked up and I watched her face go through some contortions, change color and then a slight smile appeared.

"Thank you! Oh, thank you! Yes...yes." She put the receiver down and said, "That reporter from The Star Ledger said a kid called in for the $50 news tip to tell him there's a man up on a ledge at some abandoned buildings out past route 32."

"So?"

She looked at me like I had just asked the wrong question. "Black man with no clothes on!"

I saw Andy throw a perfectly good BLT down on Elaine's desk.

"Y'all coulda' taken it with you, Andy."

"Elaine, try to reach Mojica and tell him we're headed out to the abandoned Palmer Estates. Sharp, are you armed?"

I frowned. "Let's go, goddamn it!"

■ ● ■

Mojica

"Heeks! Slow down, bro!"

"Sit tight, Raoul. I can handle these roads okay."

"That ain't it. How are we handling the Troopers if we get pulled over?"

"There is no getting pulled over tonight. They'll have to follow me and just try to keep up."

I could feel Raoul seething next to me, but he didn't say anything so he knew I was serious. It took us forty minutes to get to the abandoned housing complex. When I slowed down to fifty we could see a flashlight scanning the side of a building.

"It'll take them forever to check out these buildings like that."

"Maybe that's all they got, Heeks."

I jumped a curb in a weedy parking lot and heard Raoul curse when his head hit the roof. I ran my Skylark through the brush and slid up close to where Andy was shining his light on windows one at a time. Andy suddenly directed his light along the base of the building.

"What the hell is he doing? He's going to be up high or he would have gotten down by himself."

"Brother, you need to calm down. You're not thinking right.

■ ● ■

He might be on the ground already. Andy's checking for every-thing."

I swallowed hard and knew Raoul was right, but I replied with as much certitude as I could raise, which didn't seem like much. "He's still up there. He's not on the ground. He wouldn't give up. He knows we'd come to get him. He knows that."

Raoul grabbed my arm loosely, like he was trying to reassure me. "You right, man. You right. Let's go find the boy."

I got out and went around to the trunk. I handed Raoul a two foot long flashlight and then moved some things around.

"Lord…"

It sounded like Raoul was doing a scale, starting at the lowest G possible for human hearing. I swung the battery backpack over my shoulders. I picked up the lamp by the two handles I had welded to it and plugged it in. When I turned Raoul was staring hard at me.

"I got it off a ship."

"Uh huh…"

Raoul followed me over to where Andy and Sharp were standing. Sharp was holding his cane in his right hand and a .38 in his left. Andy lowered his flash.

"What buildings have you checked out so far?"

"We just got here about ten minutes ago. We've only been able to do two sides of this building."

"I'll hit the next building. You three can do this one." I could see the outlines of their heads nodding.

I moved off to the left. When I turned on my lamp it was like the sun had come up in fluorescent grey. I was able to easily scan the building, but my lamp was going to get hot quick.

There were eight buildings out here. For a brief moment I wondered how much the investors had lost on this project. For a shorter second I cursed them and their extravagant wastefulness.

■ ● ■

And then they slipped from my mind and I was immersed again in finding my friend.

Working my way to the next building I suddenly noticed eyes out in the brush. I turned off the lamp and then heard Sharp's voice. "It's just deer, Heeks. I got you covered."

Ten minutes later I moved into a large field and I saw him. Motionless, with his head between his knees.

"Sharp!" He was next to me before I could turn around to look for him. I pointed. "He's there. I'm going up. Go get the guys."

I took the stairwell steps two and three at a time. Somewhere, about half way up I tripped and managed to bang up my elbow and my shin. "Motherfucker!" I got back up, skipping and hopping along the stairs up to the top floor.

There was some ambient light in the room from my ship lamp, but I had to feel along the edge of the plywood hoping for a weakness. There wasn't one. "Bro! We're all here. Hang on. I'll be right back and we'll get you out of there."

I ran back down the stairs, passing Andy and Raoul on their way up. A couple of flights down I passed Sharp, who was rubbing his leg. "Be right back. Need a drill."

I ran to my car and pulled out a power drill, a canteen, medical kit, a blanket and the small hit of morphine I had stashed in the thumb of my baseball glove. Running back up the stairs I passed Sharp one flight from the top.

Andy and Raoul held the plywood while I extracted the screws. Carefully they pulled the plywood sheet away from the window and leaned it against a wall.

Andy grabbed our boy's arm, but he didn't move. "C'mon, man. Let's get out of here." He still didn't move. Raoul grabbed his other arm and they lifted him to the floor. I took a small dose cup from the medical kit and filled it with water. He gulped it down and choked. We repeated the ritual about ten times until I

■ ● ■

was sure he wouldn't choke to death with the canteen.

Raoul pulled the canteen away when he started gagging. "We need to get you to a hospital."

"No hospital."

"We have to have a doctor look you over."

"No hospital!"

His voice was raspy, but his emphatic determination was crystal clear. Andy was trying to wrap him in the blanket.

"Put the board back up."

I wasn't sure I heard his rough whisper correctly. "What'd you say, bro'?"

"Put that fucking board back up. Just like it was. Same holes. Were you guys looking for me?"

Sharp was still rubbing his leg. " 'Course, we was all looking for you."

"I want you to keep looking for me."

We were all quiet watching Andy struggle to get his best friend wrapped in a blanket. Then Raoul rumbled, "Sharp, help me hold this wood up for Heeks. Heeks…you still got the screws?"

"What?! Of course I have the screws. They're in my pocket. Why in hell would I get rid of perfectly good screws?" I thought I heard "fucking Mojica," but it was so faint I thought maybe I imagined it. Then the other three started laughing so I knew I wasn't hallucinating, I was just farther away.

Just when we finished with the plywood Andy called for help. "Guys…give me a hand. He's out on his feet. Going to need help getting him down the stairs."

"I got it." Raoul picked him up in his arms like he was his favorite son. "I have a house you all can stay in and a bed that will fit this boy for some decent dreams."

We slipped down the stairs quietly and packed up. None of us said a word.

■ ● ■

Awake

"Don't worry. I'm a fantastic teacher. You'll be able to fly. You'll have one glorious flight through the air, just like Icarus." He waved his arm across the sky and smiled at me. But his smile sounded like laughter. It was sticky laughter. The kind of laughter you want to wash off in the shower. "It will be a miraculous flight. You'll savor it." He keeps laughing at me. What's so funny?

"You don't want me to tell Andy about the water." I turned to run, but my legs wouldn't move.

"See? You can't run. That's why you should fly."

I looked at the sky. It had turned black except for the stars. All three of them. Where'd the sun go? It was sunny just a minute ago.

"I always liked Chesterfields, myself. They're road-toasted. They're…"

I opened my eyes. They were burning. Where the hell was I? I didn't recognize the room. I rubbed my eyes with the base of my palms. I propped myself up on my elbows and then lay back down dizzy. Where the hell was I? I could have sworn it was the guys got me out of the window last night. Where the hell were

■ ● ■

they? Where'd they bring me?

I stared at the ceiling. Coffee. There's a friendly smell. I sat all the way up. A wave of nausea slid through my stomach. I closed my eyes and swung my legs over the edge of the bed trying to be as quiet as possible. I wasn't quiet enough. Some odd footsteps started coming my way. I pushed myself off the bed but my nausea and a giant size headache helped sit my ass back down to wait for the footsteps. They appeared in the doorway accompanied by a man I recognized, who was holding a Thompson submachine gun.

"Sharp."

"Glad you're awake. How do you feel?"

"Headache, nauseous, stiff, like I've been a hard-on for about five weeks."

Sharp laughing. It was good to hear.

"Drink that water next to you. You need to work on that hydration thing."

"Is there a swimming pool nearby?"

He smiled. "Seriously, Bro'. We need to keep working on the fluids."

"What time is it?"

"Just about eleven o'clock."

"Damn. I thought I'd sleep longer than that."

Sharp looked at me funny. He kind of groaned. Then he smiled.

"You been out two days, partner."

"Two days?! Really?! And nobody took me to the hospital?!"

Sharp's mouth opened and his eyes widened. We both started laughing.

"You guys really didn't come and get me last night?"

"Couple nights ago. Your neighbor, Mrs. Culletti got in touch with Raoul as soon as you were taken. She is a monu-

■●■

mental pain though. She only called us about fifty times to find out if you were okay. She called the police too, but she said they didn't want to hear it. She did sit down with Raoul and Mojica for a couple of hours giving them descriptions of the men who snagged you. Anyways, I was going to make you some Cream of Wheat. How's that sound to your stomach?"

"Cream of Wheat? You couldn't think of anything more bland than Cream of Wheat?"

"Thought about grits, but we're out. How 'bout I cut in some bananas and a little honey with a slab of butter?"

"Whatever…where the hell is everybody? Where's Andy?"

"He's in court with Elaine."

"Court? What're they doing in court?"

"A judge ordered Marty back to her parents. Cops took her. Elaine's lawyer finally got Child Services woke up, so they're trying to get Marty out."

Rage always seems to be blurry. The floor was jumping up and down. I couldn't even tell what color it was. I could feel tears forming.

"Heeks and Raoul's boys are still out looking for you. Actually they're looking for any of the guys who took you based on Mrs. Culletti's descriptions. We're hoping to get a trail to DeFord."

I nodded.

"Drink that water, dude. Ah'm a get some Cream of Wheat goin'."

I nodded again, but raised my head in time to see Sharp's back moving away.

"Sharp. Anyone seen Cheike?"

Sharp stopped, but he didn't turn around. "Yeah. Elaine saw her over at her studio." He disappeared toward a kitchen I assumed was where the coffee aroma came from.

■ ● ■

As I pulled on a pair of jeans I yelled down the hall. "Where the hell are we?"

"One of Raoul's places. We're out past Jukette. Nobody's sleeping at home now. We're all going to be moving around a bit."

"So who's been sleeping here?"

"Mostly me and Andy. Raoul has Heeks and Elaine movin' around to friends. And then we actually didn't really sleep too much after Mrs. Culletti called. Mostly we stayed in the office at night. Brother, stop with the chatter and drink some damn water."

"Yeah. Yeah. Okay."

"And then come on out here and sit the fuck down so y'all can eat something."

"You going to join me?"

"Sure. Ah'm a fix me up some scrambled eggs, home fries, bacon…maybe a little French toast."

"You bastard. You're making my stomach flip, goddam it."

I brushed peeling skin off my left arm as I walked toward the kitchen. I raised my head and saw Sharp looking at me with a grin as big as Mojica's. "It's good to see you, Sharp."

"You know, that reporter from the Star Ledger told us where you were. Some kid called in for the fifty dollar hot tip money."

"So one of them actually had a brain."

"One of who?"

"Nevermind. Is there a car here?"

"Yeah. An agency car, but you're not going anywhere yet. Let me cut some bananas in this and…"

"Sharp. I need to see Cheike."

Sharp turned around with a knife in his right hand and half a banana in his left. "Bro, it can wait."

"She's with DeFord, isn't she?"

■ ● ■

Sharp looked at the floor and shook his head. "I don't know that. But her timing for packing up and leaving town is mighty peculiar."

"Leaving town?!"

"Elaine stopped over there and it looked like the moving van was already at the door."

I started to sit down, but I stood back up and stared out a kitchen window. "Gimme the keys, Sharp."

"Dude, you can't be running around town. You wanted De-Ford to think you were still up there. He's gotta have her place staked out."

"Don't care. Two days later he knows I'm gone. I'm hoping he just doesn't know how. Gimme the keys. You don't give me the keys, I walk! You'll have to fight me to stop me."

Sharp turned his back to me and then I heard him sigh. "I'll drive you. You can't go alone."

"Drive me then. One way or the other I'm going."

"You drink two more cups of water, put on a shirt and some shoes…eat some Cream of Wheat and we're gone."

"What's with you and Cream of Wheat? Give me the keys and I'll warm up the engine."

Sharp started laughing. "Did you get elected to Congress while you were gone? Drink some water. Eat some cereal. Then go get a shirt on." He shook his head. "If my brain was that pitiful, I would'a been the object of an infanticide a long time ago. Give you the keys…you been out in the sun too long." He shook his head laughing and I laughed right along with him.

We were both silent on the drive into the city. Colors in the trees seemed off to me. I couldn't understand why. None of the buildings seemed to register, even when we got close to Cheike's apartment.

■ ● ■

There was a small moving truck in front of her building. I passed two workers coming down as I was on my way up.

The door to her apartment was wide open, but I knocked anyway. I had never been here before, but it seemed there wasn't much left inside. I saw her leaning over a drafting table by a set of frosted factory windows. She didn't look up as I approached. I could see she was looking at blueprints, which she rolled up and slid into a black tube.

"You were leaving without saying goodbye?"

"I was going to. I probably still will."

"It's that simple? I thought we had something…something really special. I don't want you to leave my life no matter what's happened. I think you're wonderful."

She finally looked at me.

"So? Wonderful, huh? What did you think? Did you think you were going to carry my halo for a while? Give me a rest from my perfection? Where were you for the past three days? Wasn't there a phone where you were? Was it some place where you could be heroic? Was it a place of myth and legend…and maybe stories…stories you can tell your grandchildren if you live that long."

She strode for the door with her jewelry singing. I watched her walk through the door while I stood frozen in place in the grey light from the old factory windows.

On the way back to Raoul's safe house Sharp didn't say a thing. I stared out the window at scenery that still didn't seem to be the right color. It felt like the hills weren't the right shape. The sun seemed dark in a clear off-blue, greenish-grey sky.

When we pulled into the gravel driveway Sharp said it looked like Andy and Elaine were here. I saw their car parked behind a hedge away from the house.

■ ● ■

"I couldn't ask her."

Sharp sighed. "About DeFord?"

"I didn't care what she'd done. I just wanted her to say she'd be with me."

"Dude, I don't even know what to say. I'm sorry."

"There's probably nothing to say. I'm a fool. I shouldn't care. But…"

"Well, if you didn't care, you and I probably wouldn't be friends. You're no fool and just because you were willing to give yourself to someone who doesn't want you doesn't make you one. We can talk later, but we need to go in and see what's up with our partners."

Sharp squeezed my shoulder and then stepped out of the car.

When we walked into the house Elaine gave me a hug that felt like desperation. I pushed back from her a little.

"What's happening with Marty?"

"The judge told Child Services there was no reason to re-move her from her parents' custody. Marty told the judge she wanted to get married and that she wasn't being forced. That creep was actually at the courthouse out in the hallway."

"The guy who's buying her?"

"With a big grin on his face."

I saw Andy coming from the bathroom with a very genuine smile on his face.

"Good to see you up and around."

"Yeah."

"You feeling okay?"

"Yeah."

He reached down and felt my ankle. Then he stood up, star-ing into my frowning face. "Just wanted to make sure you didn't pick up any shrapnel." I smiled.

"You need any time away?"

■ ● ■

"I think maybe you guys need to forget me for a little while, so I'm pulling out of the partnership."

Elaine grabbed my arm lightly. "What do you mean?"

I turned my head back to Elaine, hesitating before I spoke. "I'm going to kill DeFord. He tried to kill me and now I'm going to do him."

"I think he was trying to scare us by taking you."

"I hate to insult you, Andy, but that was close to the dumbest thing you've ever said. You can't possibly think what you just said. You found me because of some dumb-ass kids. I don't think DeFord counted on them walking through that field. The only reason I didn't get a bullet to the back of the head is because he's probably legally insane. He wanted to create a little spectacle and maybe scare you, but he expected me to end the show dead. He could have grabbed any one of us, but he grabbed me. So you're going to have to stay away from me for a while. If I get snagged when I'm done, none of you had anything to do with it."

"Ah hate to interrupt you, but that's about the stupidest thing ah have ever heard you say. You are talking to the wrong people. We're partners and we're going to figure this out as partners. DeFord made a move against all of us when he took you. If we act, he is going to come after every single one of us, you can be assured of that. Plus, if anyone wants out, they can leave for some place safe right now."

Sharp never got a chance to take a breath before Elaine was all over him. "Nobody's leaving, but murder, Sharp? We're going to sit around and plan a murder?"

"Self-defense, Elaine. We can't really trust the city cops, so we have to be able to defend ourselves."

Andy was staring at me.

"What do you have to say, Andy?"

"This isn't just some eye for an eye bullshit, is it?"

■ ● ■

"While I was up on that window ledge I remembered a feeling I had when we first found that sheet of paper out in the alley by the diner. A route to a town. Concern about water flows. Poison. It made me feel like something big was being planned and I had to figure out why. Why a whole town? Then it hit me one night after the angels…after I saw a meteor shower. DeFord is going to try to poison a whole town to influence the political climate in the country. If the country moves to the right after the election, DeFord wants it to go further. If the whole country is afraid of some kind of faceless radicals, who do crazy shit, then the FBI, the CIA, the police or whoever else is out there, can run wild in the name of national security. I think that's what the Commission wants and DeFord has to be stopped. So for that, and for him trying to do me, I'm going to kill him."

Everyone was quiet. I started counting to see how long it would be before Elaine started talking. Sharp sat down and started tapping his knuckles on a small wooden table.

"That's a pretty logical theory. A scary one. But we gotta figure this out as partners. We're all we got that we can really trust. We know we can't trust the city police. We don't know how many cops DeFord has gotten to. We can trust each other, but this is really going to get sticky. Anyone wants out, now is a good time."

Elaine moved around me and put both hands on her hips while she stared at Sharp. "Who the fuck do you think you're talking to?! I know you're talking to me. I'm right here in the room goddam it! If you want to ask me a question, don't make it third person like we're in a novel. We both know you're not suggesting the option of leaving to Andy. He's not going anywhere! On top of that, you're arguing no one should jump ship, but then you say now is a good time! What the fuck, Sharp?!"

Sharp sighed and looked at the floor. "Ah apologize, Elaine. I

■ ● ■

don't want you to be in deeper than you feel comfortable…"

"Deep?! You're not the only one who got shot when the Commission decided to take us out. I've been in the deep end with you guys ever since my interview ended. I'm getting out of the pool now?!"

I looked at Andy. His eyebrows almost touched his hairline. I felt like I had to save Sharp.

"Elaine?"

She spun on me so fast I involuntarily took a half step back.

"Keep your mouth shut for a second!" She turned back to Sharp. "And is he drinking enough water? When was the last time he drank water?!"

"What about Marty?"

Elaine's hands fell from her hips. Her shoulders drooped. She turned to face me slowly. "She told the judge she wanted to get married." Tears formed in her eyes.

I sat down in a chair by a window. There was a dead, barkless tree just at the edge of the tree line.

"The judge asked her if she was afraid and she said 'no.'" The judge just smiled, even though Marty was looking at the floor."

"Was she wearing long sleeves?"

"Yes. Probably so no one could see the bruises her father put on her."

Elaine kept on talking. Then Andy talked. The tree was becoming fuzzy. The yard was getting fuzzy. It was like entropy, but "fuzz" was a better word for it. The world decays to 'fuzz.' DeFord, Marty…Cheike. The front door opened and I jumped.

"Capitan! How're you feeling?"

Everyone was looking at me. I felt embarrassed. "I'm stiff, but I'm okay." Raoul strode in, walked up to me and clasped my hand. He put his left hand on my shoulder and it felt like it disappeared. "Brother, you had us all shook up there. We're gonna

■ ● ■

have to take care of some serious business. You up for it?"

I squeezed his hand, but didn't say anything.

"Good. Good."

"Elaine, I'm sorry. I missed some of what you were saying about the court. Did you say that the man who is buying her was there?"

"He was out in the hall. When Marty and her parents came out of the courtroom he met them in the hall with a big grin on his face. The judge slapped a restraining order on me. I'm not supposed to be within one hundred and fifty feet of Marty. If I harbor her again I'll be charged with kidnapping. Our lawyer and the child services people got into an intense whispering argument after the hearing. I was going to try to speak to Marty but Andy held me back. Calmer heads and all."

"They would have tossed your ass in the cooler as soon as you approached her." Andy looked at me like he was in pain. "Elaine started a file if you want to see it."

"Yeah. Let me have it."

"Okay, folks. Raoul and I have found a house where we are sure that two of DeFord's men are staying. Raoul has a friend watching the place."

I heard Andy's voice as I sat back down by the window. "Just one guy, Raoul?!"

"Believe me, we only need that one man down there. He's like a reflection of a shadow."

Everyone was exchanging information. The conversation was turning to fuzz. I looked out the window again at the dead tree. It was becoming blurry. A world of fuzz. DeFord, Marty and Cheike. At least I knew what I was going to do.

■ ● ■

Pull

Sharp was behind the wheel playing with the top of his cane. He'd snatch a look at me every so often, like the second hand passing twelve. After a half hour of this, I finally said, "What?!"

"Ah was wondering a couple of things…like where is Bryan Clutocher from. Every time I ask Raoul he just says, 'Out West.' That's one."

"I think he's from L.A."

Sharp looked out his side window at the building we were watching. "What makes you say that? Raoul tell you something?"

"No. I think I heard Clutocher say 'stoked' in the same sentence as 'the 58' when he was talking about route 58."

Sharp looked at me again and laughed. "You caught a couple of colloquialisms? You really are a detective, aren't you?"

"That's right, Tex."

There was a metallic sound, like garbage cans hitting each other. Sharp's heard spun back to the building again and we watched a stray dog come out to the street with a bag of something in its mouth. Sharp chuckled. "So when are you and me going to straighten out a bottle of JD?"

Sharp suddenly looked like a stranger to me. I'd had that

■ ● ■

feeling a couple of times before when a panic was coming. "Why the fuck are you playing with that cane so much and when did you get that new handle?!"

Sharp turned back to me real slow. I got the feeling he didn't like the tone of my question. For a second I thought I should apologize and then I thought, 'screw it.'

"Well…"

The cane handle seemed to come off. In the dark it took me a moment to catch the glint off the metal. The handle was attached to about 18 inches of blade.

"Heeks put it in. Don't know that it will ever come in handy, but I'm trying to get acquainted with the handle since it has a double lock. If ah ever need it ah want to be sure I don't fumble the combination. Y'all want to play with it?"

"No. I need to piss and I'm going to grab some food back at that deli."

"Hold on. Brother, what's on your mind?"

"A BLT with light mayo."

"Bullshit. What's weighing on you?"

"Nothing. It's personal."

"Uh huh. Well, if you're coming back, get me whatever you get."

I paused. "Of course I'm coming back!" Sharp didn't look at me or say anything else. I slammed the car door knowing he was right. I was going to be gone for a while.

When I finally turned onto Carey Street I could see an orange and blue neon sign that read "Dreg's." The street was quiet, but as I got about half a block away I could hear "school's out forever" pounding through the walls. I stood outside for a couple of seconds looking at the peeling paint bathed in orange light that drifted down from the neon sign. There were two, three by three windows on each side of the door. Probably the minimum

■ ● ■

for the building code. I almost laughed. At first I thought there were curtains over the windows. Then I realized the windows were so filthy you just couldn't see through them. Couldn't wait to see what the inside looked like.

When I pushed through the door, that should have pushed out, for just a moment I felt like I was sixteen again. I was in a high school sophomore's paradise. It was one of those bars you look for where the drinking age hovers around 14. I was surprised this one existed.

There were about ten tables in the room. Off to the left, in one of the corners were two tables with separate crowds of kids standing and sitting. One or two of the patrons may have been eighteen, but everyone else was as young as fifteen. For a brief eye squint I was confused. There was no bar. It was so dark I wondered where the light came from. Two pinball machines pushed up against the wall basically gave off the only light in the room.

I shook my head for one stanza of Janis Joplin and the Holding Company, finally noticing a very dim light coming from a doorway in the far corner to my right. As I passed through it I read a sign taped on one of the pinball machines. "I am brokin."

The door was the beginning of a hallway, about ten feet long, that led me to a room with a bar. I had left a room where no one cared who was in there, and entered a room where no one cared who was in there. The main difference being, this place was populated with adults only.

The room was moderately busy. Some people were moving around, but most seemed intent on being in one place and committing themselves to serious drinking for the most part.

Over to my left, oblivious it seemed to everyone in the room and vice versa, were a man and a woman sitting near a barely illuminated table, kissing. A thread of drool dropped down from

■ ● ■

one of their chins and was pooling on the woman's skirt. The man had his hand in between her legs and she had a grip on his wrist. I couldn't tell if she was trying to pull his hand away, or struggling to keep it right where it was. I really didn't care.

The underside of the bar was lit up with fluorescent lights. The mirrors behind the drink well were bordered by blue Christmas tree lights. Almost all of the stools were taken. They seemed so close together I had to look twice to make sure people weren't sitting on each other's laps. And then I realized that on one stool at least, a woman was sitting on a man's lap.

But down at the 'L' in the bar there was space. The man I was looking for had empty stools on each side of him. He was drinking beer, eating peanuts and glaring at a spiral bound, little black notebook. He had slightly long black hair, a thin mustache and a pointy goatee. He was wearing a white tee shirt and black leather jacket. It looked like one I had seen Bobby Seale wearing in a poster. Didn't look as good on him as it did on Bobby. And here I was, looking at him with as much contempt as I had ever felt in my life.

As I began to weave my way slowly to his end of the bar, it occurred to me that in some way, for some reason, he was important in this place. Either that or he was perceived as dangerous, which amounted to the same thing.

When I began to sit down he gave me a look like 'what the fuck do you think you're doing?' I glanced at him and said, "Thanks for saving my seat." I put a twenty on the bar and yelled at the bartender, "Two Bacardi doubles." His expression seemed to change when the bartender put down two drinks and I tapped for two more.

He closed his notebook and slid it inside his jacket. He was giving me the eye even when he raised his drink to his lips. He asked me why I was sitting next to him.

■●■

"I move stuff and you look like the only guy in here worth talking to."

"Oh yeah? Well I don't have anything that needs movin'."

"I was in business with someone and the partnership broke up and I'm trying to get right again. Maybe you could point me in the right direction since I'm not from around here."

"Just like that. You buy me a coupla' shots and I'm going to aim you in the right direction."

I looked at him, shrugged and picked up my drink.

"Then maybe you could at least point me in the direction of a woman worth the time and the dime." That seemed to get his full attention. "I had a girl I had to drop a little while ago. She was too young. So I kind of feel like I'm out here in the desert."

"Too young? Ain't nothin' too young."

I fondled my drink while Larry kept chuckling and repeating , "…too young…."

I tapped the bar for a couple more drinks and then told Larry I had to piss.

The restroom was bleak. The toilet seat was gone. So was the toilet paper. The urinal had paper towels in it. I wondered where they came from, since the front of the dispenser was gone. I remembered the first time throwing up in a bathroom like this when I was a teenager. And that's what I was here for now.

I stuck two fingers down my throat and brought up most of the four shots of Bacardi. While I coughed and spit I heard someone say, "What a waste." I turned around wiping my mouth with my hand and then wiping my hand on my jeans. The guy swaying in front of me had probably been drunk for more years than I had been alive. When I hit the door I heard him mumble, "Damn waste."

I took my seat again and noticed that some of my change was gone. I expected it. Five for the bartender and five for my

■ ● ■

pimp friend.

"What kind of work do you do?"

He started laughing again. "I don't work."

I gave him my best 'what the hell look.' "So are you married?"

He grinned. "Used to be. Three times."

I stared at him while he polished off the second drink. When he put the glass down and reached for the next one, I said, "What happened? You're a young guy to have been married three times."

"Fuck. The first one took off. The second one got fat, so I got rid of her. The third one cut herself up. Fucked up my kitchen. Fucking blood everywhere."

It felt like the temperature in the place went up ten degrees. I tried to sit up straight instead of leaning on the bar.

"Damn. Think you'll ever get married again?"

He started laughing with his drink about two inches from his lips. He leaned in toward me like he was going to tell me a secret. I pretty much knew the Barcardi was kicking in.

"I'll probably be gettin' married in one or two weeks."

Two stools away a head flopped onto the bar. The guy's eyes were closed, but his mouth was partially open and his tongue slid out of his mouth in between a space where three teeth probably should have been.

"I hate these fucking drunks. Can't hold their liquor. Get all liquored up. They make the place feel crappy. Used to have a guy to throw this shit out, but now it's just Bartholomew here does that stuff."

"Who's Bartholomew?"

"The bartender. Hey, Bart! You gonna take out this trash or what?"

The bartender looked at us and then lazily at the back of the head lying on the counter.

■ ● ■

"He's just sleeping. In ten or fifteen minutes I'll wake him or get him out of here." Bart turned away, and moved slowly toward the other end of the bar.

"Jesus Christ. They leave all kinds of…"

"You were telling me you were going to get married."

"Fucking bums. Yeah. So what? Gettin' married."

"You were telling me I shouldn't worry about my girl being too young. I mean my girl is like twenty or twenty-one. Makes me a little uncomfortable."

He looked into his glass to make sure there was something in it. Then he swished it around. "My wife is gonna be fifteen."

"Fifteen?! No shit?"

He grinned. "No shit. She'll keep me from workin' too hard."

"What'dya mean?"

He leaned in toward me with the smile of the stupid. This guy was a punk. A creepy, drunk punk.

"Once I get her trained, I'm set."

"Trained? What are you talking about?"

"Ass fucking, man. Do you know how much I can make a night with a fifteen year old who let's guys ass fuck her? Five, six hundred a night. That's what I was making with my last bitch until she started fucking up."

"The one who went over the edge? You tell me about this when I get back. I have to hit the john again."

"You in that bathroom quite a bit."

"You don't think I started drinking here, do you?" I put another twenty on the bar and told him to take care of the next round.

I went into the bathroom and managed to vomit again without an audience. I washed my face and then slipped out into a hall. I tried two doors. Both were locked. I looked into a storage room. Just black. I turned around, then took one step right into

■ ● ■

Jocko's chest.

"Well, well, well, if…"

"Jocko, is there a back door to this place?"

"What a surprise seeing you here."

"Is there a door out of here, Jocko?"

"Certainly. It is in the fire code that an establishment of this type should have a fire exit. Are we expecting an imminent conflagration?"

"Show me the door."

"Let me get a drink first and then…"

I grabbed and squeezed his arm hard. "I'm working, Jocko. Show me the door!"

Even through the haze of alcohol and shadows I could see in his eyes that I was hurting him. He winced and then stared at me like a frightened cocker spaniel. He led me down a pitch black hallway that I had thought was just a storage area. Boxes of empty bottles were stacked up close to the ceiling. I could see the bottles at the top reflecting a dim light, but I had my hands out to my sides to touch the cases because I was following Jocko blind. How the hell did Jocko walk down this aisle without one goddam stumble.

We made it to the end of the hall and Jocko tapped on a door. I pushed it open and stepped halfway out into an alley that reeked of garbage and urine.

"Thanks, Jocko. Here. Get yourself a drink, but you don't know me. I'm working. Don't even come near me."

"Well, that is the first time I've ever been tipped for showing some…"

"Jocko! Shut up! That's it! You don't know me. Don't come near me."

"When…"

I pushed him against the wall and left him in the hallway.

■ ● ■

There was a dim light I could follow out easier than it was following Jocko in.

When I sat back down, Larry started talking again about his 'gold mine.'

"Some nights I been able to get five or six guys…"

It felt like the lights were going out and someone turned up the heat. I rubbed my face. Five guys?! What was that on the other side of the room? I squinted and Larry slapped my shoulder.

"Walked in…" "her ass was all red"…laughter…why's he laughing…who's laughing…"boys"…black sailor in the corner…"she did all of"…little girl crying behind him…"she did"…put his arms out to keep me away…three white sailors… "so much money"…sailor between her legs… "dude, the money she"…two of them passed a bottle laughing…three white sailors… "so much money"…sailor between her legs…laughter… fucking laughter… "fifteen is excellent"…the black sailor's eyes are wide…she spread her legs so…woman on the bed with a cut lip bleeding… "made me a ton of"…she was no longer crying… staring at the ceiling…black sailor shook his head scared… "I had her"…pulled my Colt and hit the sailor on top of the woman in the back of the head he stopped pumping… "she went down"…aimed the pistol at the two with the bottle get him out of here and they dragged him out… black soldier shaking his head don't, while I throw the sheet over her legs wave my gun to get out…black sailor slides out little girl runs screaming to her mother lies down clutching her…sailor is gone I'm sick lean against the wall puke little girl is clutching her mother she squeezed child… Andy and tall guy… what's going on… stagger out to hallway…"fuck like a horse"…

I tossed back a shot of Bacardi. No one will miss him. He should leave town. I'll just beat the crap out of him so he gets the idea. I looked around the room and tried to focus. I dropped

■ ● ■

a powder-filled cellophane packet on the bar.

"Now we're talking!"

"Let's get straight and then we can do some serious drinking." I nodded my head toward the hall.

We got up and headed toward the bathroom. When I walked past it, I heard the pimp say, "Where the hell you goin'?" But he followed me out into the alley anyway.

"This is worse than the bathroom. What the hell are we doin' out here and what is this shit?" He held the cellophane bag up over his head to get a better look at the contents.

"You need to leave town."

He looked at me like I had said something very stupid that he didn't understand.

"You need to get the fuck out of town tonight before something really bad happens to you."

"What?! Yeah, let me go back inside and get my ticket."

His mouth was open when the blade appeared behind his teeth. He grabbed my wrist. I spun him around and pulled the knife across his neck. He stumbled two steps and fell down. I picked up the packet and wiped the blade on his pant leg. Walking out of the alley I dumped the sugar out and threw the cellophane away. When I got to the street I tried not to listen to the echo. 'What did you do? What did you do? What did you do?'

I was walking fast. Suddenly, across the street, I thought I noticed something darting from shadow to shadow. I stopped across from a gas station with all of its lights on to see if something would be visible. Visible. What have I done? What have I done?

Nothing. I started walking again. Marty's house was on a street where none of the houses had front yards. I looked back down the street. Nothing there. Nothing there? Nothing there.

I stood in front of Marty's house looking for a way in. Down the alley about ten feet, a window with a screen. I pulled out the screen and slid in head first. I started and froze. Something moved in the shadow. Nothing. I could hear snoring and I followed it to a bedroom with twin beds. In one bed a very overweight woman was lying fully clothed with one leg hanging over the edge. The leg still on the bed had a shoe on the foot. On the other bed a man in a tee shirt and work pants was lying on the bed with his mouth open. The room reeked of stale alcohol.

I pressed my knife to his neck and put my free hand over his mouth. His eyes suddenly jerked open and his hands swatted at my arm. I pressed a little with the knife.

"Stop. Don't do that. Put your hands down." He now had the idea. "Put both of your hands inside the front of your pants."

When he did I pulled his belt as tight as I could; cut a new hole quick and then put my knife back up to his throat.

"What'dya want? My wife is in the next bed."

Incredible.

"Jesus, don't kill me. My girl is in the next room. She's…"

I slapped him across the face so hard I thought I might have wakened the wife. But the way she was snoring, nothing was going to wake her for the next few hours. So here I was with a knife to a man's neck and he's trying save himself by offering up his wife and daughter.

"Shut up you piece of scum. You just listen. Got it?"

He nodded.

"Good. Now listen close. You will take what I give you now and that will be it. No more money. Your daughter is no longer yours. That is what you will tell the judge tomorrow. Got it?"

He didn't nod, so I pushed down on the knife. Was he that drunk? He actually started to struggle by trying to rock away

■ ● ■

from me. I slapped him again, hard. He stopped moving so I let up on the knife a little.

"I told you not to move, didn't I?" He nodded again. "After tomorrow you no longer have a daughter. You tell the judge you want the woman who approaches you tomorrow that you want your daughter to stay with her a while. Got it?"

He didn't nod so I pressed down on the knife a little more. He gasped.

"I got it. I got it." I thought I could see a trickle of blood sprout from the blade. He nodded vigorously as tears trickled from the corners of his eyes.

"Open your mouth."

"Oh please! Not that! Plea…"

I covered his mouth. The snoring in the other bed continued. What the hell? Did he think I was going to cut out his tongue? How would he be able to tell the judge anything if I did that?

"You don't speak. When I say 'open your mouth,' what do you do?"

He opened his mouth. "Wider." I crammed $1,000 into it.

"This is all you're getting. Don't make me come back. Understand?"

He nodded.

"The pimp who was buying your daughter has left town and will not be back. There is no more money. Tomorrow you give up your daughter."

It looked like he understood. When I stood up, I hoped he did.

It took me over two hours to get back to the car. When I opened the door Andy said, "Where the hell have you been?!"

"Where's Sharp?"

■ ● ■

"He called me and said he had to clean something up and it was an emergency. What the hell have you been doing?"

"Some business I had to take care of." I sat down in the car.

"You smell like someone threw up on you and 'what business?'"

"Personal business."

"Personal?! You leave your partner out here alone? That's not personal. That's bullshit. That's putting your partners in jeopardy."

"Personal."

"It's all personal! You think you're saving someone? We're in this together. We're supposed to be partners. We're facing some real danger and you're off doing something that increases that danger."

"Personal."

"Asshole."

Andy didn't understand. Neither did I.

■ ● ■

Sideways

"Our partner is off the rails."

"So when you got him home, did he go upstairs?"

"Yeah. Ah went up with him. But it doesn't mean he's going to stay there. When I got him inside ah told him that he really let us down. He said he was sorry but we couldn't expect him to be around and that we had to keep our distance. Ah said so we can't count on you anymore? We're all in danger and this is when you're going to abandon us? You're always running that 'we're not knights going down these mean streets alone. That bullshit is in the detective novels.' Ah said, you always talk about we have to have a collective effort and now you're going to run off with this individualistic, voluntarist bullshit?! I said you need to check yourself, my man. Ah told him to get some sleep and we'd call him later."

"What'd you do with the body?"

"I talked to Raoul and brought it over there. He said he has somebody who can handle it."

Andy started looking at me like I just handed him a fake twenty and told him to go get us some coffee and buy someone's firstborn child. "Jesus Christ, Sharp! So we don't know where

■ ● ■

the body is, Raoul's involved and some guy we don't know is going to handle it?! What the hell, Sharp? I mean what the hell?!"

Andy was starting to piss me off. "You can stop shaking your
head any time, Andy. What...maybe you wanted to get Udo involved?! Let him handle it? Or did you want to go down there
and stick it in your trunk until you figured out what to do with
it? You don't seem to have any qualms about Raoul coming with
guns to help us when you think we need it. And now you're not
the one on the horn and Raoul is a suddenly a problem again."

Andy leaned back in his chair and crossed his arms on his
chest.

"Or maybe we could have driven to Chicago and left the
body as a donation on the steps of some med school..."

"Okay, okay. I'm sorry. I get the picture."

We stared at each other for a long moment. We seemed to go
from very, very pissed to calm almost immediately. We needed
sleep.

"So, Andy, you have any idea of how we're going to handle
our renegade?"

"I think he has to get some full time help and some rest. Like
six months or a year."

"I was more talkin' about now."

"If he decides he's done with us, there's nothing we can do, I
think. If he's willing to deal with DeFord with us, then I think
we have to have tasks that keep him overbusy and let him know
he can do whatever he wants after we get the bastard. I don't
know if we have anything he can hold onto here at this point.
I'm kind of at a loss, Sharp. He's my best friend and I don't have
a clue. Plus, having Cheike walking definitely didn't help. I hope
he can still see the situation we're in."

"Andy...he killed somebody. Ah'm covering it up. As far
as I'm concerned you, Heeks and Elaine don't know anything

■ ■ ■

about it."

Andy locked his fingers on top of his head. "Did you fill Heeks in?"

"Yeah."

"Did he have an opinion?"

I looked at my palms for no particular reason. Maybe I could see my future. Hopefully it wouldn't include jail.

"Sharp, did Heeks have an opinion?"

"He said maybe the pimp needed to die."

"What?! Oh great."

Andy looked like someone hit him in the stomach with a riot stick.

"Did you tell Elaine?"

"No."

Andy frowned. "Why not?"

"Ah wanted to wait until the court situation cleared up."

"Damn! It occurs to me…Do you think the pimp is the only body out there? I mean, I hope he didn't try to solve all of his problems last night."

"Far as I know, just the pimp."

"So there could be other bodies we don't know about."

"Doubt it, but could be."

Andy sighed and then bent his head back staring at the ceiling.

"Did you have any idea he was going to pull this shit?"

I looked at Andy hard.

"Do you think I'd let him wander off to commit a homicide if ah knew that was his intention? It didn't even cross my mind until he didn't come back to the car. I was waiting for a BLT with light mayonnaise. When it didn't show, that's when I thought he was going to do something out of the ordinary."

"You mean stupid."

■ ● ■

"That, too. But if you're asking me questions about whether I had advance knowledge of his intentions, then ah'm thinking you need to take a nap. Plus, you know he's going to go after DeFord on his own or with us as a team. Hope it's as the team."

Andy put his hands in his lap and looked at me like he just had a death in the family.

"Sharp, I think you need to get some sleep, too."

"Ah need some breakfast is what ah need."

"Elaine is going to be wrecked if she finds out the parents won't give Marty up because there isn't a buyer and they tell the judge they're not going let Marty get married so there's no issue. Believe me, from what I saw at the last hearing, the judge is a moron and he'll just say there is no custody issue. The child is with her parents."

I stood up to leave Andy's office when I saw Elaine walk in with a smile that would rival anything I'd ever seen on Mojica. She walked back to us simply glowing. I looked at my watch. It was 11:00.

"The parents gave up custody of Marty in favor of me. Can you believe this?! You had to be there. The social services lawyer was livid. It was almost like theater. Or really a circus. The judge was going to turn her over to social services, but Marty's father freaked and he said he wanted her to go with me. And then the judge said the wishes of the parents should be respected and the social services lawyer jumped up and the judge threatened him with contempt and it was crazy!"

I glanced at Andy, who was now wide-eyed. He glanced at me and said something I didn't understand. It seemed Elaine didn't understand either and said, "What?"

He hesitated, but then said, "Yeah...that's really good news...hope this turns out right."

I could see a look of concern on Elaine's face, because Andy

■ ● ■

showed no enthusiasm at all. Andy started to speak and instead cleared his throat.

"Uh…well, it's not over yet. You have temporary custody, so this situation still has to play out. But this is great news."

Elaine looked at Andy like, 'why are you raining on our parade?'

"If you have custody, where is she?"

Elaine turned to me frowning. "She's downstairs getting a celebratory pizza at Carl's." She glanced at Andy and then locked eyes with me. "Did something happen while I was gone?"

"What Andy's trying to say, is if you need some babysitting, or help looking for a bed, both of us will eventually be available."

Elaine's smile died completely. "Cut the shit. Marty's fifteen. I doubt anyone is going to need a babysitter for her. Did something happen while I was gone?"

"Elaine, ah have some information I need to relate to you." Over the next twenty minutes I explained what I thought had happened with our partner and the pimp. Elaine was mostly quiet, sitting in her chair with her hands gripping her thighs and resting in her lap.

"So the outcome of all this may…will, affect what happens with Marty." Elaine's eyes got pretty big. "So this is probably why Marty is with me now."

"Good chance."

"What the hell was he thinking."

Andy had been quiet through my whole story. "We have this problem. DeFord and how to keep our business running. Now that you're caring for Marty, you'll have to take all of this into consideration and I feel like an idiot saying that. Sharp is right. I need some sleep."

Andy's eyes bounced from me to Elaine and then he said, "You may have custody because of what happened last night.

■ ● ■

You may also lose custody because of what happened last night. If you can try to crack his shell so that we know what actually happened, we'd be in a better position to defend everybody."

I looked at Andy realizing he had just uttered the first logical thing I had heard him say in about six hours. Elaine was staring at Andy dumbstruck.

"Me?! We barely get along as it is."

"If you talk to him, unless he's way gone, he's got to recognize the situation he's put you and Marty in. If he really thinks he's helping Marty, then he needs to talk."

■ ● ■

Intention

It was just about a quarter to twelve. I had been out of bed about half an hour. Why I didn't go to a diner and get some eggs was beyond me. Instead I was jonesing for a couple of slices of pizza. What was wrong with me? Really. What was wrong with me?

I pushed through the doors at Carl's and started to drown in the fragrance of bread escaping from an oven. Then the attack came. I barely got my hands up to defend myself and took a step back. Marty threw her arms around my waist and buried her face in my chest. I could hear her muffled mumbling of "Thank You," over and over. Her hug kept getting tighter. "I don't have to marry that creep, Larry."

I started thinking, 'What have I done? What have I fucking done?' Tears were starting to drip down my face and I noticed Carl staring at me with his arms folded and a light smile on his face.

"Why are you crying?"

I looked down at her and heard Carl say, "She hits hard, don't she? You took him by surprise, honey. He wasn't expecting someone so strong to rattle him first thing in the morning."

■ ● ■

She looked up at me like she didn't believe Carl, and was still concerned. "I'm sorry. I didn't mean to hurt you."

"He ain't hurt. Just surprised. Right?"

"I looked at Carl and choked out a whisper of, "Yeah."

I smiled at Marty and put a hand on her shoulder. "What are you doing down here?"

Marty's expression changed from concern to exasperation. "Getting a pizza pie, Goober! What the heck do you think I'm doing down here?"

I wiped the tears from my cheeks with the palms of my hand. "Where's Elaine? Shouldn't you be with Elaine?"

"Upstairs. Elaine said we could get a pizza to celebrate. Hey! Did you know Carl used to be a boxer?"

I chuckled. "Yeah. I think I knew that."

Marty wrapped her arms around my left arm. "Of course you did. I wasn't thinking. You and Carl are old friends."

"Okay, so what's on this breakfast pizza you're getting?"

"Pepperoni and mushrooms and it's brunch or something."

What have I done?

"Think I can catch a slice?"

"Course. It's a large. It's for everybody."

"Hey, Carl. I'm going to get a couple of sixers of o.j. and seltzer."

"I'm going to get a cola."

I looked at her and shook my head. "Did you have breakfast yet?"

She looked at me like I smelled bad and the bad smell came from dumb. "The pizza is breakfast or brunch."

"Well then you're going to have juice or water like the rest of us."

Marty stared at me, but didn't say a thing. Uh-oh. What'd I do? I became an authority figure in five seconds. Some authority

∎ ● ∎

figure. I can't control myself and I'm giving guidance all of a sudden to a kid I hardly know?!

Carl handed over the box of pizza and refused to take Marty's money for the pizza. I pushed a ten under a jar of red pepper.

When we got upstairs three of my partners momentarily stared at me, probably trying to figure out who I was today. Andy's gaze was like a laser. Sharp's was kind of like he was intently watching something from the other side of a river. Elaine had kind of a stunned look, but she walked straight up to me and said, "We need to have a serious conversation."

Off to the side I could hear Marty's excited chatter. What have I done?

"You're right. But I also need to speak with everyone."

Marty slid over to Elaine miming an ice skater. "Elaine, what do you want to drink?"

"I think I'll have an orange juice." Marty led Elaine over to the pizza and drinks on invisible ice skates. Marty turned around and smiled at me. "What do you want to drink?"

I almost started to cry again. My eyes shifted to Elaine who happened to catch my expression. She looked away quickly. For a second I thought she looked embarrassed.

"Seltzer. I think I'll have a seltzer."

Elaine yelled toward Andy's office. "Hey, Sharp. If you want any of this pizza, you better drag yourself back out here."

A seltzer suddenly popped up in my face.

"Thanks, Marty."

"I'll have one, too." Then she held up hers so we could clink bottles. When I raised my bottle, she pulled hers back. "What's the toast?"

"What?"

"What's the toast? We need a toast."

Elaine sauntered over waving a bottle of orange juice at me.

■ ● ■

"Yeah. What's the toast?"

Sharp was suddenly at my shoulder chewing on a mouthful of pizza. Andy was standing over by the windows with his arms folded, silhouetted by the late morning sun. It felt like he was looking at me from a thousand miles away.

Marty was tugging at my arm. "What's the toast? You have a toast yet?"

I looked at my partners and said, "Yeah. To the truth and honesty that springs from friendship." It was real quiet for longer than it should have been.

"That's it?! That's the toast?! I thought a toast was supposed to be longer than that."

"Oh, yeah? Well, what the heck do you have, lip?"

"Lip?! Who are you calling 'Lip?' Here's my toast. To the people who make friends and never turn their backs on each other because they're friends and they stick up for each other even when one of them makes a mistake and they help them get through it and, and, and it makes everybody stronger…and happy…or something, I guess. Toast."

Sharp chuckled. "Ah can drink to that one." He held up his orange juice and Marty clinked it with her seltzer bottle. Then she hit my bottle and Elaine's. She ran across to Andy. "Get a drink. We just toasted."

Andy picked up a seltzer and walked back with Marty. He bumped his bottle against Marty's and then tapped everyone's bottle. When he was done he said, "To truth and the honesty that springs from friendship."

There were two slices of pizza left when Mojica barged into the office. He stared down into the box. "You could have let me know you people had a very greasy large pepperoni and mushroom pie going."

Marty tentatively squeezed out, "Maybe we should get an-

■ ● ■

other one for lunch?"

Elaine pointed out that two slices would probably be enough to temporarily satisfy Tony.

We had all moved into my office and closed the door. We left Marty out on the sofa with a hair care magazine.

"Should I turn myself in?"

My four partners gazed at me. Sharp's head tilted to the right, but he never broke his stare. Andy shook his head.

"Have you lost your mind?! You might as well take Sharp to jail with you! Where's the body? Oh, my business partner took care of that. Are you on some kind of new drug called 'Dumb and Selfish?' No you're not turning yourself in! Especially not now!"

Sharp looked out the window when Mojica started to speak. "Dude, that pimp may have needed to be put on ice. But you have to take us into consideration. This is not the time to be off taking care of business as you please."

I could see Andy was hot. "Heeks, at no time should any of us be off deciding someone's fate like a Mickey Spillane character."

"Isn't that what we're doing with DeFord?" Heeks suddenly seemed to have fire in his eyes.

"No. It isn't. He's ready to commit mass murder for political reasons and the government doesn't seem to be ready to defend the people from an organization of madmen."

Heeks looked ready to explode. "Uh-huh! And someone we know and trust was trying to defend a fifteen year old girl from one of the scummiest pimps I have ever heard of! And the state didn't seem to care. My problem is people doing shit on their own when we need to have collective decisions made!"

"So our situation is better because one pimp got taken out last night?! The world is a better place because a despicable scumbag no longer walks among us, but we're…"

■●■

"Yes! The world is now a better place and that kid out in the waiting room reading magazines is a lot safer!" Mojica was yelling at Andy. I had never seen that before.

"So you want to hang a sign out? We can be the new progressive Purple Gang!"

Elaine stood and walked across my office. She was about eight inches from my face. "You may think you've helped a girl get out of a horrendous situation. But now you've put her life on the edge of an abyss. If you go down, her life will be a complete mess. What the hell did you think you were doing?"

Mojica started to speak but Sharp cut him off. "Sorry, Heeks, but ah'd say the girl is with you now, Elaine. If the pimp didn't, uh, leave town, who knows what might'a happened in that court. I may be talking crazy out of my head, because for the life of me ah can't remember what sleep feels like, but we have got to deal with DeFord. Marty is safe for now and if we have to defend her in the future ah'm in all the way. But we have got to get back to dealing with DeFord. And the first thing is we have to find out where we're going to hide her until this thing is over. If DeFord can kidnap one of us and put us up on a building ledge, he can certainly turn his attention to her to put some serious pressure on us."

What have I done? I could feel the knife slipping in under his chin. Everyone was quiet waiting for someone else to speak.

Andy broke the silence. "Heeks, what's the situation with our phones?"

"They're dirty, Andy. We can't use them except for in house work, if you get my drift. The offices are clean. So is the outside hallway. I don't know about the bathrooms so the only thing we should talk about out there is the Bears and the Cubs."

"Sharp, you want to get in touch with Raoul again to find out what he did this morning?"

■ ● ■

"Last night. He said he'd call me when things were taken care of."

"Maybe Marty could stay with my old friend, Margot?" Elaine looked pained.

"Maybe she could get a gig as Margot's sidekick in the diner." Mojica started to grin.

Elaine burst out laughing and Mojica followed. Andy looked at me and then we both turned to Sharp who said, "We just freed her from her alcoholic parents and now we're ready to push her out into the world of economic exploitation?"

"She has to earn her way sometime." Mojica, Elaine and Sharp exploded in laughter.

Andy locked eyes on me. "It's not funny. None of this is funny." I shrugged and got up from my chair. I looked at the box covering my new caster.

What have I done? I could feel his hair in my hand as I cut his throat.

I went to the door and opened it. I had an immediate sick feeling. My partners came out behind me and I heard Mojica say, "Fuck."

Where was Marty? Elaine pushed past me. "Maybe she's in the restroom." And then Marty came through the main office door reading a newspaper. Our twenty second scare brought home that we needed to do something about Marty for our own sanity.

She looked up from the paper and her eyes lit up. "All done with the detective stuff?"

Elaine stood next to her and asked if she wanted to get lunch before they went to find her a new bed.

"Is Goober going to come? Or any of the other guys?" Then she walked over to me and pointed to an article on page three. "You might want to read this."

■ ● ■

It was an article about a man named Larry Walker who was killed during a drug deal on the north side of town. I handed the paper to Andy and he passed it to Sharp.

I said, "Yeah, I'm going to join you for lunch. Where'd you get the paper?"

She looked up at me slightly confused and then I could see the sarcasm coming. "Downstairs. You're a detective and you never noticed the newspaper stand downstairs?"

What have I done? A cold feeling crept up my back and I could see Sharp lying on the lobby floor in his own blood.

Andy said the three of them had some work they had to catch up on and that maybe we could all hook up for dinner. I said I was going to join them for lunch and that I'd then have to come back to the office.

At the elevator Marty looked behind us and whispered, "Why is Andy so serious all the time?"

■ ● ■

Tilt

Marty and I were standing in front of the elevators collecting stares and smiles. I had shown Marty the arcade I used to hang in when I was her age. It was kind of a tunnel that went from one block to the next under the buildings across the street. The 'tunnel' had a lot of businesses on both sides when I was a kid. Now it was mostly empty. Marty laughed a lot about the place and the things my friends and I used to talk about back then. She said it reminded her of things her friends talk about now.

While we were there we slipped into Mr. Latimer's shop for gum. It was one of the last stores still open in the arcade. We were trying to decide between Dentyne Cinnamint and Wrigley's Spearmint, when Marty talked me into buying two Groucho Marx masks. They had the glasses with the mustache and the heavy eyebrows. She thought the guys up in the office would find them hilarious. I didn't think so, but they made Marty happy, so what the heck.

If we were into very early Halloween chic, I decided we needed White Sox caps. Mr. Latimer had trouble finding one that fit Marty. So while he searched the shelves in his backroom,

■ ● ■

Marty stared at a Perry Mason re-run on Mr. Latimer's black and white T.V. I don't think he had turned off the set since before I left for the Army.

Marty had a hard, serious frown on her face.

"What's wrong?"

"I thought Perry Mason never lost a case."

"I think he loses a couple."

"More than one?!" Marty looked at me like she was stunned. Then she turned back to the show and said, "That woman is going to fry in the chair if P.M. doesn't do something."

I smiled at 'P.M.'

Mr. Latimer came back to the counter with the smallest hat he could find. It still went half way over Marty's ears.

"Gee, Marty. It's a little big."

"No it's not. It's perfect." She looked in the mirror that was up on the wall so that Mr. Latimer could see what was going on over by the candy. Marty was very pleased with her fashion statement. Mr. Latimer shrugged, mumbled and walked back to his perch by the front door.

A woman came out of the elevator and stared at the Groucho Marx imitators wearing White Sox hats. A smile slowly spread over her face like she was seeing the cutest Halloween trick or treaters of all time.

"You two don't look a bit like Carlton Fisk." And with a smile so big I hoped she shared it with someone else, she strolled away.

I looked at Marty who was looking up at me. "I think we made her happy."

"Who's Carlin Fist?"

The elevator doors opened and we stepped into the empty

■ ● ■

car past my increasingly mute operator. Two men followed us in and took spots in the back corners.

My mute elevator operator was suddenly talking. He pointed at me and said, "I know where you're going. Where are you two gentlemen going?"

"Ten."

"Nine."

"Thank you. So I don't think Evans is going to work out. I mean I am so glad Avellini is through, but I have no faith in Evans. He's going to lead the league in interceptions. If you want to bet on the games again, you won't have to give me a Christmas tip."

My head tilted slightly to the side. "Gee, don't get cocky." I felt Marty's arm wrap itself around my arm.

"Cocky? How much did you lose last year? You want to raise the bets?"

Marty pulled at my arm. "Mom is going to freak when we walk in like this. I'll go on her left and you sneak up on the right and we can scare the heck out of her."

In my head I kept hearing, "Fuck, fuck, fuck…"

"I don't think Mom will appreciate us scaring her."

I watched the elevator glide past four and wondered where the man in charge thought it would be safe to get out. We stopped at seven. "Okay, Mr. Corinelli. See you later."

We walked straight toward the glass doors that read "Corinelli's Photo." I slid my hand slowly under my sport jacket. Marty was trying to get behind me and I pulled her back to my side. The elevator doors closed and I grabbed Marty's hand hard.

"Come on!" I heard the elevator start to go up and then stop. We raced down the stairs from the seventh floor to our offices on the fourth. I stuck my head out of the stairwell door. No one there.

■ ● ■

"Wait here until I get the office door open. I unlocked the door and pushed it in. Andy and Mojica were both bent over Elaine's desk.

A smile lit up Mojica's face. Andy raised his eyebrows and then frowned. I looked back at Marty and said, "Come on. Quickly." She ran from the stairwell to the door and slid into our office space. Mojica was instantly laughing. Andy frowned harder and said "What's up with you two?"

I took off my Marx mask and Mojica stopped laughing.

I put my hand on Marty's shoulder. "Are you okay?"

She looked at the floor and twisted her hands together. "That was bad, wasn't it?"

"Yes it was. But you're okay and nothing is going to happen to you."

Andy and Heeks were standing right next to us now.

"There are two of DeFord's men in the building."

"What?!"

"They came up in the elevator with us and our silent operator tipped us off. Then Marty went into a routine about her Mother and I think they weren't sure who we were with the masks on."

Mojica moved toward the phone. "I'll call Elaine and Sharp."

Andy crossed his arms. "Are you sure there were only two? Could there have been others in the lobby?"

"I honestly don't know. I never picked up on the two who got on the elevator with us. There could have been someone else down there." I felt like the biggest ass south of the Canadian border.

Andy's frown was as severe as I had ever seen. "It seems like, for the most part, DeFord's men work in pairs. But we should go out when Heeks gets through to Elaine and Sharp."

"Where are they?"

"Getting a bed delivered to one of Raoul's outposts for Marty."

■ ● ■

"We have to get her out of here."

Andy glanced at Marty and then looked at me. "You're right."

Marty was sitting on the couch by the window. Her hands were being rung red. I sat down beside her and pulled her hands apart.

She looked at me and then back down at our clasped hands. "Are Larry's friends pissed at you? Did they come to get even with you?"

I squeezed her hand. "It has nothing to do with Larry."

"Then who were those guys? I saw you and I heard you. Don't tell me a bull crap story."

"What story? What do you mean you saw me and heard me?"

Marty looked around the office trying to appear like she wasn't. Then she whispered, "I saw you when you talked to my father with the knife. I heard what you said to him."

I was stunned. "Oh, Marty…I'm so sorry."

"Don't be sorry. You kind of saved me, but I just wish Larry's friends weren't looking for you."

"Larry didn't have friends. Those guys have nothing to do with Larry."

"It's other detective stuff?"

"Yeah. It's other detective stuff."

"Oh." I had almost forgotten I was holding her hands when she squeezed mine. "I won't say anything to anyone."

"That's good, Marty." I was trying to think of something else to say that would make sense, but I couldn't. Instead, "Okay. Okay. But what the heck were you doing trying to walk behind me?"

"I thought they wouldn't do anything if a kid was between them and you."

"Oh, boy. Look, Marty, I don't want you to ever try to shield me with your body. Okay? That is a strict rule."

"Well what were you going to do if they wanted to fight?"

I wished it was that simple. "If they got off the elevator I was going to push you to the side and…and have it out with them."

"Oh." She slapped her hands on her thighs. "I'll bet you could take them, too."

I nodded. "Maybe." This could have been very bad. On top of it all, she had heard me threaten her father.

What have I done?

Mojica said he'd caught Sharp in the car. He told him not to come into the building until one of us signaled by the lobby doors.

Andy came back out of his office checking the cartridge on his .45. "Ready?"

I nodded. Mojica was at the door. I turned to Marty. Her eyes were big, taking in the image of Andy moving past Elaine's desk to the door with a gun in his hand.

"Marty, don't open the door for anyone. Understand? Even if it's Elaine, you do not open the door, okay? This is important."

"Got it. But what if you don't come back?"

I noticed a potential tear in one of her eyes. "We will all be right back. I promise." I stood up and Marty grabbed the bottom of my jacket. I looked in her eyes and I could see how scared she was. On a scale of 1-10, a definite 9.

"We'll be back in about ten minutes."

"If you're not back in ten minutes, I'm calling the police."

I glanced at Andy and Mojica. It felt like they were both wearing hurt on their faces while they gently looked at Marty.

I bent over and looked in Marty's eyes. "Honey, those guys probably are the police."

Marty's mouth opened about half and inch and then closed. She stared across the room and just nodded.

■ ● ■

"We will be back, but if we are taking too long there is a number on Elaine's desk on her notepad for Raoul. You call him and leave a message. Tell him what happened. Okay?" It looked like her shoulders relaxed. She let go of my jacket. That seemed to make her less tense. I hoped it did.

I walked quickly over to Elaine's desk and checked the monitor to make sure the anteroom was clear. I gave Andy and Heeks a thumbs up and they stepped out toward the elevators. I joined them while Mojica was ringing for the elevator and said, "I'll take the stairs."

I had a .38 special in my jacket pocket. I was holding it and wondered for a second if I should have pulled something larger. When I got to the ground floor I cracked the door and I could see both of them standing by the phone booths.

An elevator door opened and DeFord's men started moving toward Heeks, who was acting like he didn't have any particular place to go. I came out of the stairwell, grabbed the guy in the light brown suit by the collar and pushed my .38 into the small of his back by his spine. His partner in the light grey suit turned as Andy came out of the elevator with his hand in a paper bag and walked right up to the grey suit and whispered, "Keep your hands empty." Mojica walked over to us with a smirk on his face.

"You fellas need to think a little. We can take you down-stairs…" Grey suit started backing away from Andy.

"You ain't takin' us nowheres, bitch." Then his eyes got big and then they squeezed closed tight, and then he choked and fell down on his hands and knees.

"That was a nice swing, Sharp." Andy was smiling. Sharp was smiling back, running his fingers up and down his cane like he was looking for a crack in a baseball bat.. Elaine walked past us silently to the elevators.

Mojica chuckled and leaned over grey suit.. "As I was say-

■ ● ■

ing…we could take you downstairs, but if you just give up your toys and go away, class can be over for the day… uh, oh…" Mojica stood back up straight.

Two police officers came through the lobby doors. The elevator supervisor and the mute operator approached the police.

The supervisor was not laid back like Ivars used to be. His head went red. "These two have been loitering in here most of the day. Then they started bothering tenants and visitors. I think they have guns. I want them out of here."

I let go of the collar of the man I was holding and backed away from him. The two cops asked why one of them was on his knees. The man in the grey suit said something no one could hear. One of the cops bent over and said, "Whatd'ya say?"

"Tripped."

"Well, get up then. Are you hurt?"

He said "no," but he was having a hard time getting upright.

I moved toward the elevators with Andy and Mojica. One cop started to give the guy in the grey suit help and then I heard Sharp say, "He's going for a gun." I looked at Sharp and he smiled and raised one eyebrow. Then he walked over to join us while the spectators moved away, but not so far that they couldn't see. The guy in the brown suit said, "We have permits."

The helpful cop asked to see them. As the elevator doors closed I could hear the other cop say, "Can I see some I.D.?" There was a pause and then the same cop said, "What do you mean, 'no'?"

I had noticed the building manager over in a corner of the lobby shaking his head. I was thinking this was not going to help the eviction process.

As the elevator went up I tried to thank our now eloquent operator. Without turning his head he said, "Huhh." I almost started laughing, but I didn't want to hurt his feelings after the

■ ● ■

heads up he gave me.

When we filed into the office Elaine was sitting on the couch next to Marty. I sat down next to Elaine. Marty looked at me and then concentrated on her hands that were clasped in her lap.

"I was just talking about Marty visiting Helen in Chicago for a little while."

"Yep. You guys are going to dump me with Helen."

Elaine looked hurt. "It's not like that. We're worried about you getting hurt. It would only be for a week or so. Like a vacation."

"You're just trying to get me out of the way. It's not a vacation. You're just getting rid of me."

Elaine started to speak, but I put my hand on her arm. "Marty…you know what I did." Elaine glared at me. "I didn't do that to shuttle you off somewhere and we're not doing this to get rid of you. It'd be great if you could be around all the time…after school is out, of course…" Marty's head snapped up.

"School?!"

I smiled. "Yeah. School. You'll be going to school every day when summer is over. But let's get back to a little reality here. Those men from the elevator are insane. They don't give a darn about…"

Marty interrupted me with, "You sound ridiculous. 'They don't give a darn?' That's stupid. Why don't you be honest and say 'They don't give a fu…'" Marty caught Elaine's eye and blushed. "A damn."

Elaine smiled now. And then she looked at me with a smirk, like 'let's hear some more honesty.'

"We can't be worried about your safety if you stay here. Those men don't give a fuck about whether, or how much they hurt you or me."

Marty was looking at her hands with her head bowed. Then

∎ ● ∎

she mumbled, "That's more like it."

Elaine elbowed me in the ribs with her teeth clenched. "Language."

Marty raised her head. "You guys are funny. I'm not a kid. I'm fifteen. I've heard all of the curses. Want me to recite them for you?"

Elaine broke in. "Look, Marty. Helen is not a stranger. As soon as it's safe we'll have you back down here."

"I've never been to Chicago. Might be good." She was staring at her hands again. "But what do I do? I'm going to be worried about all of you."

Elaine put her arm around Marty's shoulder. "Someone will call you every day and give you a report."

Marty's eyes slipped from Elaine to me and back to Elaine. "Every day. With no bullshit. A full report. I want to know who got punched, who got shot and who got killed…" Tears started dripping from her cheeks.

I felt terrible. Let's screw up some young girl's life even more. "No one is going to get killed. And someone will call you every day."

"Every day. Promise?"

Elaine squeezed her tight. "Every day. Promise."

While Marty was drying her eyes, Andy stood in front of us and said, "I don't know if this is a good time, but we need to have a talk." He walked away with a grimace on his face.

■ ● ■

Storms

His wave made me sad even though he was smiling. I waved back harder with my own fake smile. While I watched him get into Sharp's Barracuda I started to feel a little lonely, which I thought was stupid. In my head I started chanting, "Black Barracuda, Barracuda, Barracuda. Black Barracuda, little Cuda, little Cuda." I watched Sharp's car disappear into traffic, and then behind me I heard Elaine. "Let's go catch a train, Marty."

I followed Elaine onto the platform carrying my new green army backpack. I looked up and down the platform at all of the people.

A train was coming at us. I backed up. I felt excited, never having been on a train before. I saw them in the movies like the one with Washington and Lincoln carved in a mountain out west somewhere. It was that movie with the anorexic blonde and the guy with the goofy smile.

I had never been to Chicago either. I hoped Helen wouldn't get mad at me for being there. She seemed cool when I met her back at the office, but when Elaine leaves, what if she goes off on me? I won't take another beating like my father gave me. I'm not going to let someone beat me with a piece of rubber hose or a broom handle. I'll just take off.

I have money now. I've never had so much money. I have fifty bucks. I'll get a hotel room if I have to. But then how will everyone be able to call me? Shit. I have money. I'll call them and give them my number at the hotel.

The train stopped. People got off. We got on and I followed Elaine down the aisle, looking at the people who stayed on the train. Elaine took my bag and threw it up on the rack over our seats. I wondered how many people were going to Chicago.

"Want to sit by the window?"

I couldn't help smiling. The train lurched, I lost my balance, but managed to sit down and smile some more. For a couple of seconds I felt like I was on a ship leaving to go on a glamorous adventure. That didn't last long. We passed somebody's backyard and I saw a dog chained up to a tree barking at the train. I couldn't hear it, but it didn't feel like I was on a ship any longer. I kind of felt bad for the dog, but I wasn't quite sure why.

The train was exciting enough once it got going. We passed through a couple of towns I had never heard of. They looked sunnier than where I lived. Except for the park. Our park was just as sunny as these towns.

"So you have a birthday coming up. What do you think you'd like to get for your birthday?"

Elaine was smiling at me.

"But my birthday..." It was hard to understand. She was asking me what I wanted?! No one ever asked me what I wanted. I looked out the window feeling really weird.

"No ideas? Nothing you've been thinking of?"

I kind of muttered, "I've been wishing my birthday wouldn't come, so I wouldn't have to marry Larry."

Elaine didn't say anything for a while. I saw a woman hanging clothes in her backyard and then Elaine said, "If you think

■●■

of anything you've wanted, let me know. But don't wait until the day before your birthday, okay? Or maybe I should just surprise you?"

I could feel tears starting to run out of my eyes. I couldn't stop them and I didn't want Elaine to see.

"Cake."

"What?"

"I want cake for my birthday."

"Well of course you'll have cake."

"And friends to help me eat the whole thing." I pretended to stretch and yawn and then wiped my eyes with my arms hoping she didn't see.

"Tired?"

"A little." I glanced at Elaine and she was smiling. Or was she laughing at me?

"You know, one of the presidents once said, 'The only thing better than cake…is more cake.' Maybe we'll have two."

"Two?!"

"Why not? Is there a rule against having two cakes for a birthday?"

I was starting to think Elaine was crazy. If she's crazy, I'll be crazier. "Three."

Elaine started laughing. "I'm not making you three cakes."

"Why not? Is there a rule against it?"

"Yeah. In the labor laws. We're not having three cakes on top of the ice cream?"

A conductor came and stood right next to us.

"Tickets, please." The train was slowing down.

"Why are we stopping? How many more stops before Chicago?"

"For us, just one."

"Really? I thought Chicago was farther than that."

"We, are getting off at the next stop. We're going to drive the

■ ● ■

rest of the way."

"Why? Did we get on the wrong train?"

"No. This was the plan. In case we were being followed."

"Oh." I thought about the men in the elevator. The train started moving again. Someday I wanted to ride a train all the way to California. I didn't want to go by bus. I guess it doesn't matter, but I'd really like to take a train and see the Rocky Mountains and the ocean. I wonder if Kennedy would go with me? She's been to California before and said it was great.

When we pulled into the next station Elaine shook my arm and said, "Let's go."

We followed a line of people off the train and I followed Elaine out into the parking lot. I was surprised. Andy was standing there. We walked right up to him and he handed a set of car keys to Elaine.

"Have a safe, smooth trip. See you soon." Then he got into a car with somebody I didn't know. Andy waved and they pulled away.

"I get it. If someone was following us they won't have a car. Right?"

"If we are lucky, you would be right."

"We're lucky." I looked around the parking lot. "We're lucky, aren't we?"

"Yep. And good." Elaine tossed the keys up in the air and caught them." She looked at me and laughed. "We're good. Let's get in."

"In this?"

"What? Not nice enough for you?"

I didn't know what kind of car it was, but it was different from the ones everybody in the office drove. It was damn shiny.

"Throw your bag on the back seat, get in and get comfortable."

"What kind of car is this?"

■ ● ■

"It's a Chrysler...Le Baron, I think. Hey. Find a radio station."

The static made me jump. The volume was up pretty high. Finally I found a station playing Rod Stewart, but I didn't recognize the song. Only the voice.

"Elaine, is this Rod Stewart?"

"Yeah. With the Faces."

"The Faces. Who the heck are the Faces?"

"They were Rod's band before he was with Jeff Beck."

"Huh?"

"Jeff Beck the guitarist. From the Yardbirds."

"Oh." I looked at Elaine and then out my window.

We did a pee break at a Sinclair gas station. They had green dinosaurs everywhere inside. You could get little ones for thirty-nine cents. You could get a blow-up one for $1.29. I decided I didn't need a dinosaur.

When we were back on the highway it started to drizzle. I felt tired and the rain wasn't helping to keep me awake. I thought I started to feel dizzy so I shook my head a little. For a second I thought I saw a little dust tornado out in a field. It kind of felt like our car went up in the air. Our road was a two lane highway but everything seemed to be right next to the road. We passed a house with a woman sitting on her front porch petting her cat. Off in the distance I could see a cow all by itself. I thought that was weird. It looked like it was floating. Then we were going across a low bridge and I could see two men fishing in the river. They waved at me. I felt stupid but I waved back. Up ahead a woman in weird clothes was riding a bicycle with a basket on it. She looked mean. Elaine moved over to the passing lane and I noticed the bicycle was coming up behind us very, very fast. But it wasn't a bicycle. It was a motorcycle with the same kind of

■●■

basket on it coming up behind us very, very fast. There were two men riding on it. At first I really couldn't see them. But when they pulled up next to us I could see it was my Father. I didn't even know my father could ride a motorcycle. I couldn't tell who was next to him until he turned his head to look at me. He was laughing. It was Larry.

"Will nightmares last forever, Dorothy?"

"Dorothy? What?!"

"You sleeping a little?"

"I guess so…what did you say?"

"Sorry I woke you. I thought we had company but I'm sure I was wrong. They were just pacing us for a while. They've turned off."

"Oh."

An hour later I could see Chicago in the distance. I started to get nervous. It was bigger than I expected. I wondered how Elaine knew her way around so good. At least it seemed that way.

"Have you been here before?"

"Chicago? A few times."

"What for?"

"Days of Rage…Chicago Eight trial…Bobby Seal…"

"What was that?"

Elaine gave me a quick look and then she smiled. "I'll fill you in on that stuff a little later." Elaine started to park and said, "This should be it."

"You mean you're not sure?"

She laughed. "Actually, I'm totally sure."

I got out of the car looking around. Elaine said, "Heads up!" She tossed me my backpack and then ducked back in the car.

I heard someone say, "Marty!" I turned around and Helen was squeezing me with both arms. "It's so good to see you." Then

■ ● ■

she and Elaine hugged. When they finished Helen wrapped one arm around my arm and took my backpack away.

"Come on up and check out the crib." Helen asked Elaine about the drive and how everyone else at the office was doing. I saw Elaine hand Helen a letter from Heeks and then Helen grabbed my arm again and led me into her apartment.

"Wow. This is your place?!"

"No. This is a friend's apartment. But she's in Africa for a year and she thought it would be good to have someone stay in the place. So here we are. This is your room…comes with a T.V. and a Garrard turntable…and a ton of records."

I was fascinated by all of the books on the walls. How could someone have so many books? I looked out one of my windows at the street and noticed the men getting out of their car. They were looking up and down the street and then they started to cross. They were coming right at our building. I went to get Elaine.

■ ● ■

Dice

Andy and I drove north on a gamble. We were hoping we could talk to one of the town's three deputies about the Sheriff and the men the Sheriff had been meeting with. We knew that talking to the Sheriff would be a waste of time. He was either bought and paid for, or else he was a true believer. We wanted to find a sympathetic deputy who would at least listen to our story before he called the psychiatric folks. It seemed like a long shot, but we didn't like the idea of going up against local law when it was time to stop DeFord.

We knew we could get one of the town's three deputies alone. Whether he would take the time to seriously listen to us before he ran us off was another matter.

We were heading to the town diner where we were pretty sure the deputy we wanted to talk to would be taking a lunch break at eleven o'clock. The diner only had a few patrons inside when we sat down at the counter. The place seemed very clean, which didn't surprise me. The waitress was very professional, which did.

"Would you gentlemen care for coffee or tea while you review the menu?"

■●■

She placed two cups of water in front of us with a really nice smile.

"Ah don't think ah need to review anything. Ah'd like some pancakes and scrambled eggs with some nice, crisp bacon and an endless stream of coffee."

She smiled at me. "We're not a twenty-four seven diner, so the endless stream of coffee will eventually end. Everything else will be fine and up in just a few minutes."

She didn't have to wink at me, but she did. It made me feel kinda good that early in the day.

"And do you know what you would like to order this morning, sir? Or do you need a few moments more?"

Without raising his head from the menu Andy said, "About half of what Tex here ordered. One fried egg, short stack and one, just one, cup of coffee."

"Yes, sir."

She walked away and I felt Andy staring at me.

"I didn't get a wink. Why'd you get a wink?"

"It's my eyebrows, Andy. Some women find my eyebrows infatuatin'."

Andy's face seemed to go blank.

"Damn. I never noticed you had eyebrows. Wow. Could you turn this way? Wow..." Andy winked at me, stood up, grabbed a newspaper that was three stools away and then sat back down just as our coffee arrived along with the deputy Sheriff we were hoping to talk to.

"Good morning, Officer Mazeroski. How are you?"

"Hi, Ethel. I'm fine thanks. The regular please."

"Sharp, I'm going to introduce myself to the deputy to see how receptive he is to talking." I watched Andy engage the deputy out of the corner of my eye.

The waitress brought our food and I had to admit to her,

■ ● ■

"That was pretty fast." She smiled again and said, "I hope you enjoy your meals. And I hope I'm not being rude, but where are you from originally?"

"Amarillo. And ah hope I'm not being rude, but what do you do when you're not here?"

"Do you mean am I married?" She held up her naked left hand and turned it around a little like she was looking for something. "I don't have children and I'm the town's volunteer librarian. I'm also a volunteer fire fighter."

"What do we do if you have to run off to fight a fire?"

"Yell for Wallace out back and leave the money on the counter with your number." She winked again and strolled purposely down to the other end of the counter.

"Sharp. Hey, Sharp."

I turned to find Andy and the deputy moving to a booth. I picked up my plate and coffee and half way to the booth I said a silent "Damn." I turned back to get Andy's plate wondering how I'd balance that with my cane. Ethel was already there holding Andy's order. I shrugged. She kind of grinned and I went to sit down next to Andy.

"This is Officer Mazeroski."

"No, I'm not related to Bill. You can call me Clint. So what's so important to our town?"

Ethel showed up with Officer Mazeroski's burger. He bit into it like he hadn't eaten since the day before. Maybe he hadn't, but I appreciated his appetite nonetheless.

Andy told him who we were and where we were from. We began to lay out our theory that his town's water supply was going to poisoned. That put him on pause with a mouthful of hamburger. When we told him that we thought his Sheriff was involved he started chewing again, very slowly. He finished his burger without looking at us. He drank about half of his cherry

■ ● ■

coke and then his eyes kept moving between Andy and then me.

"Fella's, I have to hit the can. I'll be right back."

We watched Officer Mazeroski head towards the men's room.

"What do you think, Sharp? Could you stop eating for a second?"

"Course, I can…what do I think? The pancakes here are excellent and that man has gone to put in a call to see if he can get some information on us."

"Do you think he believes anything we've told him?"

"You gave him a very convincing story in a logical manner. But it's got to be hard to have two strangers walk up to him and tell him his town is going to be the potential site of a mass murder…and immediately believe them. Now if you don't mind I'm going to finish off these pancakes."

"I'm sorry. You just said 'mass murder' and 'let me eat my pancakes.'"

"Do you have a point, Andy?"

Officer Mazeroski came back and said he thought we should go outside to continue our conversation. When we were out in the parking lot near his car, Mazeroski asked us to stand aways just a little. Then he went into his car and got on his mic.

"Giff…this is Clint. Can you meet me down at the diner?"

When he hung the mic back up he put his right hand on his weapon and told us to back up a couple of steps. When the other officer pulled in, he got out of his car with a smile on his face. He saw Mazeroski with his hand on his pistol and his hand immediately went to his. His eyes were locked on us like a cobra. He positioned himself about fifteen feet away, off to our side.

"What's going on, Clint?"

"I want you to listen to a story."

"What? What story?! You called me all the way back here to

■ ● ■

listen to a story?"

"Just listen. These two guys are going to tell you a story. They're private detectives."

We gave the same information to the second officer. He didn't ask a single question. When we were finished, he turned his head toward Mazeroski.

"Do you believe this? This is crazy. Did you check these two out?!"

Clint looked at Giff like he couldn't believe what he was hearing. "Of course I checked them out!"

I couldn't help myself. "Uh, he went to the men's room, slipped out the back door and went to his car. I was on my pancakes when he came back in. Are you two brothers?"

Andy elbowed me.

"It's okay Andy. We're all on a first name basis here."

Clint took his hand off his pistol and crossed his arms on his chest. He looked down at the ground. "I don't know what to believe here. Hatchley's sending his wife to Florida in two days to visit her sister. He got us a new water cooler. Then those FBI agents he never let's us meet."

"Y'all didn't have a water cooler?"

Clint raised his head and stared at Sharp. "We used the sink in the kitchen."

"Oh."

"Knock off the Mojica shit, will you!"

"Sharp? Where the heck are you from anyways?"

"Anyways or anyway…Texas. Ah'm originally from Texas."

I noticed Giff suddenly get a very serious frown on his face.

"And I saw those FBI agents out by the lake."

Clint's head snapped toward Giff. "When?!"

"A couple of days ago."

"I don't know how we figure out if this is real or we have two

■ ● ■

lunatics on our hands."

"Clint...you think they'd drive all the way up here...know that Sheriff Hatchley has been meeting with the FBI if there isn't some truth in this?"

"I just don't know, Gifford."

Andy took a step forward and both officers put their hands back on their weapons.

"Look. First of all they might be FBI, but how do you know they are? They...let me go over and talk to the Sheriff and see what happens."

Both officers looked at each other.

"Clint, what do you think are the chances Hatchley would just shoot him?"

"Zero to none. White man walks into his office and Hatchley just shoots him down in the middle of the day? If he was Black, maybe. But not a white man... Least not in the office."

The four of us were silent for about fifteen seconds. Finally Clint said, "You sure you want to do this? Your partner with the quips and the cane can stay here."

Andy was gone for over half an hour when Clint said, "As soon as Gifford comes back I'll go over to the station house and see how the conversation is going."

Ethel came and poured me another coffee. I smiled and she smiled. Clint watched her walk away.

"You know, Romeo, she has a white belt in judo."

I couldn't help grinning. "Ya' don't say..."

"How long were you over there?"

I gave Clint a hard look. "About four years too long."

"Why do you say that? You didn't feel like you were proud to serve?"

■ ● ■

"How long were you in country?"

"Long enough to get shot three times and then they sent my ass home."

"Uh-huh…brother, you and I probably have a big chasm in what we believe we were doing over there, so maybe we…"

"You don't think we can have a civilized exchange of views? If we can't, how the heck is one side going to understand the other side? I apologize for interrupting."

Damn. He had me there, that's for sure. "No apology necessary, ah guess."

"Well, I'm going to do it again and then I'll shut up a while. Why do you sometimes have this heavy twang in your voice and 'I' becomes 'ah'? Other times you talk like you just got done teaching a class at the University of Chicago."

"Damn. I'll have to work at getting rid of that educated dialect and leave my panhandle accent in place. Mostly when I'm hungry or frustrated my Texas accent really takes over. But let's get back to the more important topic. You got hit and I'm glad you made it back. Me, I never got touched. Ah didn't even get jock rot. But I saw some stuff that turned my stomach and changed my view of the world. And then I went to Central America and it was worse. It occurred to me they were related. When I…"

"Sorry. There's my brother pulling in. I'm going over to the station house. And don't think this conversation is over. It's just started."

He put out his hand to shake and I grabbed it and said, "Any time, brother. Any time. Hey, Clint. Didn't y'all have three deputies?"

"Hatchley fired the other one last week."

Clint met his brother outside. They spoke for a few seconds and then Ethel reappeared with the coffee pot. I started laughing.

■ ■ ■

"Why are you laughing? You wanted coffee. You get coffee. Question is, when the hell do you use the Men's room?"

"Ah was thinkin' this might be a good time. If you would, could you tell Gifford I'll be right back. Don't want him to think Ah'm hightailin' it."

Ethel squinted her eyes. "Are you under arrest?"

"Nah. Protective custody."

She laughed. I took that laugh as a good sign.

Gifford and I were having a nice conversation about the benefits of being a police officer in contrast to being a private eye. About fifteen minutes after Clint left; Clint called. I could hear him on Gifford's walkie talkie.

"Giff, better come over to the station house. Bring that suspect with you, and put some cuffs on him."

That didn't give me a warm feeling. I could feel Gifford's demeanor change. At least the cuffs were in front and I could use my cane. Ethel had kind of a sour look on her face when I said I'd be back to tidy up my bill.

As soon as we walked in the station I saw Andy sitting at a desk. Clint looked up from something on another desk and said, "You can take those off now."

Gifford unchained me and looked around. "Where's Hatchley?"

"He's back there."

"You put him in a cell?!"

"Yep. When I got here he was on the phone to his wife telling her he had changed her flight to tomorrow. He already had Andy here locked up. He told me that Andy was a terrorist with the Weather Underground and that he was going to poison the town's water supply. Then he told me that he was going to call the FBI and have him picked up. I asked him if he was calling the two agents he had been meeting with. He tried to look at

■●■

me and couldn't and said that the poisoning is what he'd been meeting with the FBI about. When I asked why he hadn't introduced them to me, he said it was classified. When he picked up the phone I told him to put it down. He didn't, so I shot the phone. I told him the next shot will be an accident and he went back to a cell with a lot of mouth but very peacefully."

"I'm not going along with this because you're my brother. I think there's something very wrong going on. But if this blows up we're going to be doing a lot time…you shouldn't have shot the phone, Clint."

"This is serious shit, Giff. We have a lot of stuff to talk over… I shouldn't have left you over at the diner with the guy with the cane."

I looked at Andy, who was looking at me. I think we both had a look on our face that said, "Didn't expect this."

"We'll have a couple of the mechanics from Foley's pick up your car and then later we'll drop you at it just outside of town in case we're being watched."

"So we won't be able to make a stop at the library before we leave, will we?"

■ ● ■

Rungs

This particular phone booth was clean and shiny. Clean, like somebody stopped every morning to wipe everything down. Even the light worked. I wished they all could be like this.

Outside the booth Elaine was pacing back and forth, and pantomiming looking at a watch she wasn't wearing. I was starting to feel like she might slice me a phone on the side of my face if I didn't give up the receiver soon.

"Yes. Everything is fine here. Do you still like Chicago?"

"It's so big. I don't think I've seen most of it. Raoul's friends still say we have to be careful about where we go. But they took me to this place to hear music one night and I got to meet this incredible guitar player named Buddy. He was really nice and we had ribs and greens. Oh my gosh, they were fuc…uh, they were so good. And they said I need to learn history so I've been learning about Fred Hampton and the meat packing strike and Eugene Debs like the poster by Elaine's desk and May Day and…"

"Marty…"

"…the eight hour day and I'm learning to play chess and going to play Andy when I get good…"

Elaine was making faces at me now that I think she thought

■ ● ■

were threatening. I almost started laughing.

"…was thinking that…"

"Marty."

"What?"

"Elaine wants to speak to you."

"Oh? Okay. I miss you guys and I miss you."

"Miss you too."

After I stepped out of the booth and handed the receiver off to Elaine, I leaned against the booth kind of eavesdropping. Though I couldn't make out the words, I thought I could still hear the teenage excitement at the other end. I couldn't help smiling. The conversation sounded like short, staccato machine gun bursts. When I heard Elaine say Andy and Sharp were out of town, I could feel the smile disappear from my face. I drifted down the sidewalk a little wondering what would happen if Andy and Sharp didn't find a sympathetic ear up north. Were we going to have to fight the local police to save a lot of lives in their little town?

Elaine and I were riding back to the safe house in silence. The car felt crowded by things that weren't being said.

"Marty sounds good."

Nothing.

"What do you think?"

Silence.

What do I do to break through? I glanced at Elaine with some concern. She mumbled something.

"What was that?"

"What if one of us dies?"

"None of us is going to die?"

"We don't really know that, do we? I mean we really don't know how dedicated DeFord is to pulling this insanity off. Last time we were lucky. Three of us were shot and we were lucky

■ ● ■

Sharp didn't die. What if one of us dies?"

"Nobody on our side is going to die."

She slammed her fist into the dashboard. "This is not fair!"

"What's not fair?"

"This isn't fair to Marty."

Now the car felt empty. It was like the windows and doors were all open and the windshield was gone. I didn't even have to think about it. Elaine was right. I wanted to say she's better off with us than with her parents or a pimp, but I kept my mouth shut.

I kept my eyes focused straight ahead. The headlights made me feel like they were cutting through the truth. And the truth was all dark.

When we got back to the house the living room was filled. Andy and Sharp were back. Ryan Byrne, one of the guys from White Lightning was sitting in a corner. Mojica was next to a window looking at a knife with a man I thought I recognized, but couldn't place. Where was Raoul? Was he a boxer? When Raoul came into the room from the kitchen, it struck me as funny how the room seemed to shrink. A six foot six, three hundred pound human can make that happen. He motioned Elaine and me over toward the boxer.

"This is Oz. He's going to do a little recon for us tonight. He'll try to find out the exact number of people DeFord has at his compound. If we're lucky, maybe we'll find out why DeFord is not at his farm."

Elaine and I shook Oz's hand and watched him put his knife away. Everyone found a place to sit and then Andy began to brief us on the trip up north.

"Sharp and I were surprised. We didn't expect such a warm

■ ● ■

welcome. The two deputies we met were brothers. They didn't seem to need much persuading. They had a feeling that something was wrong."

"Ah think Andy is understating our reaction. We weren't 'surprised.' We were shocked and stunned. Course it was the new water cooler the sheriff had installed that sewed it up for them."

Andy was looking at Sharp like he sometimes looked at Mojica. "Anyway, Sharp can tell you all about the water cooler in a second. This is my theory. They are going to poison the stream that comes out of the lake. Sometimes the water treatment plant actually uses the water from that stream."

Elaine, our water flow expert jumped in. "That's probably a diversion. They couldn't be certain the poison would get into the water system. They probably need to go to the purification plant."

Andy was nodding his head. "Sharp and I were wondering if that was the case. Poison in the creek would make it seem like any water supply is vulnerable if there's a lot of dead fish or animals. That, and some dead humans would definitely freak some people out. We talked to the two deputies and they actually put the Sheriff in a cell. He's clearly in on it. They'll have men at the plant and a group down at their lake when they need them. Sharp will go back up there to be with the group at the plant. Raoul."

Raoul's voice was thick and heavy. It seemed to lay on the floor and climb up to our knees and then just rumble.

"I've introduced you all to Oz. He'll be going into DeFord's compound tonight to get as much information as he can about their defenses and how many men they have. When it's time to act Mojica and I will lay down a barrage to get them moving. Once they evacuate the compound the White Lightning men

■●■

will split DeFord's entourage on the road that leads to the farm. Andy and Udo's boys will be at the farm waiting for DeFord. Sharp will leave for up north as soon as we're finished here."

Of course, Elaine had to start with the what-ifs.

"And what if they decide not to move?"

Andy and Raoul looked uncomfortable at the same time. I almost started laughing.

It was the Irishman who responded first. "Well, darlin', we'll have to have it out right there at the spot."

Elaine's head went red and then her face turned dark.

"Mr. Byrne, you don't call me 'darlin', understand? I'm not your darlin', or sweetie, or love. You talk to me like you talk to any of the men in this room."

"Well, you are the only woman in our group. If ya want, I could refer to Mr. Whitfield as darlin' so you wouldn't feel so put upon."

"Yeah? I'd like to see how long that lasts. This is serious shit and we don't have time for your sexist bullshit!"

Ryan Byrne's eyebrows were almost in his hairline. Then he smiled kind of meekly. "My apologies, madam…uh, madam comrade."

Mojica had to jump in. "You know, 'Madam Comrade' has a cutesy kind of ring to it. Maybe 'comrade' would be better. But I've also noticed that if you call her Elaine you can get her attention."

On the other side of the room I heard Oz say to Raoul in a very low voice, "These guys are going to do what, tomorrow?"

Andy must have heard him too. "Look, if they decide to stay and fight, I think they'd be fools. They have buildings for men to sleep in at this compound. At the farm they'll have cover they know they can fight from. But they won't know we'll be waiting for them."

■ ● ■

"And we've been assuming all of this happens at night. What if they decide to do the contamination in the daytime?"

Sharp responded. "We'll have a couple of men at the treatment plant all day. We can have more men there in just a few minutes if something is going down. Their object should be to expect not to be seen. If they want people to think lefties did this to the water, they have to pull this off under cover of darkness."

It was my turn. "Our job is to stop DeFord, and if we can, destroy his little organization. We want no casualties on our side. So no one try anything crazy. If we stick to our plan we should all be fine. Andy, Elaine and I will be at DeFord's farm. There are only four men there. Udo and his men will meet us there and we shouldn't have any problems being ready for DeFord and whoever is with him. No casualties on our side."

As I looked around the room everyone was nodding their head except Andy, who was frowning, and Elaine, who was staring at me. I heard someone say "that's it then."

Everyone was standing up. Oz said something to Raoul and then he walked across the room to Elaine.

"Those were important questions you asked. They needed to be made clear." He held out his hand to shake with Elaine. He nodded at me and left.

Ryan Byrne drifted over. "I want to apologize and hope we can still be comrades of sorts. I didn't mean to be offensive. I seen you shake hands with that tattoo fellow, so I hope yul' do me the same." They shook hands and then Byrne offered his hand to me. "Tomorrow then, mate." He smiled. I smiled. He grinned, and then he left.

I noticed Sharp talking to Andy. Andy was holding Sharp's arm and shaking his head. Sharp seemed to end their conversation with a nod and an okay. As he limped by me he punched me in the arm lightly and waved to Elaine as he went out the door.

■ ● ■

I almost yelled ,"You forgot your cane."

I turned toward Elaine and held out my hand. She looked at me like her feet hurt from standing on tacks. "You haven't apologized for fuck." She turned away and I slid my hand into my pocket and wondered if I had done something really wrong. I knew my list of transgressions was long, but I didn't really know what to say.

A huge, vise-grip hand landed on my shoulder. I turned to find Raoul looking down at me with a question on his face.

"What's up, Raoul?"

"Why were you emphasizing 'no casualties'? Is there something on your mind that's bothering you?"

"I just don't want anyone to do anything stupid…anything beyond what they need to do."

Over my shoulder I heard Elaine. "Bullshit. What he was doing was trying to placate me in some condescending way. Right?"

Raoul let go of my shoulder. "If you two have a private beef going, I'll just step out of the way."

I was focused on Elaine's eyes. "I didn't know there was a problem until a few seconds ago. Why don't you stick, Raoul? We might need a mediator."

"All of that nonsense about 'no casualties' was all because of my concern with Marty. Do you think saying that makes Marty's situation better? Will I be less anxious? Does Marty deserve this…to be hiding in Chicago with Raoul's bodyguards?"

Raoul looked at me waiting to see what I was going to say.

"I'm sorry, Elaine. She didn't deserve the pimp or those people who claim to be her parents, either. But…"

"And she doesn't deserve to have murders hovering in her background. She's a kid!"

"I know." I didn't know what else to say. I felt like the floor

■ ● ■

dropped out from under me. I walked out the door into the darkness. I heard Raoul's rumble of a whisper start up as I looked up at the stars and pulled the door shut. My feet slipped through uncut grass as I headed for the tree line. I sat down on a fallen log and stared into the woods hoping to see nothing but black. Something moved in the trees. I thought maybe it was a deer. Some light. Like a pinprick. Firefly? Was someone standing out there in the trees? I started to stand up, but Andy's voice made me sit back down.

"How're you doing?"

"I don't know. I've really been a fuck-up lately, haven't I?" I was hoping Andy would lie, but he didn't.

"You sure as shit have."

"Was I always like this?"

"Come on. You know damn well you weren't. You're asking the question because you know you weren't. Once we get through this craziness you'll get your shit straightened out."

"I don't know, Andy."

"I do."

"Maybe I'm in the wrong fucking job."

Andy didn't answer at first and then he said, "Maybe…but we're going to figure it out."

We sat there a few minutes staring into the darkness. I think both of us were trying to pretend we weren't afraid. In the next two or three days something bad was going to happen. Maybe Elaine had a spot-on premonition.

Raoul's voice cracked the darkness like a boulder tumbling down a cliff. "Andy, you better come in here."

I looked back out in the woods. I thought I saw something moving away. The thought crossed my mind…'trust your friends…trust your friends.'

Andy came back from the house and sat down on the log

■ ● ■

again.

"Ryan Byrne is dead. He was shot down in front of Colm O'Brien's house."

"What the hell were they doing there?! I heard Raoul myself tell them to move somewhere safe."

"They're kids to this."

"And now there's a dead kid…are they still in?"

"Maybe they thought O'Brien's was safe, and yeah, they're still in."

"So much for me mouthing off about 'no casualties.'"

"What the hell was that all about anyway?"

"I don't know. I guess I wanted Elaine to feel less anxiety about what we have to do. It was stupid I guess."

"It wasn't stupid…it was arrogant and demeaning…and thoughtless and insensitive…and…"

"You could throw in controlling."

"I was going to get to it after self-centered and self-serving."

It was really quiet. It was as if someone grabbed the dial and turned off the crickets. I felt like something wrong was sitting on my shoulder.

"Now why the hell haven't you just said 'fuck off, Andy?'"

"On our way back from our daily kibbitz with Marty, Elaine said, 'what if one of us dies'…what are we doing to Marty?"

"Yeah. That's a tough one. But Elaine's not ignorant. She knows how dangerous this can all be. And now she's made a commitment to a kid that she really doesn't know…that she may not even be able to hold on to. She's stressed. We're all stressed. In a few days something will happen that we don't know the outcome of. The best thing you can do for her is hold up your end and make sure everything goes smooth."

"But it's not going to go smooth, Andy. If it was, Byrne wouldn't be dead right now."

■ ● ■

At 3:30 a.m. I heard voices outside the front door. I sat up on the couch where I was sleeping to try to listen. One of the voices belonged to Raoul. I was pretty sure the other one belonged to Raoul's friend, Oz. I walked shoeless and shirtless to the front door. The night air felt good on my skin when I pulled the door open. Oz stopped speaking.

I couldn't really see Raoul's face in the dark. "Couldn't sleep?"

"Raoul, every time you stop speaking the floor stops vibrating. After a while that will wake somebody up. You're like Walter Cronkite's voice on steroids, or a talking tuba."

I heard Oz chuckle, and then he started speaking again. "They have twenty-four men at the compound including DeFord. Six of them will be leaving first thing in the morning for the water filtration plant. They have three men on night duty. Two with dogs circling the buildings. On the west end they don't take the dogs out far enough to complete a search of the full perimeter. There's a thicket of blackberry bushes out there and I think they feel no one would try to get through at that point. Or they're just lazy, which is my guess. DeFord has a bodyguard. A young kid who sleeps in a chair with his eyes open."

"I think we've seen him before."

"Slightest noise and he tenses up. I counted six vehicles out in the open. DeFord's building has a four stall garage. One stall is empty. Two stalls have Jeep Renegades in them. The other stall has a vehicle with a tarp over it. This is a map of the compound. This building stores barrels of gasoline. I couldn't find anything that suggested there's a storehouse of weapons. I assume all of the men keep their weapons on their person."

Oz handed the map to Raoul. "I'll see you tomorrow. I'm going to catch some sleep."

"That was good work, Oz."

Suddenly he was gone. I kept staring at where he used to be,

■ ● ■

but he was gone.

"Raoul, what does that guy do?"

"Tattoos mostly."

"Wasn't he a boxer?"

"Yep. Top ten light heavyweight before he went to war. Tomorrow morning we have to get in touch with Sharp and let him know what kind of company he can expect. You want to fill in Andy when he gets up?"

"I'm up. Heard the whole thing. Going to be a busy night tomorrow. Raoul, I can relieve you at the door."

"I got it, Andy. I won't be able to sleep."

Raoul just said, "Okay, be cool, brother." Then Andy and Raoul lumbered off to bed. I sat down on the stone stoop fingering my weapon, hoping no one got hurt the next day.

■ ● ■

Tocsin

The echoes of the first explosion rippled through the night like thunder. Lights that had been on suddenly retreated into darkness. I had missed the house and hit the garage and I cursed myself. Raoul did not miss his target. The building where the gasoline was stored went up with a roar. There was no echo. It was like the night had gasped and didn't bother to exhale.

I aimed my RPG at DeFord's house again while listening to a dog feverishly working its way toward me through the brambles. My second shot hit DeFord's house dead on. The glow from the gasoline fire was so bright I was sure they could see me now. The German Shepherd certainly could. It was coming right at me. I pulled my pistol and shot the dog three times dead.

Bullets were ripping through the underbrush very close to me. They stopped when another explosion lifted one of the Broncos up in the air and dropped it on its side.

My last grenade went into the building farthest away from DeFord's house. Men were screaming and running in opposite directions, but now I could hear car engines starting. One Jeep and a Toronado pulled out of DeFord's garage and raced down the dirt drive past the guard near the road. Other vehicles filled

■●■

in behind them. I guessed DeFord was in the second car, the Toronado.

Through the smoke I thought I saw something going in the opposite direction of the other cars. Bad time for illusions. De-Ford's garage suddenly blew up and I could barely see the outlines of his compound through the smoke.

"Heeks! You okay?"

"I'm alright. Thought I saw a vehicle going that way."

"Oz said that's rough territory out there. What kind of vehicle?"

"A jeep."

"You see anyone that got in it?"

"No. I'm not even sure I saw it. There were two jeeps in the garage, right?

"There was, but it'll be a while before that fire is low enough for us to check on it, and we have to go."

We were lying on our backs, blind in a 1964 Dodge station wagon. I thought I was going to gag. The fake seat paneling Mojica put in was about three inches from my nose.

"Fucking Mojica should have checked out the goddam exhaust after he stripped out the fold down seats. We might be asphyxiated before we get to DeFord's farm.

"We're close. Just hold your breath for a minute or two."

"Fuck you, Andy. You know if this doesn't work, we're helpless."

"Notice you didn't say dead."

"Yeah, that too."

"Ow! That hurt! Jesus H. Christ, Elaine! Could you drive around the potholes please?"

"Andy, will you quit complaining about every little thing?"

"You know where…"

■ ● ■

"Hey back there. Here we go."

I imagined Elaine sweating, trying to get ready to make three soldiers sexually curious.

"Hey, sexy! Free blowjobs for everybody!"

"Hey, you! Stop! Stop!"

A burst from an automatic.

We made it past the guard without him shooting up the station wagon. I could feel the car rocking and sliding around the curves that Elaine was taking too fast. Andy and I kept bumping into one another. Finally the engine roared and the car came to a screeching, fishtailing stop.

Men were screaming at Elaine to get out of the car.

"Hey, boys. DeFord sent me over to break the monotony. How're you doing, tiger?"

I could just barely hear the men discussing making a call over to DeFord's compound. One of them said they should just shoot her. That gave me a sick feeling in my stomach. Andy squeezed my arm. One of the station wagon doors opened.

"Nothing in here. Reeks of booze though."

"Just like her."

"C'mon guys. I don't stink that bad. Get a coupla' shots in ya and ya won't even notice. Ya'll got any alcohol inside?"

"Where the fuck do you think you're going?!"

The car shook and it sounded like something slammed onto the engine hood.

"Ow, goddam it! I can get kind of frisky, but I don't like it that rough. Ya know?!"

"Shut up! I'll take her inside and call over to the compound to see what's what. You call down to McAvoy to see if he's still awake. She never should have made it up here like this. C'mon, bitch."

"Ow, goddam it!"

■ ● ■

"Shut the fuck up!"

Footsteps disappearing. I pushed the panel that Mojica had built in the floor to one side. I slowly sat up and looked around. Nothing.

"It's all clear, Andy." I wondered if the Greeks were this nervous. I climbed out the side door so that Andy could slide over and follow me. We circled to the back of the house where we knew a communications room had been set up. Andy went up the stairs first and reached for the door which opened before he could touch it. Andy's Colt was under the guard's chin while I was still climbing up the steps.

"If you're quiet you may live to see a sunrise." I said the wrong thing. As soon as I finished my sentence he turned his head to yell, "Jake…" Andy hit him twice in the side of the head. The guard fell to the floor in a pile, but his partner had heard him.

"Loomis? What's going on?"

Silence.

"Loomis?!"

More silence and a footstep. And then he opened up. The hallway was filled with automatic weapons fire. It seemed like his plan was to keep the hall clear, work his way to his partner and drag him back to somewhere. Not a good plan.

Andy let off one shot that wasn't close to hitting anything but a wall. The guard must have realized how ridiculous his plan was. The shooting now came in sharp cover bursts as he backed out of the hallway.

I motioned to Andy that I was circling to the front. We had to deal with the two men inside before the guard down by the road made it up the hill to the stone farmhouse. If we didn't, we'd really have problems. I raced around to the front door. It was reinforced oak. The windows all had bars on them. I ran to the station wagon hoping the key was still in the ignition. It was and

■ ● ■

as the engine turned over I thought of the television program, "The Untouchables." I floored it and aimed at the front door. The porch in front only had one step. The station wagon jumped the step and slammed through the door. From somewhere down a dark hall I could see fire spitting at me from the darkness.

He's going to call DeFord's compound. There's shooting all around me. I can't sit here pretending to be a passed out prostitute. I opened my eyes just far enough to see that the communications man was the only one in the room. He picked up the shortwave mic. I pulled Mojica's knife from out of the back of my platforms. The communications man looked at me upside down with very wide eyes. I had a handful of hair, a knife at his throat and he was still inching his hand toward his gun.

"Please don't do it." I pressed the knife until blood began to trickle from his neck. These guys must be true believers.

The front of the house seemed to explode. We both jumped and he made the decision to reach for my knife hand. I pressed harder. I couldn't die like this! I just couldn't. "Drop your fucking hands!" His hands slid away from his neck. I was hoping I hadn't killed him.

"Put both of your hands under your ass. Sit on them. Now!"

His hands disappeared. I could see a steady stream of blood running down his front.

"I'm going to kill you, cunt."

The automatic seemed to be shooting in the opposite direction and then it went quiet. Andy's face popped in and out of the room. Then I had both faces staring at me from the hallway.

"Don't move." I pulled the knife away and picked up the communications man's Beretta. They were still staring at me.

"What?!"

■ ● ■

"Colm. They're on the way. Mr. Raoul says to cut em' at the third car. He said they'll be coming in right behind them…five or ten minutes back."

"Then tell the boys to get ready with the fire works. Fifteen minutes."

Andy was looking at the cut Elaine had inflicted on the phone operator. I started to go down the hallway to pick up the guard Andy had dumped on the floor. I was concerned that the other guard from down the hill hadn't shown up yet.

I turned into the hall and immediately jumped back. In a whisper I yelled, "Men!"

Andy reached for a light switch and the room went black. Car lights flooded the hallway from the front of the house.

"Shit…you think the Irish missed?"

"Nothing should have started yet."

We waited.

"GM! You in there?!"

"God damn…it's Udo." Andy exhaled like it was a long word.

My heart rate started to drop back to about 120 beats a minute. Andy flicked the lights back on and stepped out into the hallway. "Glad to see you…but I thought you were going to wait for a call."

I turned around and saw that Elaine had the radio man's Beretta pressed against the back of his head.

"I had two men hidden down on the road watching things. After they took out the guard, one of them got back to me and said there was all kinda trouble goin' on up in here. So we came on up and seen all this damage. Looks like we missed everything."

Two men came up behind Udo holding the guard from the

■ ● ■

doorway. "Louie, what you want us to do with him?"

"Tie the motherfucker up." Udo looked at Andy and hooked a thumb at the guard. "He ain't with you, is he GM?"

Andy shook his head. "Louie, you should park your cars behind that barn across the yard where they were laying concrete."

Udo turned to one of his men. "Alvin, you hear that? Can you take care 'a that?"

Alvin nodded and walked out toward the back door. I heard glass crunching under someone's feet from the front of the house.

"Whyn't you have us come up here with you, Andrew? We coulda…and, oooo, looka that cut. Who did that?"

Andy nodded his chin toward Elaine. Udo was beaming. "That's surgery, there. Boy, she about to cut you a new oral cavity, motherfucker. Yes she was!" Udo chuckled. "You cain't trust no woman with a knife. Uh uh. Not with a knife." Udo started laughing. He got right in the phone man's face and said, "And I bet you serious money she got your gun, too. Don't she? Serious money."

I looked at Elaine and gently shook my head. Her eyes caught mine and her face remained expressionless.

Udo looked at me. "I got those two dogs, Loco. Where you want em?"

Andy stared at me. "Dogs?"

I ignored him. "Can you keep them in your van for a little while?"

Udo shrugged. "Yeah. We can do that."

Then one of my ten worst nightmares entered the room. Daveed stood in the doorway swaying back and forth, wearing a cut-off black tee shirt, jeans cut off just below the knees and high top black Converse. Except for the Mac 10 he was holding and the Walther tucked in his jeans, and eyes that were popping out

■ ● ■

of his head, he looked like he could be heading to the beach.

Udo turned to another one of his men, "Melvin, let's get the one the chica fucked up tied down, too."

"Uh, Louie, we need him to answer the other compound on the short wave if they call."

"Huh? Okay, GM. Daveed. I need you to watch this punk. He get a call on the radio you holler for me. He does anything stupid you bust a cap in his ass."

Daveed moved into the room and I looked at his eyes again. They were moving back and forth like he was watching goldfish in an aquarium.

"So GM…you got everybody in check without us."

"The main event hasn't started yet, Louie. We'll be having some trouble in about twenty minutes…maybe less. We're still going to need a man down on the driveway to make it look like nothing's wrong."

"Okay, Andrew. I'll get a couple of men down there. A couple to hide and one to act like a guard."

"Heeks, where'd you get a pair of waders big enough to fit me?"

"A guy in a shop near Chesterton had them. He agreed to meet me half way so we'd have them tonight."

"They saved a lot of pain. This blackberry patch is something else, but these rubber pants are hot."

"Raoul, that jeep is bothering me."

"So we'll try to see if Oz saw it. He'll probably beat us back to the van. Damn! These prickers just pull at your legs."

"Ready boys?" My two friends in the back of the truck nodded. I walked back to the cab and climbed in, slamming the door shut.

"Sorry."

■ ● ■

"Fer what?"

"For slammin' the door."

"What...you think someone'll hear ya? We're miles away from anybody."

"Why'd you put four of our men down on the road alone?" I sucked on my cigarette and saw Colm's face looked angry. Certainly sounded like he was when he started talking.

"Put yer fuckin' fag out, Thomas. I coulda sworn on the bible that was you at the meetin' that we discussed this. The four of us'll be bouncin' round in here. We need some steady eyes, too. On top o' that the four are not alone. Each of them has three other comrades with him. That's not alone."

"Why not have everybody down there?"

I thought his stare would burn a hole in me. I took a last drag on my cigarette. From the glow I could see his face.

"You paddy motherfucker...what if...you know what? We been over this whole thing and where we are is where we are. Like when you said why don't we just park the lorry in the road? Cause they'll see it a quarter and three half miles away. When... this is where we're at, Thomas. We play from here."

I tossed my cigarette out the window and felt stupid.

Ah didn't like the sound of the news that was coming over Clint's walkie talkie. From the looks on the other faces, that was true for everyone else who could hear except for the three men introduced to me as the Douglas brothers. Where everyone else seemed to get tense, these three seemed to relax. I noticed that the eyes on the one named Murray, turned into very narrow slits. He patted his brothers on their shoulders, then sat down by the wall and stared at the main treatment plant door.

"Was anyone hit?"

■ ● ■

Over the talkie ah heard, "Just Delbert Chidester. The shot hit him in the arm and the bullet sliced along the side of his chest. We have the bleeding stopped, but his brothers refuse to take him to the hospital."

"Of course they do. Miss the action if they did that…how many were there?"

"Three. Don't think we hit any of them considering how much shooting went on after they shot Delbert. Do you want us to come up there?"

"Giff, I have the Douglas brothers up here, right?…and your attackers might try for a second chance. There's supposed to be six of those bastards up here somewhere. Over."

"Over."

Ah put a toothpick in my mouth and said to Clint, "Ah take it Douglas and Chidester don't mix."

Clint looked over his shoulder and then shook his head. "The Douglas brothers are crazy. The Chidesters are wild. For whatever reason they just hate one another. If we had all of them in here, and any shooting started, as likely as not someone would have a bullet in their back."

We were up on a platform over the main floor of the plant that had pipes running through it parallel to each other. Ah had no idea of what they did but they made a constant loud humming sound.

Clint stood up and said, "Fellas, the men at the lake just had an exchange of fire with three intruders. We should assume they're going to try something here. Probably soon."

I heard one of the Douglas brothers mutter, "I wish they would."

Clint sighed, "Yeah, well…don't forget. John is outside. He'll rap on the door first if he needs to come in. Nobody, nobody fires until I say so. Nobody."

■ ● ■

As if it was staged, there was rapping on the main door. The man closest to the door looked at Clint. He nodded and the door swung open. One man came through the door and I heard the man outside say, "Shut it."

"Connie, what the hell are you doing here?"

"Clint, you need to get some men up the station house. Three men with automatic weapons came in the front door."

One of the Douglas boys said, "And you went out the back."

"Damn right! I got this." He held up a .38 police special.

"Goddam it! Sharp, I'm going to take Connie, if he'll go back, and one other man over to the station. Hey, Murray. Can you go with me over to the station?"

"Fuck, yeah."

"Clint, you know they're trying to split us up, right?"

"Yeah. But I've got to try to keep the Sheriff in custody. He could create some serious problems if they get him out."

"You're right there, ah suppose."

"Listen up. Connie, you willing to go back the station house?"
Connie nodded.

"Okay then. Murray, Connie and I will see what's going on up there. Nobody fires unless Sharp says to. Understand?"

"Heads nodded all around. Then one of the Douglas brothers said, "Who's he? He ain't nobody to be givin' me no orders."

Murray Douglas stood up and walked over to his brother who was lying stomach down on the platform. He kicked him in the leg. His brother looked up at him, said "okay," and turned his head back to watching the main door.

Where the hell are they going? If they get to a road it's going to be hard to close the distance in the dark. Shit. Especially without lights.

■ ● ■

"Here they come, Colm."
"I see 'em."

Four of us were standing on the farmhouse back porch. Louie's men were busy moving cars. I watched Elaine staring off into the distance. Andy and Louie were discussing where the men should be positioned. Andy kept emphasizing that we couldn't let anyone get out. And then I heard a burst of gunfire. Everyone turned toward the house.

I heard Andy say, "Fuck," and then he walked back in. Udo sauntered after him. Elaine and I followed and ended up looking over their shoulders at Daveed. Udo was shaking his head.

"Andrew, did we really need him?"

Right on cue we heard a distant voice requesting a check off on the shortwave. The dead communications man was holding a .45 in his hand with packing tape hanging on it.

"Where he get that gun, Daveed?"

"Taped under the table." Daveed kept stretching his eyelids like Jackie Gleason would when he fooled Norton.

The shortwave asked again for the check-in. We all looked at each other, except Daveed. He was still working his eyes.

Elaine suddenly spoke. "Udo kind of sounds like the dead guy."

Udo smiled. "Daveed. Go out and cover the front porch. First car that comes in, give it a welcome." Daveed's eyes were popping out of his head again, but he left immediately.

"So let's see what my man got to say." Udo sat down like he'd been here before. He raised his voice. "Who is this?!"

The voice on the other end paused, and then said, "What?"

Udo smiled. "Who the hell is this?!"

Another pause. "What are you screwing around for?"

■ ● ■

"Just doesn't sound like you."

"Who the hell did you think it would be? Hey...what's my name, asshole?"

The sound of an explosion came through the speaker.

"What's going on over there?"

"Came from the garage. Is everything cool over there?"

"Very quiet. Very quiet. Chilly. Everything is good."

A louder explosion. The connection ended. Louie stood up beaming. "Put 'em on the defensive. I don't sound right. You don't sound right. But it sound like the shit is on, don't it?"

Our truck had hit the rear of the third car and spun it into a ditch. Colm had hit his head on the steering wheel and was unconscious. The other boys up the road were already firing and I wasn't sure what to do. I jumped down from the truck and walked over toward the car and said for everyone to get out. Instead, they started shooting at me and then all of a sudden my legs wouldn't hold me up. I was on my knees pumping rounds into their car wondering if I hit anything beside the windshield. Kerry and Gregor were off to my side shooting into the car and the shooting stopped kind of sudden. I fell forward on my face.

Colm turned me over.

"What have ya done, Thomas? You went and got yerself shot. Christ a mighty...you'll be okay. You'll be okay."

"Colm..."

"Yes, Thomas?"

"Call my boss t'morrow and tell him I'm gonna be late for work."

I heard Colm laugh. "Shut yer mouth, you."

We couldn't wait for Oz and we left to hook up with the White Lightning boys. Raoul was visibly upset. We couldn't

■ ● ■

reach Oz on the talkie and Raoul was worried that everyone might not have left the compound. He was feeling that we had bungled that part. Too late now. The damn jeep. What if the toxin was still in the compound?

"We needed two more men."

I just nodded. When we came up on the truck we could see that one car had smashed into the side of the International. A couple of the Irish were standing over five men who were lying facedown in the road. It looked like most of the cars had been abandoned. There was gunfire out in the field. Raoul told the two men to go get their friends. It was time to leave. They moved off into the tall grass bent over and Raoul walked around all of the vehicles shooting out the tires.

The headlights of another car were coming down the highway. The car slowed down and Raoul stepped behind one of the cars from the compound. I slipped partially behind the truck while warning my prisoners not to move.

When the car was at a complete stop, Raoul stepped out. The car had four teenagers in it. I could hear Raoul answering their first question. He didn't allow a second.

"You can't get through this way. I need you to notify the police. Two drug gangs are shooting it out down here. We need help. Turn around and drive to a phone booth. Don't go so fast you have an accident. Go."

The car turned around and took off while the White Lightning men were coming out of the field. We quickly made our way over to the other side of the truck.

"Colm, you alright?"

"Jest a bump on me head, Mr. Raoul. But Thomas was shot in both legs."

"I have someone who can help him and is up expecting to see some casualties. Let's get the boys in my van and I'll get you

■ ● ■

to your vehicles and give you the address where you can take Thomas."

"Elaine, what's on your mind? You keep staring off into space."

"What was our backup plan?"

"Huh? I guess we really didn't have a backup, per se."

"You guys always operate like what you expect to happen is what will happen."

"Usually it does."

"Well, other people aren't as cocky and don't operate like that. Go in the glove compartment of the station wagon and pull out the map."

"Okay. Why?"

"Because DeFord is not coming here. Something happened he didn't expect. He's going to his backup plan."

I passed Daveed on the porch hoping he would remember who I was and not shoot me. I stumbled through the detritus and I heard Elaine yelling for Andy. I ran back with the map frustrated that I knew Elaine was right again.

"You're thinking DeFord is going for a second target?"

"When we were trying to find his target we thought this might be the place." She pointed to a town on the map about a half hour away. "I'll bet he's headed there because he knows we're on to his play."

"On to his play? Where the hell have you been hanging out?"

"What's up?"

"Andy, we need one of Udo's cars. Like right now." Andy's gaze shifted from Elaine to me and back.

"We'll tell you in the car."

■ ● ■

Clint was standing on the stairs leading up to the platform. "The Sheriff is dead. They shot him in one of the cells."

One of the men asked, "Why didn't they just let him out, Clint?"

"Don't know. Maybe they felt he was responsible for this thing being screwed up. Maybe they didn't trust him anymore. I don't know."

Ah knew we were in for trouble when the side door exploded.

Andy had driven like a madman. It had taken us a little over twenty minutes to get to the facility we thought DeFord would try to hit. The town was dead quiet as we passed through. After Elaine explained to Andy why DeFord wouldn't show up at his farm, the car was as quiet as the town. When we pulled up at the treatment facility a jeep was already there. We were confused by the fact that it had two flat tires.

"I guess someone will have to go in. I guess it'll be me."

Andy and Elaine were looking at me like I was a silent movie actor and they were waiting for the dialogue to pop up somewhere.

"I said I'm going in. Try to find a side window that you can use to give me some cover if you can."

Elaine said, "That's the plan?!"

"We don't really have time for Plan B, they're already inside."

"How do you know that you can get in?"

"Well, the lock cylinder is lying on the ground at the bottom of the door. Getting in should be easy. Find a window."

Andy grabbed Elaine's arm and pulled her toward the side of the building.

I opened the door and immediately heard DeFord's laugh. The two of them had their backs to me. One of them was carrying a five quart metal container. DeFord started laughing again

■ ● ■

and turned around just as I felt the gun barrel on the back of my neck. DeFord's body guard started up some concrete steps and then stopped. Oz was standing at the top of the stairs. The bodyguard didn't seem to have a gun, but DeFord did.

I felt the gun at my back disappear. Andy walked past me saying, "I'd put that shit on the floor, DeFord." DeFord jumped so high I wanted to laugh. Instead I turned around to find that Elaine had her pistol securely placed inside the man's ear.

"You two couldn't find a window? And you, face down on the floor." He didn't hesitate and I picked up his weapon.

Elaine's eyes got big. I turned back to find DeFord on his knees and the bodyguard moving up the stairs. When he was almost at the top, Oz faked with a right and threw a left hook that snapped the bodyguard's head and made him stumble down two steps. He stood up and climbed the steps again, but this time the rod he used on my legs was in his hand. I thought he'd take a swing with it, but instead he charged Oz. It was obvious that DeFord's bodyguard was trained in martial arts. They traded blows and then Elaine said, "We don't have time for this." She marched to the stairs to pick up the metal container. Then I watched her climb the rest of the stairs and simply shoot the bodyguard in his leg. Oz followed her quietly down the stairs.

We pushed DeFord out the door and into the car. This time Elaine drove following Oz on his motorcycle. The first time DeFord laughed I hit him in the mouth. We rode the whole way to DeFord's farm with his hands over his mouth trying to suppress his laugh.

Ah wasn't expecting this kind of attack. There were too many of us for them to kill everyone. There were too many of us for them to play this off as a leftie conspiracy. And by now it was ob-

∎●∎

vious that we weren't retreating. Too many bullets in the air for me to be pondering anything other than trying to put a couple of them down and to guess what they might try next.

Murray Douglas was off to my side. I saw him run down the stairs and pound out the front door. The noise inside the place was bouncing off the concrete ceiling and walls. It was almost as loud as the explosion. Bullets were ricocheting all over the place. One of the Douglas brothers yelled, "Fuck!" I glanced over. It looked like he got hit in the back of his leg.

I could hear what sounded like fire engines screaming toward us from the other side of town. The shooting on DeFord's side stopped and then we stopped. Fifteen seconds later Murray Douglas and John, the former deputy, came in through the wrecked side door dragging a man by his arms. I assumed he was dead by the way they dropped him. Apparently John and Murray had DeFord's men in a cross fire and they eventually broke off.

"Is everyone okay?" Everyone was looking at each other kind of stunned. Maybe this was like Northfield. Clint's voice was more insistent. "Is anyone hit?!"

"I took a bullet in my fucking leg."

His other brother laughed. "You probably took a ricochet if it got you in the ass. You okay. Probl'y no worse than a bee sting."

"You ain't no fucking doctor!"

From across the room Murray yelled, "Can you walk?"

"Yeah?"

"Then you're okay."

The other brother switched sides. "But he's bleedin' some, Mur."

"That don't do me no nevermind! That happens when somebody gets shot. Put a rag around his leg."

Ah started to laugh, but held back.

■ ● ■

Clint broke up the dialogue. "Murray, get your brother over to the hospital. After they deal with his wound, I'd appreciate it if you'd stop over at the station. Anyone else injured?"

A chorus of "no" broke out.

As the Douglas brothers left, the Fire Chief came in looking around almost in a daze. "Clint, what the hell is going on?!"

"You men meet me at the station house."

"What's with all the guns?"

"Donald, we had a serious problem tonight with some out of town drug dealers. Give me a moment and I'll fill you in."

When I heard that, I did a double take. Drug dealers?! Why is he going to sell this as drug dealers? I decided I should start walking toward the station house.

John walked up to Clint. "What about him?" He pointed to DeFord's dead mercenary lying on the concrete floor on the other side of the room.

"Hey Clint, where's Sheriff Hatchley?"

"Please Donald, give me a moment. Okay?"

Fire engine lights were cutting through the night. The sky was starting to lighten. Ah wanted coffee, but the boys said the diner didn't open until five. When I walked in the station house I smelled coffee brewing in the kitchen. I realized what I really wanted was to look at a friendly, sympathetic face with a confident smile.

We followed Oz up the dirt driveway and pulled up in front of DeFord's farmhouse. Raoul was the first person we saw standing in the yard. Mojica stepped out of his shadow and walked toward the barn. We all got out of the car with me holding DeFord by the collar. I looked around and it was obvious that Udo's men had the situation under control.

■ ● ■

DeFord started laughing and I let him laugh. He was a disgusting lunatic and I wanted everyone to know it. Raoul walked up to us with his eyes on DeFord. Louie Udo strolled over like he was the mayor and stood next to Raoul.

"I would have used you for breeding."

I had never seen Raoul stare at anyone like he stared at DeFord. When he spit at Raoul I almost lost my grip on DeFord's shirt. Raoul continued to stare and suddenly DeFord began an almost hysterical laugh. Udo looked up at Raoul and then at DeFord. "Uh-uh." Udo took two steps toward us and kicked DeFord in the groin. Raoul put his hand on Udo's shoulder and gently pulled him back.

"Loco…I'ma meet you inside."

I nodded and watched Raoul walk away. Andy was at the far end of the yard now. I could still hear sporadic gunfire out past the field in the tree line.

"This way, asshole." I pushed DeFord toward the farmhouse. "There's a cellar in here isn't there?"

DeFord started laughing again. One of Louie's men passed by and I told him to tell Louie I'd meet him in the basement. We went inside and when I found the stairs, I pushed the scum down them.

"Don't get up until I get down there. You were going to poison most of a town of innocent people for a really bad reason. You want to create a world where people who have next to nothing, have even less so you can have more. You want a country full of paranoids so that your idea…"

"What a nice little speech. Did you…"

"Get up you piece of scum. It's nice down here. You were having it all redone for your troops? Your fellow lunatics and Nazis?"

"No. For men who understand what must be done to save

■ ● ■

the nation from socialists."

I pushed DeFord down a hallway until I saw a room with no windows. "Get in there."

DeFord giggled. "Take your clothes off."

"Why? I have a lot of money. You can be very rich."

"Take your clothes off."

"How much money would…"

I raised my Colt and fired at a spot just above his head. "Take your clothes off. Everything. And now, goddam it!"

DeFord was undressing as Louie Udo came through the door with two very nasty looking dogs.

"Louie…the man stripping over there is the man who had your girl beaten to death."

DeFord was in his socks.

"I said everything." One dog was growling. The other one stared, kind of like Louie was right now.

"I handle it from here unless you want to watch."

I stepped out through the door and closed it. The last words I heard from DeFord was, "But I can make you rich."

The screams started. I could hear the dogs going wild. I walked slowly down the hallway rubbing my arms. Going up the stairs, listening to the fading screams, I felt very, very cold.

■ ● ■

Fracture

"Happy Birthday, Happy Birthday, Happy Birthday to you."
"Blow out the candles, Marty...on both cakes."

"You want help?" Mojica had a grin about the diameter of one of the cakes.

"Nope. I think I can do this."

She did it with a beaming face. Mojica handed her a knife to cut the cake. Sharp took a phone call and had a very serious expression on his face.

"How're you feeling?" Andy was holding my arm. I could see he really wanted an answer.

"Relieved. I feel relieved. All I can say right now is that I feel relieved, I guess, and worried. There are some crazy people in this country." And then I started feeling nervous, like there was a large, black, dark spot hovering in front of me.

"Yep. Me too."

Sharp strolled over to us holding an orange juice. "I just got off the phone with Clint. He's the new Sheriff. The FBI and the State Police finally realized they weren't going to shake the drug gang war story."

Andy shook his head. "Yeah, because the FBI already knew

■ ● ■

who DeFord's people were."

"Ah think they were trying to figure out who was helping Clint so they could run the story that lefties were killing people out in the street."

"Raoul told me that the man who was shot in your office was a DeFord man. He…"

"Hold the phone! When did you and Raoul become best friends?"

"The man who went through the window was the brother of the shooter you tracked down in the bars."

"Don't ignore my question."

Andy crossed his arms and shook his head. "The window jumper was involved in creating the toxin. Anyway, he and his brother got religion and they turned the whole thing into a clusterfuck."

I could see Andy was not going to answer me. "Okay… Wait a minute. Did you just explain something, because I just missed it." I watched Marty opening her presents with a flushed face. Her friend, Kennedy, looked a little jealous. The three of us moved closer to the party table. I felt tears were forming so I faked a yawn and rubbed my eyes.

"Goober! You got me all these gift certificates to the movies?! Thank you! Kennedy and I are going to have to use them up quick."

I noticed Elaine immediately pinched Marty's arm. Helen distracted me by placing a kiss on Mojica's cheek. I liked the way they looked at each other. It made me feel like I was part of something special.

Sharp was looking at the main office door. "If that don't make the corn reach for the stars on a warm summer night…" He walked away to greet a woman who had just come through our door.

■ ● ■

Andy was smiling. "That's Ethel."

"Oh, yeah? Who's Ethel?"

"She's a volunteer librarian fire fighter judo expert."

Andy turned back to the table when he heard Marty scream about a chess set.

"Ethel? Could you give me just a little more information? Just a little?"

Andy gave me a hard look in the eyes. "She works in a diner up north." Andy turned back to the celebration like he had just explained everything.

"And what was that faux Texas witticism he just spouted?"

"C'mon. You know he just made that up. It sounded half stupid."

"One of Marty's bodyguards from Chicago gave her a Bulls jersey and a couple of history books. Marty hugged him, went to pause, looked around the room and then started crying. Elaine draped her arm around Marty's shoulder. Kennedy was holding her hand. Helen was rubbing her arm. I had to yawn again.

"I'm really, really happy and I can't stop crying."

We had found a two story office building for our new crib thanks to my favorite waitress, Margot. She had heard two men discussing the place at the counter and got in touch with me as soon as they left the diner.

We looked at it and had decided to buy it. Sharp and I were on the second floor in the common area discussing which rooms we would take as our personal office space.

Mojica walked in grinning. "This place is great. Our security will be so much better here once we take it over." He raised his arm pointing. "I gotta have that room. Those walls are perfect." He trotted into his new space, his head snapping left and right,

■ ● ■

imagining how his office would look after he remodeled it.

Sharp had moved over by the stairway and was leaning against the wall with his shoulder. I heard an unusual swish, bump sound and then Sharp was staggering across the common space like a baby trying to learn how to walk. His feet couldn't catch up with his head and he crashed to the floor with his mouth open.

"ANDY!! INTRUDER!!"

The rod had entered Sharp in his back and was poking out the side of his chest in front. "Heeks, call an ambulance!"

The shooting started downstairs. I had a .38 in my hand. Everything seemed dark. I shook my head.

"You'll be okay. I know it hurts, but I can see you'll be okay."

Sharp panted out, "Jeeezus, it really hurts."

Andy and Elaine came up the stairs. I looked at Elaine. Her face was ashen.

"Andy?! What the fuck you doing up here? He'll get away!"

"It's DeFord's bodyguard with a fucking little crossbow. He went up in the ceiling through the access tunnel, that's why we're fucking up here! He won't be able to get back out. The door is blocked."

"Did you detain him?" Sharp's eyes were huge.

"Elaine hit him, but he still managed to get up there."

"We both got him, didn't we?"

Andy looked at Elaine like something more than Sharp being shot was wrong. "Yep. We both got him."

"At least he didn't use poison or shoot me in the heel."

"Bro, you have to be quiet. Quit trying to move around."

"We have to get outside so the fuck doesn't get away. I'm going up in the ceiling to see if…

Mojica was walking back to us and suddenly fell down. He crawled to a wall and sat up looking at the ceiling, pointing.

■ ● ■

He was holding his hand over a wound that wasn't caused by a crossbow.

"Well I don't think we need to worry about him getting away. He wants to kill all of us. I'm going up."

"Let's wait for the police."

"Fuck that, Andy! I'm going up. I'm going to get that son of a bitch!"

Elaine suddenly said, "I'm going up on the roof in case he tries to exit. I may even be able to see him."

"How…Yeah." If our assassin made it to the roof then Elaine ought to be able to get there.

"Elaine…don't try to stick your head in the access tunnel." I thought Andy was going to say, 'Why don't you stay here with Sharp and Heeks,' but this was no time to appreciate a small victory for women.

Everything seemed to have a dark pallor even though it was mid-afternoon. I thought I saw a dark shadow outside one of the windows. I flinched. Everyone turned.

"What's happening?"

"Nothing, Sharp. Nothing."

Elaine and I jumped up at the same time. She almost flew down the stairs. I ran toward a service ladder at the end of the hall that went up to a panel in the ceiling. I pushed the panel and immediately wood splintered and a hole appeared a couple of inches from my hand. I jumped down from the ladder. He had a suppressor so I'd never really be sure of where he was firing from. I grabbed a fire extinguisher and climbed back up the ladder. I pushed the panel again and heard two thuds hit the wall. Without raising my head above the ceiling, I started spraying foam in every direction I could. Faintly I heard "aagghh!" Now! I dropped the extinguisher and pushed up into the crawl space. I could see the bastard now and I opened up. He was moving

■●■

toward the roof access. Elaine started firing. He curled at the waist. I fired again from my knees and knew he was finished. I spit in his direction and started crying. What the hell was wrong with these people?! What the fucking hell?!

I heard the ambulance siren and police cars, but they seemed so far away even though I knew they were in the parking lot.

I yelled, "He's finished Elaine! He's done!"

I climbed back down the ladder just in time to see the medics walk in with Andy.

The first medic kneeled down. "It's a good thing you didn't try to pull that out."

The second medic was on the floor with Heeks. I heard Heeks say, "I probably don't seem it, but I am in a heck of a lot of pain. What do you guys have?"

Andy was talking to the medics as they put Sharp on a stretcher. I couldn't understand what he was saying even though I was only two feet away from him. The police were everywhere it seemed. I couldn't seem to answer anyone's questions until Elaine started holding my arm.

We were in the hospital and I was wondering how we got here. Which car did we take? Who drove? I couldn't remember who drove!

"What are you frowning at so hard?"

"Huh? I don't know, Andy. Everything. Everything I guess."

Mojica walked up to us on crutches smiling. "The doc says Sharp came through the surgery fine. We can't see him until tomorrow. He's going to be out."

"Someone should be here with him. We don't understand how these people think." Andy was looking at me funny, like he was on the verge of panic. "I'm going to talk to that doctor to see

■ ● ■

if one of us can stay in the room tonight." Andy walked over to the nurses' desk.

"You okay, Capitan?"

"Yes. Just worried about Sharp."

"Once we move into our new building, that kind of bullshit won't happen. I guarantee it."

"You guarantee it?!"

Mojica looked embarrassed. "C'mon Bro, you know what I mean. There won't be anyone slipping in and taking shots at us from the ceiling."

Somehow the tension left my body. "Sorry, Heeks. I didn't mean to sound like that. I know exactly what you mean, but I'm nervous that these Commission creeps are going to keep popping up."

"I'm worried that someday they're going to be running around with a significant part of the population behind them."

That stung. Heeks was right and right now all I could do was nod my head.

"Hey, Ray."

"How's Sharp?"

"He'll be fine after a long stretch in bed and a little bit of vacation."

I was confused. "How did you find out about Sharp?" Raoul looked at me like I just told a bad joke.

"I got my people. I got my sources. Andy called me."

I must have blinked my eyes and shook my head at the same time. Mojica started laughing. Raoul put his hand out to shake. I started to raise my hand when Andy's hand grabbed onto Ray's.

"Ray."

"Andy."

"The doctor gave us the green light to have someone in the room with him all night. Maybe we can come up with a rudi-

■ ● ■

mentary schedule."

Raoul looked at me with a peculiar smile. "So you took one of the enemy out with a fire extinguisher?"

"Didn't expect to. I was just trying to confuse him a little so I could figure out where he was. I got lucky."

The four of us started laughing.

I stretched and sat down, watching Sharp sleep. It was funny that he said 'at least they didn't get him in the heel.' I wondered how it was that the strongest man in our crew kept getting dealt the heaviest pain. The door opened. I looked up at Raoul hovering over me.

"Ray, what are you doing here so soon?"

"I need to talk to you."

"Uh-huh. So talk."

"Out in the hall. I don't want to wake Sharp."

"Y'all can forget about that."

"Damn, Sharp. I'm sorry. Thought I was whispering."

"Raoul, y'all whisper like a diesel."

"What's going on?"

"I finally have all of the information you wanted on that woman, Cheike. She had nothing to do with DeFord. Her only sin is that she designs nuclear fission reactors for the Nuclear Regulatory Commission. If you want an address…" Raoul handed me a sheet of paper with an address in Laguna Beach. "You sure you want that?"

I nodded.

Sharp was snoring.

"I'll sit with Sharp. Y'all take care of your business."

I went back to the office to grab a couple of things and an overnight bag. The elevator operator actually spoke. It made me

■ ● ■

nervous for a second thinking maybe someone was waiting for me on one of the floors.

"I hear you guys are leaving the building."

"Yeah. I guess we are."

"Be a lot calmer around here…why don't you leave me some business cards with your new address…in case someone comes in who wants to shoot somebody. I can just give him your card. Of course I'd give you a ring to let you know to expect company."

When he opened the door I couldn't tell if he had a smile on his face or a smirk.

Entering the office I saw Andy hovering over Elaine's desk. He looked up as I approached. I didn't like the expression on his face.

"Raoul is sitting with Sharp."

Andy nodded, but his expression didn't change.

"You need to read these." He handed me two sheets of paper and then walked over to the big window by the couch.

The first paper was a letter from the court stating that Elaine was to appear with Marty so that she could be turned over to the custody of Social Services. I read the second page, re-read it and read it again. It was like I was waiting for magic words to appear even though I knew they wouldn't. "We love you guys. Don't try to find us."

I felt like the world was either getting so small it was going to crush me. Or the world had gotten so big I was going to be completely lost in it. I ended up across the room next to my best friend, Andy. We stared out the window in silence.

"Andy, I know this is not a good time, but I…"

"You take care of what you need to take care of. We'll be able to handle anything that comes up here." He slapped me on the back. Then he walked off to his office.

I went into my office and looked out the window. I turned

■ ● ■

and scanned the room. A desk with a putty filled bullet hole on top. One grey file cabinet. Two wooden chairs and a desk chair with a box on one wheel that looked like "Finnegan's Wake."

I picked up the phone while Andy leaned in my doorway.

"What's up?"

"I booked you a reservation on the 6:10 to San Francisco. There you switch…I didn't book you a return flight." He strolled back to his office.

The plane took off on time, which pleasantly surprised me. We were fifteen or twenty minutes into the flight before I really noticed the woman sitting next to me. She had shoulder length braids with a gold bead in each of them. She was wearing a black, brown and gold dashiki with carpenter's jeans.

Since it didn't matter to me, I said, "Do you want the window seat? I'd be happy to switch seats with you."

"No. I'm fine right here."

I turned back to the window, wondering what Cheike would say when she saw me.

"Acrophobia."

I turned to look at her with a frown on my face. "You know, there are trains down there."

"Kinesphobic."

"What the…"

She broke out in a brilliant smile.

I smiled back and shook my head. "Okay, what is…kinesphobia? Is that the inner ear problem?"

Well, kinesphobia is fear of movement. It could be related to an inner ear problem. Could be…"

"I was wondering about that scar on your hand."

She scrunched up her lips. "Soccer. Two operation injury.

■ ● ■

Also had a broken nose if it comes up. Other than that, I'm still in one piece."

"Where'd you play?"

"Hamilton College."

"Upstate New York?"

"Yep." As she said that she took two bracelets out of her bag and put them on. They made just a little metallic click and then she rested them quietly in her lap.

I tried to hold up my end of a conversation but I kept blanking out parts.

"…Burkina Faso…mother ill…Berkley…tried to play in Europe…Phd…well what did you do immediately after Vietnam…uh…friends…Big Sleep…"

Did I tell her about Vietnam? What did I tell her?

The 'Fasten Your Seatbelt' sign went on. The stewardess was passing. I had never taken mine off.

She handed me her card…'Ariel Simpson: Clinical Psychology.'

"I have a shrink already."

She looked embarrassed. "I teach. Wow… I really wasn't very impressive I guess."

I felt ashamed.

"I'm sorry. I'm worried about my friend who was shot."

"Sharp, right?"

"Um…yeah." I pulled out one of my cards and handed it to her. "We're moving in a couple of weeks, but we'll still have the same phone number." Why the hell am I doing this?

"Will you still have the same name?"

"I…" I scratched the side of my face. "I'm really sorry. I must have been pitiful company."

"Not really. You just seemed distracted. I'd love to get the chance to talk to you some time after Sharp is okay."

■ ● ■

"I have a connecting flight I have to make."

She smiled, stood up and moved down the aisle with the other passengers.

My connection was twenty-five minutes late. It drove me crazy. I spent the entire flight rehearsing what I'd say to her… and what I hoped she'd say to me. At one point in the taxi I thought, 'This is ridiculous. What am I doing?' A voice that sounded like the narrator from "Industry on Parade" yelled back at me, 'You're in love. You have to do this."

I paid the driver and walked up to a black door with a brass knocker. I turned to look at the view. I thought Cheike would live closer to the water. But it was really a stunning view of the ocean from up here. I turned back to the door and used the knocker.

The door opened. I could hear her jewelry. Her eyes locked on mine. I should have rehearsed 'silence' while I was in the cab. I started to take a step forward. Her jewelry made a discordant sound as she put her hand on my chest and held me where I was standing. Her eyes fell. She started to slowly close the door. Her hand came off my chest with her jewelry singing. The sound disappeared when the door closed.

I put my left hand flat on the door. Then I leaned my forehead on it. I stared into the black. Finally I closed my eyes.

■ ● ■

Notes

Child Marriage

Between 2000 and 2010, 248,000 children (17 years of age and younger) were married in the United States. Of those, the majority were girls married to adult men. Due to legal exemptions twelve states have no minimum age for marriage. As of 2021 twelve year olds with "parental consent" were allowed to marry in the State of Massachusetts. Though children may legally marry in most states, they may not file for divorce until they become 'legal adults' at eighteen.

On July 23, 2021 New York State became the sixth state to ban child marriages without exception (joining Delaware, Minnesota, New Jersey, Pennsylvania and Rhode Island).

■ ● ■

Michael Townley

Michael Townley was an agent and assassin of the Chilean secret police and an operative of the CIA.

In 1973 the CIA helped organize a military coup (led by General Augusto Pinochet) against the democratically elected government of Chile. Townley (born in Iowa) was recruited by Pinochet's secret police, the DINA, after the coup. In 1976 Michael Townley planted a bomb under the car of former Chilean ambassador Orlando Letelier. The bomb was detonated in the center of Washington, D.C., just blocks from the White House, killing Letelier and his co-worker, Ronni Moffitt. In a 1978 plea bargain, Townley pleaded guilty to both murders in exchange for immunity to all further prosecution. He ended up serving 62 months in jail for the double homicides.

In 1975 the U.S. helped organize and coordinate "Operation Condor," a program created with the intention of eliminating political opposition to U.S. backed military governments in South America. Townley was a DINA agent directly involved in the Condor operation. In 1993 Townley was convicted in abstentia by an Italian court for the attempted murder of former Chilean Christian Democrat Vice-President Bernardo Leighton and his wife. The attack failed, though Leighton was seriously wounded and his wife ended up a paraplegic.

The 1983 government of Argentina requested Townley's extradition from the U.S. to stand trial for the 1974 murder of Chilean General Carlos Prats and his wife. They were exiled opponents of Pinochet's coup and proponents of democracy in Chile. They were assassinated in a bombing similar to the one used to kill Letelier. The U.S. refused extradition.

Townley also worked on a team led by biochemist Eugenio Berrios. Berrios reproduced sarin and other poisons that were subsequently used on political opponents. At one point the Berrios/Townley team was developing a plan to poison the entire water supply of the city of Buenos Aires.

We're living in a time when someone who is elected to Congress believes California forest fires have been started by Jewish space lasers.

We're living in a time when an elected member of the House of Representatives says that she is tired of "this separation of church and state junk."

We're living in a time when elected officials are willing to let their citizens drink water they know has been poisoned by lead, if it saves the municipality money.

We're living in a time when a President of the United States can say there are good Nazis.

We're living in such a dangerous time...the danger of civil war...the danger of fascism...of climate collapse.

We're living in a time that calls us to educate, demonstrate, organize in our communities and workplaces...to stand up to misogyny and white supremacist ideology. It is a time to stand up for our children's and grandchildren's future...One that should be healthy, humane and free of blind hate and ignorance.

Acknowledgements

There are many people I want to thank for helping me get this project to completion.

First of all I'd like to acknowledge Linda Hanlon who reviewed and criticized every chapter almost as soon as it was written. It was almost like she was reading over my shoulder as I typed. My sister-in-law writer, Mary Brown, gave me a lot of things to think over and I truly appreciate her reading and take on the story. Greg Mojica made some very important suggestions about the 'action' sequences and weaponry. (I will always listen closely to someone who has been stabbed as many times as Greg has.) I want to extend special thanks to my daughter, Kira Manso-Brown, and Len Warner for the effort they put in criticizing the final draft. They spent more time with this than I could have expected.

I want to thank Amy Manso for her excellent work in designing the cover and the interior of this book. I don't think I can thank her enough.

I wish I could personally thank Amine Wefali, my next door neighbor, who has passed on. She gave me some gentle and enthusiastic criticism of NYCTOPHOBIA and my short stories. She was working on a new piece when she died. From what I saw, it seemed like it would be a great book and I wish she had the chance to finish it. But I'm also glad she had the opportunity to begin it.

Finally I want to thank all of the people who read DARK and then encouraged me to finish NYCTOPHOBIA so that they could find out 'what happened next.' My favorite line of encouragement was, "Will you hurry the fuck up?!"

About the author

LEE BROWN

Lee is a former trade union organizer. Before moving to New York City from Binghamton, N.Y., he was the founding president of Local 994 of the International Chemical Workers Union. In NYC he worked with the ILGWU, organizing shops in New York's garment center and in Brooklyn. As a community organizer he was active in housing issues and in the anti-apartheid movement. Before taking up writing fiction, Lee led a rock band called "Patterns of Grace," and he owned a coffeehouse for fifteen years. If he were forced to pick three favorite current writers, they would be Mosley, Mieville and Modiano. He loves watching the NBA. Lee has two wonderful daughters (who he shares with one of his best friends, Amy Manso) and his first grandson, who he hopes, in his future, will continue the struggle for the rights of workers everywhere.

Praise for Lee Brown's DARK

Dark *by Lee Brown takes off with a running start. Strange and mysterious at first. Slowly the narrative comes into focus while at the same time the events barrel ahead. Each personality is well tended to and engenders affection from me, including the un-named narrator. I was sorry to leave them as well as the world the novel builds behind.*

Harry Roseman
Professor Emeritus of Art, Vassar College

This is not your usual detective story...always something new poppin' out in your face.

Sleuth Pro
author of *Hip Hop Tales* **• Poughkeepsie, New York**

Brown's novel constructs compelling character driven webs of story you don't want to free yourself from. This is the new noir- elliptical and challenging in the best ways, with flashes of light and dark-ness- befitting our age but referencing and refracting others. If you like Mosley, Butler, diners, intrigue, blue notes, or the scent of books at any age, there's something here for you in this complex and re-warding read.

Mind Bullets Collective • Brooklyn, New York

www.ingramcontent.com/pod-product-compliance
Lightning Source LLC
Chambersburg PA
CBHW031951060726
47497CB00016B/1296